I let go, and time cl____ ____ ____ me like the case for an old pair of spectacles. The moment passes, and I stumble for a couple of steps, feeling more meat slop out of my belly and back, more scraps on the floor. There's a hard thud as a hundred and fifty pounds of flesh that used to be a human being crashes onto the concrete.

I walk gingerly around the stacked crates and have a look. His legs and arms are thrashing, his eyes rolled back in the sockets. His skull is cracked and bleeding. His fragile, fractured eggshell skull.

And the tasty yolk within.

And all of a sudden –

– all of a sudden my head is pounding and there's a hot metal taste in my mouth and I don't have anything better to do than think about –

brains!

An Abaddon Books™ Publication
www.abaddonbooks.com
abaddon@rebellion.co.uk

First published in 2008 by Abaddon Books™, Rebellion Intellectual
Property Limited, Riverside House, Osney Mead, Oxford OX2 0ES UK.

10 9 8 7 6 5 4 3 2 1

Editor: Jonathan Oliver
Cover: Mark Harrison
Design: Simon Parr & Luke Preece
Marketing and PR: Keith Richardson
Creative Director and CEO: Jason Kingsley
Chief Technical Officer: Chris Kingsley

ISBN: 978-1-905437-72-6

Printed in Denmark by Nørhaven Paperback A/S

Distributed in the US by National Book Network, 4501 Forbes
Boulevard, Lanham, MD 20706, USA

TOMES OF THE DEAD

I, Zombie

Al Ewing

Abaddon
Books

WWW.ABADDONBOOKS.COM

PROLOGUE

The Time of The Ghost Sun

Sun sank over the western plain, down into the depths of Ghost Country.

Ar-rah was he, man and hunter and son of no father, strange thoughts in his head, strange talk in his mouth. Father was in Ghost Country, under the earth. The country without light where only Ghost Sun shines.

Sun sank, Sun died. Tonight was the light of Ghost Sun, bright white as bone, shining the land white-blue. The night of the Ghost Sun. Night of ghosts, night of strange thought.

Alone of the tribe, Ar-rah hunted by the light of Ghost Sun.

Father was laid down in Ghost Country before Mother bore Ar-rah. Mother-thought brought thought of eyes cold blue, sick in heavy shadow. Sadness in those eyes, beneath the ridge of bone that Ar-rah had run fingertips over when small. Sometimes those eyes lay inside him, and when he closed his own those eyes were there, secret eyes that looked into him and all his secrets. Ghost eyes. Mother was in Ghost Country too.

No man had taught Ar-rah to hunt. Sons and fathers walked to the bush together, backs bent and stone teeth in hand, eyes sharp for the long-tooth, the killer. Fathers teaching sons, sons helping fathers, hunting together, dying together if long-tooth came upon them. It was the way.

No shame in dying by long-tooth. Shame in dying by teeth of men, shame and weakness. Un-guh drove his stone tooth through Father's neck in the time before time when Ar-rah was not. Un-guh led. Un-guh was strong and Father was weak. Father challenged Un-guh anyway.

Ar-rah understood. Mother was weak, sick. Even if she bore, Mother would be left behind, not to slow the tribe. Un-guh took dominion over Mother when he killed Father – Un-guh took responsibility. To fail in that would be the end of Un-guh. Who follows a leader who does not protect his own? Mother grew sick and died, but was never left, never abandoned.

Ar-rah had seen fourteen winters, as his Father had when Father died. Ar-rah's thoughts were quick, under the ridge of bone that shaded his eyes. He understood. Father had been quick too, and brave for all his weakness. Father had bought his child's survival with blood.

Even after Mother died, when fingers pointed at Ar-rah, strange and silent Ar-rah who hunted alone and took no mate – Un-guh took *responsibility*. Ar-rah was not left, though Un-guh never spoke to him. Un-guh had seen thirty winters, now, and was old and sick. He had days – illness would take him, or death by long-tooth or heavy-tread, for he still hunted with the tribe as a leader must.

Or the stone tooth would take him in shame.

Ar-rah had seen lips curling to bare teeth as Un-guh walked by. Hands holding cooking-stones grasping tighter, dull eyes under ridges of bone wanting to smash them down on the head of the old man as he shuffled past. But that was not the way.

The next dawn, or the dawn after, there would be a challenge. Ar-rah should be the one to challenge, to plunge his stone tooth into the old man's heart, to take leadership of the tribe, to never be abandoned and left for the long-tooth. But Ar-rah wanted only the security of the fire to come back to, the security of the tribe to belong to. And more – Un-guh had given him protection. To kill Un-guh...

Ar-rah searched for the concept in his mind, eyes squinting beneath the ridge of bone as he stooped lower, dragging fingertips over dusty ground.

To kill Un-guh... would not be...

It would not be *right*.

Such a concept would take more thinking about, but Ar-rah felt sure. He would find another way.

There was movement in the trees.

Ar-rah started, looking left. For a moment he saw a face in the trees, blue-white and pale, like the light of the Ghost Sun itself, eyes hooded. A member of the tribe?

No. There was nothing recognisable in that face. A ghost, then? Father, from Ghost Country, come under the light of Ghost Sun to watch and advise?

Ar-rah blinked, once. The face was gone. The trees were still.

Ar-rah reached up, instinctively rubbing his upper arms with his hands.

He felt cold.

Ar-rah hunted night-creatures, the things that walked and crawled and flew in darkness. A thrown stone tooth could find one of the black, shrieking flap-wings that nested in the caves, breaking bones and sending it down to the rock floor. Or a long sharpened pole of bamboo could be thrust down a burrow, impaling one of the dig-furs sleeping within. The meat was spare, but good –

tender and nourishing. Along with the roots and berries gathered in the light, it made for good eating. Ar-rah was strong, if spare himself. There was no wasted flesh on his frame.

Ar-rah had hunted the swift-legs, once. But he'd learned the hard way that the swift-legs could not be hunted alone. They were too fast for that. The swift-legs had to be chased by the weaker hunter into the arms of the stronger, caught and slit from throat to belly with stone tooth. Even then, it was easy to miss the catch, or be kicked with a hoof – perhaps maimed or killed. The meat of the swift-legs was rare, and wearing its skin was the sign of a superior hunter. Mostly, the tribe fed on smaller game or gathered roots and nuts.

Ar-rah knew better than to hunt the swift-legs alone, even though they often grazed on the plains at night and there was no member of the tribe awake in those hours to see him fail. It was a waste of energy to run like a fool after the swift-legs, when there was easier and better game to be had. And yet Ar-rah found himself standing at the edge of a wide clearing, grass shining blue-white under the light of Ghost Sun, watching one of the swift-legs bending to graze. For a moment, Ar-rah allowed himself to think that the swift-legs was close enough to catch – but no. As soon as he lumbered forward, the swift-legs would be at the opposite side of the clearing, hooves pounding the dirt as it vanished forever.

Let it go. It could not be caught. It could not be reached.

Ar-rah eyed the sharpened bamboo in his right hand. His thoughts were quick, coming one upon the other like water in a stream. He felt the eyes of the ghost-man he had seen earlier on his back. If he turned, he felt certain he would see the man's shadowed eyes under the blue-white, almost translucent jut of his forehead.

He did not turn.

Instead, he concentrated on the bamboo stake he used to catch dig-furs. It was long, but it would not cover the distance between him and the swift-legs. Perhaps if he stretched to his utmost, he could poke the creature in the side and set it running.

He considered throwing it for a moment, but the bamboo was too light. Even sharpened as it was, it couldn't pierce the beast's hide without some weight behind it...

Ar-rah felt the eyes of the ghost on him. He hefted his stone tooth in his palm, then reached down to quietly pull up a swathe of the long grass at his feet. The swift-legs heard the sound and bolted, running for the bushes. Ar-rah nodded to himself, grunted softly, and continued wrapping the grasses around the stone and the bamboo, binding them together.

The thought was in his mind now.

Ar-rah turned, studying the forest behind him. If the ghost had been there, it was gone now. He turned back to his labours. The grasses would have to be tightly bound, to keep the stone tooth on the end of the bamboo.

Somewhere in the trees, there was a glimpse of bone-white flesh.

Once the swift-legs had vanished, Ar-rah worked slowly, taking his time. When he stood again and lifted the bamboo, the stone tooth bound to the end made a pleasing heft in his hand. It felt right. Ar-rah turned, slowly stalking back the way he had come.

It would be useless to wait here for the swift-legs – none would return to that grazing ground for at least another night, perhaps a night after that. But there were other clearings, other grazing grounds where the swift-legs knew they could feed undisturbed at night. Ar-rah knew the likely places.

He couldn't help but smile. The whole idea was foolish – a stone tooth at the end of a stick, of all things – but he felt a surge of excitement despite that, a flush of pride that he, strange, silent Ar-rah, had thought of it. If it worked... if he could throw it hard enough to pierce the hide of the swift-legs...

Everything would change.

Everything.

He shook his head, laughing at his own thoughts. It was the Ghost Sun putting these ideas into his head, the Ghost Sun with its strange light, bringing strange dreams and madness – and this *was* madness. This long stick with its stone tooth, against muscle and grace and speed. Beautiful madness, made solid by the blue-white light of the Ghost Sun, and the eyes of the ghost-brother who watched him.

Ar-rah walked out into the next clearing. No swift-legs here. Perhaps it would be better to leave it until the next night. That would be time enough for his... his... his stone-tooth-on-a-long-stick.

Ar-rah laughed like a boy.

He laughed at the most complete novelty he had ever known, the wonderful novelty of naming something. Something that was his own, that he had made, created, invented from nothing but the thoughts in his mind and the light of the Ghost Sun. Stick-tooth? Thrown-tooth? Long-stick-with-tooth? Long –

Long-tooth.

Ar-rah froze, eyes narrowed.

A dark, knotted shadow of liquid muscle and fur slinked into the blue-white light in front of him.

Long-tooth.

In the blue-white light, the monster was like a ghost itself, an ever-moving mass of grey and black stripes, a coiling river of flesh and killing power. The long fangs that gave it a name glittered as it padded closer, closer. The eyes...

The eyes were green, blue-green under the Ghost Sun's light. Ar-rah took a step backward. He always thought the long-tooth's eyes would be red as blood. No man had ever seen those eyes and lived.

This was the long-tooth, the killer, deadly spirit of muscle and speed, claw and cruelty and death. Ar-rah had called the swift-legs graceful, but their grace did not save them from this. The grace and speed of the long-tooth was infinitely greater and more profound, all the more beautiful and terrible because it was so deadly.

Ar-rah could not look away. He could not run. He knew that if he ran, he would die – ripped and torn by those claws, his entrails spilled on the grass, blood black under that terrible, awful light. He knew why the ghost-brother was watching him through the trees, now. This was the night that he would die, head severed from body, innards crushed and burst between vicious jaws, his life and strength stolen to feed and build the infinite life and strength of the long-tooth. This was Ar-rah's ending.

The long-tooth growled, sniffing the air. Scenting fear.

Ar-rah's bowels voided, spilling down the backs of his legs. But he did not move.

This was Death, then. This was the end of breath and warmth, the entry into Ghost Country. This was the end of love, the end of warm skin on skin and laughter. The end of splashing in streams, of feeling the Sun, the true living Sun on cheek and back, the end of all things good.

Then let Death come.

He would look it in the eye.

Slowly, he raised his stick-and-tooth.

One moment long-tooth was still. The next it was fluid lines of muscle and motion, arcing in the air, sharp claws and fangs and weight, leaping to the kill. Ar-rah smelled the breath of the long-tooth, deep and foul and stinking of meat and blood. It was to be the last scent in his nostrils, his final experience, this scent of death and meat.

Ar-rah half-jumped, half-stumbled backwards. At the same time, he thrust the stick-with-tooth upwards at the monster on top of him. He felt claws swiping at his chest, smelt the hot raging hunger washing over his face. Then he felt the weight, the mass of the beast, pushing down on the pole in his hands.

The long-tooth snarled and bit, thrashing in rage and pain. Ar-rah felt a sharp, stinging pain in his face and his vision went flat, one half dark. He felt something spilling down his cheek.

Then the long-tooth stopped moving.

Ar-rah sat on the cold grass, feeling the dead weight of the monster on top of him. After a time, he shifted, letting the long-tooth stopple sideways and scrambling out from underneath. He lifted a hand to his face, feeling the deep gash there, the hole where his left eye had been. Blood trickled down his belly from the claw-marks on his chest. The pain was coming now, in great, slow, throbbing pulses.

And Ar-rah was alive.

The stick-with-tooth was jutting from the monster's heart.

Ar-rah stood, holding his palm to his missing eye, for what seemed a very long time. The marks on his chest were not deep, and the blood slowed, then stopped. But the gash on his face continued to trickle when he took his hand away. He would have to pack it with mud and grass, and soon. Even so, perhaps he would sicken, the flesh around his missing eye turning yellow, then green, giving off the stink of rot and corruption. Perhaps he would grow slowly weaker until he died. He had seen it happen often. It was rare for men to survive such wounds. It didn't seem to matter to Ar-rah.

He stood and looked at the long-tooth.

It was massive. Big as three men at full growth. The teeth were as long as his forearm. Ar-rah placed his palm on the monster's flank, feeling the fur, the muscle and sinew. Cooling in the night air.

Soon it would be cold.

There had been life there once – the essence of life, life and strength in all its great and terrible glory. More than men, who hunted and gathered and shivered and died in the winters, who needed fire and skins to survive, who banded together in tribes to hide their weakness. Men were half-alive, shadow-creatures who needed to walk and talk and make things simply to avoid being torn to shreds by creatures like this. Things that were truly alive. Truly real.

Stood against the long-tooth, all men were ghosts.

Ar-rah watched a fly buzz and settle on the long-tooth's fur, then move to its eye. Staying to feed. The creatures needed to be skinned, the meat cooked and stored. The long teeth could be kept and used somehow, as weapons. He should get to work.

He stood.

He tried to recall how the long-tooth had moved.

Where was that life now? That strength? Where was that slow, liquid majesty of movement?

It was as though he had killed the wind and the rain. He had come face to face with something very like the Sun itself.

And now flies were eating it.

There was a flash of white from the trees. Ar-rah waited.

His shoulders slumped as the ghost-brother stepped into the clearing. He did not even feel surprised. It seemed natural that the ghosts should be here, after this. He had ended a life – a life that possessed a power and magnitude he could barely comprehend. This was the death of awe and terror, fear and wonder. The death of everything Ar-rah knew.

Of course the ghosts would mark the passing.

The ghost-brother walked slowly, eyes lost under bone, skin the colour of the ghost light that shone from the Ghost Sun above. Ar-rah's remaining eye was sad and wet as he turned to look back. He was suddenly very tired.

The ghost-brother grunted and nodded to the dead long-tooth, and the shaft of bamboo jutting from its chest. It was an acknowledgement. This was the first time such a thing had happened.

Ar-rah knew he should feel something. Pride, perhaps? Shame? Instead he simply stood, allowing the ghost-brother to place one strong hand on his bony forehead, the other at his neck. A ritual gesture, a ghost ceremony. His reward for killing the world.

Ar-rah felt nothing, even when the ghost-brother tore the head from his body in one impossibly strong, savage motion, blood spattering the grass and the corpse of the long-tooth.

The body took a couple of steps backward, gushing from the neck, and collapsed in a heap. Under the light of the Ghost Sun, the blood was jet black. The ghost-brother said nothing.

Carefully, he took the severed head, the one remaining eye rolling back in the socket, lips twitching, and brought it down hard against his knee. Hard enough to shatter the thick, bony canopy of the skull.

The ghost-brother reached into the skull with his blue-white fingers and scooped out a handful of the grey-pink matter inside, raising it to his lips. He tasted it, then tore into the rest, chewing, swallowing, pieces of brain and skull fragments sticking to teeth and chin.

When the feeding frenzy was over, the ghost-brother casually tossed the severed head onto the grass, then stood and looked at the long-tooth, and the stick-with-tooth in its heart. If there had been a thought in the ghost-brother's ghost head, then perhaps he would have been disappointed. Perhaps he would have expected more from Ar-rah, with his strange thoughts, so quick and sure.

Perhaps he would have wondered when the time would come.

When they would be ready.

But there were no thoughts.

The ghost-brother turned and padded off towards the trees.

CHAPTER ONE

My Gun is Quick

Time slows to a crawl.

The broken glass around me hangs in the air like mountains of ice, floating in space in the science-fiction movie of my life. Like healing crystals in a new-age junk shop, hanging on threads, spinning slowly. Beautiful little diamond fragments.

For five minutes – or less than a second, depending on your viewpoint – I drift slowly downwards, watching the glass shimmer and spin. It's moments like this that make this strange life-not-life of mine seem almost worthwhile.

Moments of beauty in a sea of horror and blood.

I'd like to just hang here forever, drifting downwards, watching the shards of glass spin and turn in the air around me, but eventually I have to relax my grip or get bored. And I'd rather not get bored of a moment like this one.

I let go.

Time snaps back like a rubber band.

The moment passes.

Time perception is a trick of the human mind. The average human perceives events at a rate of one second per second, so to speak, but that doesn't make it the standard. Hummingbirds and mayflies perceive time differently. It's much slower for them, to match their metabolism – I'm pretty sure that's the case. I read it somewhere. In a magazine.

New Scientist, I think. Or *Laboratory News*. Maybe *Discover*.

I read a lot of scientific magazines.

It might have been *Scientific American*. Or *Popular Science*. Or just plain *Science*. I go through them all.

I look for articles about decomposition, about autolysis and cell fractionation, about the retardation of putrefaction. About the factors that affect skin temperature or blood clotting.

Things that might explain my situation.

I know it wasn't the *Fortean Times*. Unless it was talking about an alien hummingbird kept under a pyramid. Or possibly building the pyramids. I read that one for the cartoons.

Anyway. Time perception is a trick of the human mind. It's possible to slow down the perception of time in humans, to perceive things in slow motion, experience more in a shorter time. Shorten reaction time to zero. Anybody can do it with the right drugs, or the right kind of hypnosis.

I can do it at will.

I concentrate.

Time slows.

The glass hangs in the air.

I look for articles about the basal ganglia and the superchiasmatic nucleus, about neurotransmitters and the subconscious. I've done research when I can. Heightened time perception burns a lot of adrenaline, apparently. A lot of energy stores. You can't keep it up for long periods without needing plenty of sleep.

But I don't need to sleep.

I don't need to eat either.

Or breathe.

Time rushes back in, like air into an empty lung that's never used.

The moment passes...

...and then the soles of the converse trainers I wear to look cool slap loudly onto the concrete floor of a disused warehouse in Hackney and four big men in badly-fitted suits are pointing guns at me. But that's okay. I've got a gun too. And if they shot me, I wouldn't bleed.

My heart doesn't beat, so the blood doesn't pump around my body. My skin is cold and clammy and so pale as to be almost blue, or green, depending on the light. My hair is white, like an old man's. My eyes are red and bloodshot and I keep them hidden when I can.

Let's see, what else do you need to know before we get started?

Oh yes.

I've been dead for the last ten years.

I don't have any memory of not being dead. The earliest thing I can remember is waking up in a cheap bed-and-breakfast in Stamford Hill. The room was registered in the name John Doe – the name generally used for an unidentified corpse. I'm sure somebody somewhere thought that was hilarious.

Still, it was the only name I had, so I stuck with it. To all intents and purposes, it was mine.

To all intents and purposes, the gun sitting by the sink was mine as well.

It's strange. I don't have any memory of feeling different,

of anything being out of the ordinary. I got up, brushed my teeth even though they never need it, took a shower even though I never smell of anything. People hate that more than BO, I've noticed. That smell of nothing at all, that olfactory absence. Cologne can't cover it, because there's just the cologne on its own, with that huge blank void beneath that rings all the subconscious alarm bells. Even your best friend won't tell you.

I don't remember being surprised that I was dead. I'm actually more surprised now than I was then, surprised at not being surprised. What sort of person was I, that I woke up dead and took it in my stride?

I remember that the first thing I did that day was shoot a man in the back room of a dingy pub in the Stoke Newington area.

Why did I do that? What sort of person was I then?

Obviously, I had a reason. I mean, I must have. I just can't remember quite what it was.

I had a reason. I had a gun. I had a mobile phone that was a bit clunky and crap and didn't even have games on it, never mind anything useful, and occasionally it rang and then I had a job to do that fit someone who was dead but still moving around. I had a bank account, and I had plenty of money sitting in it for a rainy day. I had a low profile.

No matter what, I always had a low profile. I always knew how to fit in, even though I was dead. Even though I killed people.

Even though I have occasionally...

Just occasionally... I may have...

I may have *eaten*...

You know what? I have better things to do right now than think about that.

For a start, the bad men are pulling their guns.

They're pulling their guns. My legs uncoil and I sail up, arcing forward, the first bullet passing through the space I've left behind me. I hold time in my mind, keeping it running at a reasonable speed, not too slow, not too fast. Behind me, the last shards of glass from the window hit the floor. At this speed, it sounds like wind chimes clanging softly in the breeze. The gunshots sound like the bellows of prehistoric monsters. The shells clang against the stone like church bells.

Did you ever see *The Matrix*?

Bit of a busman's holiday, I thought.

My own gun roars and I'm almost surprised. The bullet drills slowly into the head of the nearest man, already fragmenting, leaving a bloody caste-mark in the very centre of his forehead, the flesh rippling slightly under the pull of an obscene tide. I watch the exact moment when the look of surprise freezes on his face, goes slack, and then the back of his skull swings open slowly like multi-faceted cathedral doors, and the pulsing chunks of white-pink matter float out, carnival-day balloons for a charnel-house Mardi Gras.

Slow it down enough, and everything fascinates. Everything is beautiful.

Little chunks of brain, flying through the air. Scudding like clouds. Floating like jellyfish. I'm casting about for a better simile here because I don't want to admit what they really look like to me.

Tasty little hors d'oeuvres. Canapès.

The trouble with being able to slow down time for yourself is that it gives you far too much time to think. And I have better things to do right now than think about that.

I speed things up a little, force myself back on the job

as the bullets move faster, one cutting the air next to my left ear, another whispering against the leg of my jeans. My empty hand slaps on the concrete ahead of me and pushes my body up through space, somersaulting until I land on my feet behind a wall of stacked crates. I'm not sure what's in them, but hopefully it's something like dumb-bells or lead sinkers or metal sheeting or just big blocks of concrete. Something that'll stop small arms fire. I don't want to patch up any more holes in myself.

There's a sound coming from close by. It's not wind chimes or church bells or a prehistoric monster. It sounds like some kind of guttural moaning, like a monster lost in an ancient dungeon.

I let go of time and it folds back around me like bad origami. The moment passes.

The sound makes some sense now.

It's a child. Sobbing. From inside the crate I'm hiding behind.

That's where they put Katie, then.

At least it wasn't paedophiles. At least it wasn't SAY A PRAYER FOR LITTLE KATIE SAYS OUR PAGE 3 STUNNER. That's something in today's world, isn't it?

It was an old-fashioned kidnap. Scrambled voice mp3 file, two days after she went missing, nestled in amongst the inbox spam with the fake designer watches and the heartfelt pleas from exiled Nigerian royalty. "Give us the money, Mr Bellows, or we give you the finger. Do you see what we did there? It's a pun." Then a time and a place and an amount to leave and no funny business, please.

Mr Bellows runs a company called Ritenow Educational Solutions. He's the one who prints the certificates when you do the adult courses. This is to certify that MARJORIE PHELPS has achieved PASS in the study of INTERMEDIATE POTTERY. Marjorie won't get any kind of job with the certificate, even if she achieves DISTINCTION in the study of ADVANCED SHORTHAND. It's worthless, but she'll pay up to a couple of hundred pounds to have it on her wall and point it out to the neighbours.

Mr Bellows doesn't run any of the courses. He doesn't make the sheets of china-blue card with the silvery trim and 'This is to Certify has Achieved in the Study of' written in the middle, with gaps. He just has a list of who's passed and what they got, and he runs that through a computer and then his big printer churns out ten or twenty thousand useless certificates a day. He has a staff of three single mothers and a temp who's just discovered The Specials and thinks that makes him unique, and all they do is collate the list of the gold, silver and bronze medal winners in these Housewife Olympics and then print them onto china blue with silver edging and sell them on for exorbitant amounts of money.

Mr Bellows runs a company that does essentially nothing to make essentially nothing. He's the middleman for a useless end product. He's living the British Dream.

And now, the British Nightmare.

Doing nothing to make nothing is a profitable line of work. Mr Bellows has two houses and two cars, neither of which have more than two seats. He also has a flat in Central London which he's working up the courage to install a mistress in. Little Katie Bellows is going to Roedean as soon as she's old enough. If she gets old enough. Mrs Bellows collects antique furniture as a hobby. And Mr Bellows has my mobile number.

That doesn't come cheap.

"Find them, John," he said.

He had whisky on his breath and his voice came from somewhere deep in his throat, rough and hollow, choked with bile. "Find them and kill them. Bring her back safe." There were tears in his eyes that didn't want to come out. A big, gruff man who could solve things with his fists if he had to, but not this. Standing in the drawing room he'd earned with graft and grift and holding my dead hand and trying not to cry. The echo of his wife's soft sobbing drifting down from an upstairs bedroom. An antique clock on the mantelpiece that hadn't been wound, silent next to a photo turned face down because it couldn't be looked at.

Frank Bellows had my number because he'd used me in the past to do things that weren't strictly legal. He hadn't always had the monopoly on doing nothing to make nothing. He'd needed someone who didn't strictly exist to break into a competitor's office and burn it to the ground. Because if the perpetrator doesn't strictly exist, then it isn't arson, is it? Not strictly.

I smiled gently behind my shades, a non-committal little reassurance. Then I stepped back and nodded gently. He only sagged.

"Get them. Kill them. Get out." His voice was choked as though something was crawling up from inside him, some monster of grief that had made its nest in the pit of his stomach. I felt sorry, but what could I do? They only make promises in films.

But then, they only make this kind of kidnap in films. If they'd been real crooks, well, she'd be vanished still. HUNT FOR MISSING KATIE CONTINUES PAGE EIGHT. "Saucy Sabrina, 17, holds back the tears as she keeps abreast of the news of Little Katie – and speaking of keeping a breast!" MISSING KATIE BINGO IN *THE STAR* TODAY.

These weren't 'real' crooks. They were fictional. The script-written ransom note. The suits from Tarantino, the bickering and sniping at each other with perfect quips that they'd spent months thinking up, while I stood on the warehouse skylight, the one they hadn't even bothered to check, picking my moment to crash through the glass and kill them all because the customer is always right. The lack of any covering of tracks, because they were too busy being 'professional' to actually be professional.

There's nothing more dangerous than a man who's seen a film.

The police would have found them eventually, but by that time Katie, age six, probably would have been killed.

They're keeping her in a crate and shooting at her, for God's sake.

It can't be healthy.

Bullets smashing wood, sending splinters and fragments into the air, puffs of shredded paper. The crates are full of catalogues, thick directories of dayglo plastic for schools. 'Teach your child about disabilities. Neon wheelchairs help kids learn.' Most of the bullets thump into those, gouging tunnels and trenches until their energy is spent.

One comes right through the crate I'm hiding behind. Right through, and there's a little yelp. A little girl's half-scream, too frightened to come all the way out.

The silly bastards have hit her.

Instinctively, I grab time and squeeze it until it breaks. Dead stop.

This is the slowest I can go. I look at the bullet, crawling from the hole. Slightly squashed but unfragmented. No blood on it. It missed.

Oh, thank God.

I'd never have managed to explain that.

Time rushes past me like a tube train and my legs hurl me backwards, firing over the top of the crates at them. *Follow me. Shoot at the catalogues. No father's going to mourn a listing of expensive fluorescent dolls with only one leg. Shoot the crates over here, you silly bastards, you wannabe film stars.*

And they do.

I squeeze off a couple of shots at them, but they've found their own cover. More crates, more catalogues. Right now they seem to just be blazing away with their guns held sideways like they're in a music video. When they run out of bullets they'll probably chuck them at me. The trouble is, they're such rubbish shots, because of their crappy sideways gun shooting and their stupid unprofessional Tarantino mindset that thinks all they have to do is blaze away and the bullet will magically find its way into my face if they can only look cool enough doing it, that they're going to blow Katie's head off long before they put a hole in me.

It's time I got a little bit creative.

One of the advantages of being dead is that you can do things that people who aren't dead can't do. Actually, most people who are dead can't do them either, but never mind that for now. The important thing is that I can do them.

For example, my left hand – the one not sporadically pointing the gun over the crates and keeping them busy – is severed. It's held on with surgical wire.

I have no idea when this happened.

I mean, it must have been done after I woke up ten

years ago. Surely. Nobody living has their hand chopped off and stuck back on the stump with surgical wire.

I mean, you'd have to be insane.

What sort of person was I?

My memory is a little fuzzy on things like that – whether I'm insane or not. I do kill a lot of people.

And I do eat... occasionally, I do eat people's...

But I have better things to do right now than think about that.

I shoot off three or four rounds to keep them busy, then put the gun to one side and grip my left hand in my right. And I pull. I'm a lot stronger than the average person, even the alive ones. Since I feel no pain and never need to rest, my muscles can work much harder, strain much longer. The wire snaps easily, link by link, and my hand pops right off in a couple of seconds, like a limb off a Ken doll.

Now I'm holding my left hand in my right, feeling the dead weight of it. Only it's not dead. Well, it is, but it's still wriggling. Twitching. Flexing.

I can still move it.

I wiggle the fingers on my severed hand. I snap them, and the sound is like a dry twig snapping. Then I toss it over the wall of crates like a grenade – a hand grenade, ha ha. The fingers hit the floor first and skitter like the legs of a giant beetle. I can feel them tapping the concrete. And then – it's off. Racing across the concrete floor as the wannabe film star boys widen their eyes and make little gagging sounds in their throats. They know what kind of film they're in now. Oh yes.

I can feel it moving. I can feel the fingers tapping. I'm reaching to pick up my gun, but I know exactly where my other hand is. Moving quickly across the floor, skittering and dancing, a dead finger ballet. I can see it in my mind's eye. Is it me, drumming my fingers, that's propelling it along? Or is it my hand, moving further away from me now, a separate entity crawling and creeping on its own stumpy little legs?

The further away from me it gets, the more I think it's the latter.

The more it moves on its own.

That's pretty weird, if you think about it.

What sort of person was I?

I can still feel the fingers tapping, but I'm not directing it any more. It's close now. Skittering around the crates as they lower their guns and stare in horrified fascination. I can't help but hum to myself at moments like these.

Their house is a museum... when people come to see 'em... they really are a scree-um... the Addams Fam-i-ly.

Ba da da DUM.

It leaps.

I mentioned how strong I am. And when my hand is this far away from me... there's really no human impulses to hold it back. The fingers flex and push against the concrete and launch it forward like a grasshopper, onto the face of the nearest cinema tough-guy. He's in a film now, all right. He's in *Alien*.

Where's your Guy Ritchie now, you tosser?

Fingers clutch, sinking into cheeks. I can feel his lips against my palm, squashed, pleading desperately, trying to form words. I have no control over my hand, my evil hand. But I still enjoy feeling it squeeze... and *squeeze*... and squeeze... until the fingers plunge through the flesh and crack the bone, crushing the jaw, the thumb and the forefinger alone mustering enough pressure to punch through the temples, cracking the skull, sending ruptured brain matter seeping out of it.

Brain matter.

I've got better things to do than think about that.

My hand drops away, sticky with blood and juice, as the last one starts blazing away at it, shrieking like a little girl. He misses with every shot. It's a hard thing to hit, a scuttling hand, and besides he's probably still holding his gun sideways. I'm trying not to laugh, I really am...

Does that make me a bad person? Does that make me a monster?

What sort of person am I?

Crushing a man's face with my severed hand that crawls around on its own when I let it off the leash, that probably makes me a monster, I'll admit that. But I can be forgiven for the occasional chuckle at the death of a would-be child murderer. *The News Of The World* would canonise me.

His gun clicks out. He's fumbling for ammo. He's in a whole other world now, the silly bastard. There's nothing so important to him as killing that *thing* that's come scuttling around the corner of his little school-catalogue fort and broken everything he thinks is real into little pieces. He's forgotten everything else in the world, which is stupid, because *I'm* in the world.

And I'm coming for him.

Grab time. Slow it down. Gunshots flatten and stretch into whale songs and I'm floating, somersaulting over the crates, converse trainers smacking the ground, propelling me forward as the gun comes round...

And there aren't any bullets in the gun.

How did I miss that? The slide's all the way back.

Do I even have any ammo on me?

How could I possibly miss something like that?

What sort of person am I?

He's seen me. He turns like a cloud formation revolving in a light breeze. The gun lifts like the thermometer in an unsuccessful TV telethon, one atom at a time. So slow. But so am I.

That's the trouble with compressing time. It looks great, but there's no use in slowing time down if you're already too late.

The gun goes off, slow and beautiful as sunrise, and here comes the bullet. Cross-cut head this time. I throw my weight off, but he's too close...

You need a bit of space to dodge bullets.

I don't feel pain, but still, it hurts. It hurts because there's no real way to patch the holes up when I get shot. I've been shot a fair bit, although not as much as I should have with the life I lead. In my arms and legs there are little tunnels and trenches where I've been shot with 9mm ammunition, a couple of nasty exit wounds packed up with clay. In my left breast, there's a big ragged hole from where some crack shot tore my heart open with a well-placed sniper round. I stitched up the hole as best I could, packed it with gauze... but my heart is sitting in my chest, not beating and torn apart. And that does hurt.

Because I do try to know what sort of person I am.

I do try to be normal.

I really do, with my severed hand and my time senses and my strength and my speed. I try and be a normal guy, as much as I can. I drink. I eat. I go to the bathroom, though it's just to sit and think for a while – there's no pressing need for me to be there, if you get my meaning. I go to the cinema and watch the popular films. I get popcorn. I used to watch *Big Brother* but now I've stopped, like everyone else. I buy *The Sun* but I get my actual news from the Internet. I listen to Radio 2. I make up opinions about religion and music and television and political parties and I try to stick to them even if they aren't very logical or intelligent. I want to be like everyone else.

I want to fit in.

I try.

I can feel the bullet press against my gut, then pierce the skin, boring into me, fragmenting, splitting, shrapnel shredding my intestines, cutting and tearing. Slowly and carefully, like surgeons' scalpels in a random operation, the surgery dictated by the roll of dice.

My arm moves forward, pushing against time. It's like I'm underwater. The gun begins to arc slowly through the air, my empty, heavy gun. Rolling and tumbling through space.

Chunks of tattered, bloody meat drift out of the ragged hole in my lower back. My T-shirt has 'The Dude Has Got No Mercy' written across it, and it's brown with kind of seventies lettering in orange and white. It's my favourite shirt and it's ruined. My shirt's ruined. My belly's ruined, because I was stupid and this silly film star-wannabe bastard got off his lucky shot...

I watch the gun tumble through the air, turning over and over, like a space station on a collision course with a nameless, forbidding planet.

I threw it very hard. The sound of his skull fracturing is like a great slab of granite, big as the world, being snapped in half by cosmic giants. It's a good sound. It makes me feel better about my shirt.

Stitch that, bastard!

I let go, and time closes over me like the case for an old pair of spectacles. The moment passes, and I stumble for a couple of steps, feeling more meat slop out of my belly and back, more scraps on the floor. There's a hard thud as a hundred and fifty pounds of flesh that used to be a human being crashes onto the concrete.

I walk gingerly around the stacked crates and have

a look. His legs and arms are thrashing, his eyes rolled back in the sockets. His skull is cracked and bleeding. His fragile, fractured eggshell skull.

And the tasty yolk within.

And all of a sudden –

– all of a sudden my head is pounding and there's a hot metal taste in my mouth and I don't have anything better to do than think about –

brains

– and now it's later.

How much later? How much time has passed?

It feels like a long time.

Mr Tarantino, the film star, the silly bastard, he's still lying at my feet. His position's changed. Like he's been shaken about like a rag doll.

His head is... empty.

Hollowed out. The top of it missing, cranium tossed across the room, and there's something... something is clinging to my lips. To my tongue.

Something I've been eating.

The taste is still in my mouth.

And it tastes so good.

Time is still slow, still in my grip. I look to the left, and I see a small, terrified eye staring at me through a bullet hole in the side of a packing crate. The eye slowly closes, like a curtain majestically falling, then rising, opening again. Blinking.

There's a sound in my ears like lowing cattle. It's Katie's

sobbing. I wonder how much she saw?

I try to be normal. I really do. I try so hard.
But I just can't seem to stop eating brains.
And that's the sort of person I am.
I let go.
Time wraps around me like a funeral shroud.
And the moment passes.

CHAPTER TWO

One Lonely Night

Twenty-four hours and everything sucks.

That's my golden rule. I don't care if you've just been elected the Lifetime President of Diamond-Studded Blowjob Valley, all it takes is twenty-four hours and everything in your hands will turn back to shit.

Case in point – it's twenty-four hours after that damn warehouse job, when I put down a bunch of soulless little kidnapping pricks and rescued a little girl from being cut up and sent through the post piecemeal. I should be happy. I'm not happy. I'm stiff and cranky and guilty and I'm not happy at all, not one little bit.

Is it any wonder?

I got shot, which means I got careless. That hasn't happened in forever and it's not something I want to happen again. The reason I'm stiff is because I let my head get so far into the clouds that some gangster-wannabe with delusions of adequacy blew a hole in my belly. How would you feel after something like that?

I know, I know, you wouldn't feel anything, you'd be slowly drying on a cold concrete floor as various kinds of bacteria had a get-together in your soft tissues, I'm actually very lucky *blah blah blah.*

Humour me. A couple of pieces got blown out of me and went skittering across the floor. I had to stick them in my pocket – my own spine jangling around with the keys to my flat. Imagine how that felt. Not to mention I was sagging and slumping and wobbling all the way home, holding my ribcage straight by putting my hands in my pockets and keeping my arms locked.

I didn't feel normal, is what I'm trying to say.

I hate not feeling normal.

So I ended up gluing my spine back together with superglue. It looks okay if I wear a shirt, but it feels stiff, unnatural. Every time I shift my weight, it's a reminder of what I am. So I'm cranky.

I'm also cranky because I can't get my coffee. I mean, I drank it – I have a big jar of Gold Blend in the cupboard – but ten minutes after I swallowed it, most of it trickled out of the ragged hole in me and made a mess on my sofa. Normal people drink coffee, but I can't because I'm not normal. I can't even pretend to digest anymore.

So where does that leave me? No more eating. No more drinking. No bacon and eggs, no bourbon. No steak, no champagne. Not unless I want to go and sit in the bath and watch it all slop out of me again. No more Sunday dinner at somewhere classy like a Berni Inn or a Harvester, no more McDonald's or Burger King or KFC. No more doing what normal people do.

I haven't felt this low in a long time.

Is it any wonder I feel like this? Can you blame me?

I try so hard to be normal. I mean, here I am, sitting on my coffee-stained sofa, in a studio apartment full of carefully chosen crap. In the CD rack, I have Robbie Williams, Abba, Coldplay. A little Radiohead, before they got weird. Everything the Beatles ever did. The Kaiser Chiefs. It's all good music. It's all music that people like. The Sex Pistols. U2.

I'm a big fan of Pink Floyd.

They're very important.

You see how hard I'm trying?

The DVD shelf is above the TV. *The Godfather, Pulp Fiction, Schindler's List, Star Wars* – the old movies, not the new ones – *Lord Of The Rings, Trainspotting...* I mean, I don't watch them, I just own them. I've watched everything on there maybe once, if that, but they're all carefully arranged in alphabetical order to show how passionate I am about film and cinema.

I'm normal.

I am just like you.

Behind the bookcase with the DVDs and the CDs and the John Grisham, there's an attachè case with my guns and some other equipment.

I bought the last Harry Potter the week it came out. It's sitting next to a copy of *Ulysses* that I keep meaning to read but never get around to, and the *Lord Of The Rings* that I only read when the films came out.

I am just like you.

Except I'm leaking coffee out of a ragged, badly-patched hole in my stomach, and my spine is fused together with industrial-strength glue.

And I'm cold and I'm clammy and I don't breathe.

And sometimes I eat brains.

Is it any wonder I feel like this?

I'm sitting on my coffee-stained sofa and I'm stiff and I'm cranky and I'm guilty. Most of all I'm guilty. Because I remember that little girl.

Little Katie, kidnap victim, six years old. I remember her eyes. Blank, looking straight ahead, her chest hitching and heaving to get out a scream as I tore open the crate she was in and scooped her up. She didn't make another sound all the way back to her father.

Bellows was waiting in the driveway of his big fancy house, stood next to his big fancy car. He looked happy at first. Then he saw her and all the colour went from his face, flooding back in a deep, angry purple. Katie wasn't looking at him. She wouldn't look at him, or her mother. She was only little, but she understood.

Her Daddy had sent a monster after her.

Bellows reached out to take her out of my arms and she twisted loose, toppling down onto the gravel, scraping her knees and elbows. She scampered inside like a cornered rat and hid, making little snivelling, whining sounds.

Bellows looked at me like he was going to tear my head off right there.

"What did you do to her?"

I just looked at my shoes.

What's the normal reaction to that?

I was angry for a moment – *I bloody saved her life, you muppet* – but then it all drained away. What had I done to her? I'd torn off heads and eaten brains from skulls right in front of her. I'd turned into a monster and then brought her back to Daddy and made him a monster too. I'd traumatised her for life. Mr Bellows asked me to bring back Katie, and I brought back a shell.

I'd killed the Katie that used to be as surely as if I'd put a bullet in her.

Under the circumstances, it didn't feel right asking for money.

It didn't feel right doing this job anymore.

I want to work in an office, doing nothing to make nothing. I want to work in a factory that makes cardboard boxes, pressing the same brown shape out day after day. I want to work behind a bar full of people who don't care if I live or die so long as I pour them the right kind of overpriced lager.

I want to be normal.

I want to be just like you.

But the trouble with those jobs is that they don't make allowances. Next time you go to a job interview, try soaking your hand in ice water for three hours before you walk in the room. Grab the boss in a firm handshake. Say how excited you are to be there. Watch his eyes. It doesn't matter if you're the best education certificate printer on planet Earth, you're going home unemployed.

Nobody wants to hire a corpse.

Even if I get some work down at an abattoir or a skinning yard, somewhere they just don't care – and this is after spending thousands on false papers to fake that I've got a past – eventually, I'm going to slip. Go into a fugue state.

Eventually, I'm going to get hungry.

What happens then?

What happens when it's five o'clock quitting time and all I can hear is the thunk-thunk-thunk of the belt moving past me and everything else is silent because twenty people are lying on the cold concrete floor of the factory with empty heads... eyelids flapping over empty sockets because I ate their brains down to the eyeballs...

Maybe it's happened. I don't know. The first thing I remember is waking up in a cheap hotel in Mile End, cold, clammy and dead. Before that – nothing.

Maybe when I was alive I killed people all the time.

Maybe that's all I'm ever going to do.

And as if by magic, the phone rings with another job.

"Hello?"

The voice on the other end of the line is fat and

adenoidal, with a faint northern twang. It's Sweeney.

Detective Martin Todd of the drug squad, nicknamed 'Sweeney'. He'll tell you that's because he looks like John Thaw, but it's not – it's because he's always got his fingers in a lot of very dodgy pies. If the contents of the evidence locker find their way into the pockets of a bunch of South London hoodies, Sweeney's been there. If the lab report you needed to convict a local gangster gets shredded, chances are Sweeney was using the shredder at the time. If the man from Internal Affairs gets a phone call and drops the case before going off somewhere to piss himself – who was he investigating?

Well, who do you think?

Sweeney's a nasty customer, and I've done enough work for him to know. He's mean, sadistic, ruthless when his own interests are at stake, lazy when they're not – a King Rat festering in his own little empire of rubbish. He's my least favourite person to deal with. He pays well – well enough that I can forget about killing for a month or two and just pretend to be unemployed, like normal people are – but... the man's a monster.

He says he needs help. Usually he just needs 'a hand' with something, or he wants me to do him 'a favour'. But now he needs help. I pause for a second and he starts begging.

I've never heard Sweeney sound afraid.

"Please... please... you've got to help me... just get over here, okay? Right now. Please – I'll give you anything. Anything you want. Get over here."

Click.

Dial tone.

I still haven't said a word.

Ordinarily I wouldn't lift a finger for Sweeney without money up front, but this situation isn't ordinary. Sweeney is out of his mind with fear. Someone, or something, has managed to terrify the demon copper of Fleet Street.

There's probably good money in that.

I tell myself it's about the money, anyway, as I pay the cab fare and step out into the pissing, pouring rain. There's no other reason I'd be out on a night like this – the rain slapping down hard against the stonework, splashing and running in torrents off the gutters and pooling in the dips in the pavement, soaking me to clammy bones the second I step out of the taxi. It's just money. I don't give a damn if Sweeney lives or dies.

So why is my hand shaking as I walk up the street towards Sweeney's place? A terraced house on a good street, curtains drawn across the windows. Well-appointed from the outside. The kind of place that costs a pretty penny anywhere, but especially here in Central London. You could probably afford it on a copper's pay, but you couldn't afford the big, shiny Jag parked outside as well. The hammering rain just makes it look pricier – diamond-encrusted, a slick MTV pimp-ride in ostentatious cream. I shouldn't be afraid. It's Sweeney. It's a cash payment for whatever's crawled under his bed and spooked him. Good money, a couple of suitcases full of crisp notes. Enough to buy anything I want for a couple of months. A couple of months of being normal, being just like you...

Why is my hand shaking?

Even as it reaches out for the sleek black door with gold lettering – number 10, right in the centre just like in Downing Street, a joke of Sweeney's – my hand shakes, trembles. I shouldn't be afraid. It's Sweeney. Who cares if he's in trouble? Who cares if the door's been forced open, like someone hit it with a battering ram, if the lock's been forced, if it swings slowly open when my fingers bump it...

I shouldn't be afraid.

The door swings open.

It's Sweeney.

I see him right away. He's looking straight at me, from the end of the stairs.

I shouldn't be afraid.

Even though most of him is in another room, I shouldn't be afraid.

A man's head was torn off and mounted on the banister at the bottom of the stairs, mouth wide open with the wooden spike on top of the banister poking out of it. Eyes glazed and wide in shock and terror. But I've seen worse things. I've *done* worse things.

I shouldn't be afraid.

I wonder what went through his mind, as he tasted varnished wood on his tongue and felt his throat stretched wide by his own beautifully carved balustrade, felt the phantom agony of a body that wasn't there anymore. I wonder what kind of chemicals flooded through his brain when he realised what had happened to him, in the half-second before everything in there shut down. I wonder what they taste like.

Am I thinking these thoughts to torture myself?

Or distract myself?

Suddenly being normal doesn't seem to count for as much as being alive.

There's blood in the air, the hot reeking smell of it, and something else. Wet, sodden... hair? My nose twitches as my eyes follow the slick blood matted on the carpet, a wide trail leading through into the kitchen.

The rest of Sweeney's in there, pooled on the tiles. Arms and legs torn from sockets, a strip of skin hanging from the bloody ragged mess that used to be his neck. Ribcage open to the world like a plundered treasure chest.

The air is full of wet dog hair. You could swim in it.

Something's been at him.

Some great animal has been chewing on his guts, tearing and snapping at the offal of him, crunching bones and swallowing hunks of meat. You can see it just by looking. Some great thing like a bear – a *dog* – burst in, tore his head off and feasted on his liver and lights.

The blood is still running, still flowing. The edge of the charnel tide licks against the soles of my trainers.

Did I interrupt it?

Is it still here?

The drop of blood hanging from the tip of Sweeney's finger takes seven long years to hit the floor. Am I holding back time? No. No. This is something else.

This is *fear*.

I shouldn't be afraid. I shouldn't.

I turn away from the yawning meat-larder that used to be a man and move back to the hall. Sweeney's face gapes at me, fixed in the last scream he ever made. Blood trickles down the upright. I step closer, looking at Sweeney's scream. His wide, open mouth. His teeth.

His solid silver fillings.

The smell isn't dog hair.

It's *wolf* hair.

Run.

I leave the crime scene behind, charging out into the rain and the wet, moving as fast as my legs will carry me. Let the police find Sweeney. They'll have a parade. I just need to get as much space between me and that wet dog hair smell as possible. I run for the Tube.

I need to throw it off my scent.

Remember when I said I didn't have a smell? I'm pretty sure that's a defence mechanism. But there's smells and there's smells. Even in the wet pissing rain, skin soaked, clothes dripping, there are traces.

Even when I swipe the Oyster card and barrel down the escalator, hurling myself onto the northbound train just as it pulls out, safe in my metal box with the stares of the passengers feeling like a baptism... there are ways.

Even while I'm slumped in my seat, dripping and draining, little rivers running in the grooves in the floor, I don't feel safe. Even at this speed, moving under the city in an electrified tunnel, I don't feel safe.

The silence of my heart is burning in my ears.

My hands are shaking as I fumble for my keys. I'm terrified. I should be.

I'm primed for a wave of wet wolf hair to engulf me as I open the door, but there's nothing. *Thank you, Jesus, thank you, God, whatever God could make a thing like me, thank you, thank you, thank you...*

Fingers scrabbling at the loose floorboard – no time for finesse, just punch through the wood and rip it out. The sniper rifle behind the DVDs is no use here – this is the time for the secret stash, the emergency weapons, the things I stocked and hoarded because I knew trouble was going to find me someday.

Just not trouble like this.

There's a bag containing passports for seven countries and fifty thousand Euros in cash, along with a few other papers and pieces of information I might have a use for.

Everything I need to get out of the country. And I need to get out of this country, for good, for ever. If what I think is true, it's run or die.

There's a loaded sawn-off shotgun next to the bag, in case I need to shoot my way out of trouble. Next to that...

...my oldest, most treasured possession. Something from before. It was waiting for me in a left-luggage locker when I finished my killing-tour of the bed-and-breakfasts of London just after I woke up dead – *why? Not important now* – old and shiny, with the scent of somewhere far away and long ago.

A katana. A samurai sword.

I keep it sharp. I keep it hidden. I keep it safe. It was very important once, to the person I used to be. And no matter where I go, I keep it with me.

That sword belongs to me. I'm not leaving it behind no matter how dangerous this gets. To hell with customs, I'll blag my way around it. Anyway, I might need it.

It's been fifty-two seconds since I walked in the door and I've got everything I need to disappear for good. Start again in Paris, or Munich, or Madrid – I can learn the language. I'm good with languages, dialects, accents. Just drop me in a crowd of people and I'll pick it up like magic. I can blend in. I love blending in. Blending in is like crack to me.

One last look, and out.

That flat was good to me. I had a nice collection of DVDs, some nice CDs. I was working through a Tom Clancy novel. I felt normal there. But I have to go.

I speed down the stairs two at a time, down to the ground floor. The sword is bouncing against my shoulder blades, the bag smacking against my side, the gun in my hand. If the coast's clear I'll put it in the bag and get a taxi to the airport. Get on the first plane going anywhere.

Open the door.

A gust of wind and rain blows in my face, carrying the stench of sopping, soaking wet dog hair.

The lightning cracks across the sky, illuminating something much larger than a man. A massive predator, eight or nine feet, coated in dense, shaggy fur. Its breathing is like some terrible bellows in the furnaces of hell. It snorts and flexes, moving muscles much greater and more powerful than any human being could have.

I have a vague memory of a man who killed a tiger. Or something like a tiger. I remember the tiger as all strength and power, coiled tension in each muscle, eyes deep and unfathomable. Every movement it made seemed to come from some primal animating force, some extension of life itself.

I don't remember exactly when I saw the man kill the tiger, but I remember what reminded me of it. I was sitting in a library killing time before killing people and I was flipping through some school-approved book of poetry – one of those big collections of important poems edited by Seamus Heaney or Blake Morrison or some heavyweight like that, that they hand out to A Level or Uni students to be roundly ignored.

I generally don't 'get' poetry – I'm just like you, remember? – but I found something in there by William Blake.

He was trying to describe what was in the tiger.

All this crashes through my mind in this one instant, as I look at this thing that is not a tiger, that could never be a tiger. If the tiger was filled with some primal life, this is filled with death. Every shift of muscle and flesh is calling out decay, disease, the nightmare on the dark side of creation.

This creature is anti-life, primal, terrible and old.

This is the ultimate killer, the monster that kills and eats the flesh of the dead, born and bred for that purpose.

I feel its name in the back of my mind like ice as it stares into me with red eyes, baring its fangs. Saliva hits the tarmac.

This is what will kill me.

This is *werewolf*.

CHAPTER THREE

Killer in The Rain

It's so fast.

I'm holding time as still as I can – gripping it until the knuckles of my mind bleed and the world becomes a silent place filled with statues, and still it's so fast that by the time I get my shotgun up it's almost too late.

Almost.

The force of the blast knocks it back a step, the pellets drifting lazily into the furry flesh of its chest, drilling and pushing, the impacts turning the flesh into soup as they push the monster back. I don't stay to watch beyond that. I've already let go of the gun, and the bag full of passports and money and all the other useless crap that's only going to slow me down. Only the sword on my back stays.

I break left and run.

Really run.

I don't ever feel pain. I don't ever get tired. I'm stronger and more resilient than living human beings. My muscles don't tear. My tendons don't snap. The small bones in my feet don't break from the impact against the pavement.

I can run.

Time is locked down so tight that a hummingbird would barely move, but I move. I pound forward, pushing against treacle gravity, knowing that the beast behind me is already healed, the liquid soup of its chest knitted back into fur and flesh, saliva dripping and spattering in expectation of the kill.

I know that every step I can put between me and it is crucial.

The pavement flows under my feet like water. How fast am I moving? It feels like fifty miles an hour, maybe more, but I have time in my grip, every second stretched and pulled like toffee and I know that to the endless parade of statues I must seem like a blur.

This is harder than I've ever pushed before. *Ever.* I know that with a cold certainty. I've seen so many films where the dead people shuffle and creep, and then a few years ago they started making new films where the brain-eaters and corpses run and sprint. The first time I saw one of those was in a cinema, and you should have heard the gasps, the screams, the girls clutching at boys and the boys too caught up to even notice... this was terror. This was shock. A corpse running.

Oh, you sweet, naïve cinema couples. If you only knew.

If you only knew how fast we can move when we have to.

This is really running. The speed I'm going now... this is superhuman. This is beyond the capabilities of anyone on Earth.

And it's not enough.

Let me tell you about werewolves.

According to legend, werewolves feed on the flesh of the dead. Groups of them, congregating under the silver moonlight, claws digging in grave-dirt, ripping up wood and nails and tearing at the rotting flesh in the cold coffins, maggots dripping from muzzles...

It'd be crazy to believe that. To think that packs of feral, half-human monsters are swarming over the landscape somewhere, creeping and clawing at fresh-turned earth, tearing at funeral-suits and best-Sunday dresses, snapping and swallowing chunks of foetid meat like alligators. You'd have to be insane.

But the gut, she makes her own rules. Deep down in the pit of your stomach, you know it's true. Every time you see a full moon, you wonder if buying that house near the churchyard was such a good idea, if one bright moonlit night you won't look out of your upstairs window and see dark shapes swarming between the stones, see the funeral wreath flying into the air, hurled aside by brutish paws as the sound of panting and snuffling and snarling reaches your ears... and then the howl of the wolf.

Got you wondering, hasn't it?

You're lucky. I don't have to wonder. I know.

There's a dark world outside and above the one David Attenborough points his camera at, a strange and terrible supernature where the laws don't apply. But some things never change – there are predators and there are prey. For every animal, there's another animal that's evolved to eat it.

You think werewolves have those snapping jaws to deal with bodies in graves? That those swiping claws are the result of millions of years of coffin lids that needed tearing open? That those pulsing, straining muscles that can tear through steel are for mausoleum gates? They evolved them to deal with the dead – the dead that runs and climbs and escapes, the dead that is to man what the werewolf is to the tiger.

The werewolf is a natural zombie-killer.

Converse trainers pounding on wet-slick streets, teeth gritted, straining and powering myself forward even as the realisation comes that I am straining, that I am pushing myself, that God help me, God-who-would-make-a-thing-like-me help me, *I'm getting tired...*

Is this what it feels like for you? That burning acid feeling in the muscles, that weakness at the joints? The fatigue creeping through you, at long last not pretend or affected? The sense that any second could be your last and when it comes, that's it? Dead for real this time, for ever and ever, rotting in the ground until even your million-year-old bones fall into the sun and burn to nothing?

I hope so. I hope this is how it feels.

Because even now, with the end of all that I am one split-second from my heels, I want to be normal. I want to be just like you.

But that doesn't mean I want to die all over again just yet.

Somehow, my arm finds the strength to reach up and grip the sword hilt at my back. Drawing it feels like lifting a caber made of solid steel in some bizarre Scotland's Strongest Man semi-final.

My legs are on fire, and I can feel the werewolf's presence at my back, the hot sour breath of death on my neck. London streets flickering past me in fast forward, my last sight on Earth. I'm too tired to swing.

But I don't have to swing.

I jerk left, stopping dead, converse trainers smoking in a skid on the wet tarmac, the sword held out at my right, steadied with both hands, edge facing back. The monster is as fast as me. It's heavier. Stronger. But it doesn't have my sense of time.

So its reflexes aren't as good as mine.

Seven hundred pounds of fur and sinew slams into a razor sharp edge and for a brief second I think the sword is going to break, but whoever made it made it sharper than that. It cuts clean, slicing into skin, fur, the muscle of the belly. I feel the jerk in my hand as it cleanly snips through the spine and with it, a strong rush of dèja vu that almost makes me forget where I am. I've never used this sword on a man before. Have I?

But anyway, this isn't a man.

Two werewolf-halves tumble forward into the rain, still connected by a thick spray of rich, red blood. With time gripped so strong in my mind, they look like grotesque helium balloons from an obscene novelty shop, their incredible momentum carrying them still forward, floating gently as the beast makes a last furious swipe, claws passing an inch from my open eyes.

I killed it. I cut it into pieces.

Impossible.

I hold time fast and move to a ready position with the sword. If I have to, I can cut off the head, the hands, whatever needs to be done to finish it. Split the skull. My mouth waters involuntarily at the thought. God help me.

I watch.

I watch the charnel-carnival balloons drifting and tumbling through the air, the wolf howling, an elongated call of rage and pain and savage hate that hits my ears like whale song. The bottom half of the monster collapses onto its knees, scraping the flesh down to the bone and beyond. The blood gushes from the clean-cut ends, great pulsing gouts of deep red, seeming thicker by the second.

Thicker and thicker.

No.

I watch as the blood seems to clot even as it runs, making thick ropes between the top and bottom halves. I don't dare to let go of time. I don't dare stop watching.

Oh, no. No. Please. This isn't fair.

The top and the bottom are connected now by a conduit of thick, pulsing red, drawing the two halves back together like elastic until they finally meet like ships docking in a science-fiction film. I watch the spine fuse first, a cluster of nerve endings rising like slithering tendrils from the base before the bone ends click into place like Lego.

My feet are glued to the floor. I can't move.

The muscles knit together like wicker, reweaving themselves. Organs slither back into place. The skin reseals and new fur pushes through the fine line of bare flesh where the cut once was. I almost don't notice the knees repairing themselves.

In subjective time, it takes less than a minute.

Which means the creature healed fully from being sliced in half within a split second.

I'm in trouble.

It turns. Looks at me with eyes like red coals burning in the lowest depths of hell.

It knows what I tried to do to it.

It knows I failed.

I can't decide whether the leer of its fangs is born from hate or triumph.

Then my feet come to life again.

And I run.

I travel, occasionally. It's one of the nice things about shooting people in the head, the travel. You can wind up in Sao Paulo, or Rome, or Schenectady. Security's more of a headache these days, but there are always ways around that. Often it's easier to travel by coffin, as some dead national of the country in question, being flown back for a burial on home soil. Who's going to crack open a coffin to check whether or not he might have seen the corpse somewhere before? So long as the paperwork holds up, it's foolproof.

It was in Berlin – cold Berlin, with its stone and its iron, in the depths of winter.

I was killing time, waiting to garrotte an industrialist in a penthouse apartment somewhere in what was once East Berlin. Acting like a tourist, looking at the remnants of the wall and eating terrible, poorly-cooked wurst from vans that catered to those who didn't know any better. Blending in.

I looked at the inscriptions on the wall fragments and then turned around to put the wrapper and the unfinished wurst in the bin. And halted. And froze.

A man was looking at me.

This was one face in a crowd of hundreds passing along the street. He was short, and skeletal, and completely bald – no eyebrows, even. It was as though someone had taken the foetus of some huge predatory bird and fastened it into a suit. Even across the street, his eyes shone, yellow and sickly around the pupils. I remember his suit was the same sickly yellow as his eyes.

He smiled. His teeth were long and as yellow as his eyes, the gums receded. He ran a long tongue across them, then simply grinned like a skull.

I'd been afraid before. Afraid of failure, afraid of arrest and incarceration, afraid of disappointing the client, afraid of being found out, being caught, exposed, not fitting in. But this was the first time I'd ever been afraid for my life.

I hailed a taxi and told the driver to head straight to the airport. It was just past noon, and already the light was beginning to fade, and as the taxi wound slowly across the icy roads, the driver chatting amiably in backwoods German, I could see the full moon already visible beyond the clouds. By the time I'd talked my way onto the first plane heading for Heathrow, the darkness had fallen.

I sat in my window seat, looking out over the runway, feeling foolish despite the slow curdling of my gut. I'd let the client down and run away with my tail between my legs – and for what? Because a chemo patient had grinned at me in a way I didn't like?

I was cursing myself as the plane rumbled towards the runway, and by the time the acceleration sat me back heavily in my chair and the engine roar became a scream, I'd resolved to go straight back in the morning and do the job for nothing. Disappointing the customer like that was unforgivable.

And then I looked out of the window.

Something was coming across the airfield towards the plane. It was nine, perhaps ten feet tall, an immense mass of muscle and fur and purpose. Its eyes shone a sickly yellow in the half-light, and foam ran from its muzzle. I only saw it for an instant.

Around its waist were the shredded remains of a pair of yellow suit trousers.

I fully believe that if it had caught up to the plane, it would have torn it open like a tin can to get hold of me, and if the whole aeroplane had gone up in a ball of fire, it would have walked right through the inferno to get hold of me.

As the plane rose into the air, I could hear a monstrous howl of anger and frustration following it. I never returned to Berlin.

The acid burning in my muscles is stronger now. I run back the way I came, through the silent, motionless mannequins, ready to come to life the moment I let go of time. Some of the mannequins are headless, some bodiless, just a pair of legs slowly beginning to buckle. Their only crime was to get in the way of the monster.

Some of the heads have had pieces swiped out of them. I run past a girl with a bright smile and one sparkling eye. The other is missing along with a chunk of skull. She's dead, and she'll need a closed coffin, but there hasn't been time for it to register yet. In this moment, she still has her whole life ahead of her. She's maybe on her way to meet her parents, to tell them about some new man in her life, or maybe she's going out for an evening with friends. Somewhere there are four women sitting around a table in a pub with two small white wines, a lime and soda and a vodka and tonic, waiting for their friend to arrive. And they'll keep waiting, and texting, and wondering why she's blown them off, and maybe they'll check the news and find out about the bloody swathe of horror running the length of Tottenham Court Road –

Tottenham Court Road.

I forgot where I was.

I grit my teeth and turn hard right, hoping there aren't too many people in Oxford Street. I need space to move now. I focus past the burning in my muscles, the straining of the bone tissue, the new sensations of tiredness and fatigue. I have to get some distance from the wolf if I'm going to pull this off.

I duck and weave between the late-night shoppers. In my head, I'm asking absolution from everyone I pass. It doesn't want them. It wants me.

I could save dozens of lives by stopping dead right now. By letting it take me.

I could.

But I won't.

Sometimes I feel like I'm dead inside as well as out. How could I do this otherwise?

Halfway down now and turning into a shopping arcade with what I need in it. It's open late – thank God, thank whatever God would make a thing like me – and everything's still on display.

I stop dead, trainers smoking again. This time I don't pull any tricks with the sword – I'm not going to catch it the same way twice. Instead, I swing my fist into the window of the shop, reaching through a curtain of shattered glass shards, the edges scoring my flesh as I grab for the window display.

I don't know how long I have to live now. Less than a second.

I hear the jewellery store alarm ringing, low and slow, like the tolling of a funeral bell. My hand scrabbles over the glittering knick-knacks and gewgaws, grabbing a gleaming necklace and wrapping it around my knuckles, checking the card to make sure it's what I need. I'm desperate and this is a gamble – these days, you're more likely to find platinum or gold pieces in a jewellery store window.

But occasionally, you can still find something silver.

I feel something on my shoulder – a hand, now, a paw, gripping with enough force to crack the bones of a normal man, spinning me around so fast that even with time slowed to nothing I'm staring into those dripping, grinning jaws before I know it. I have a split-second, a nanosecond, a picosecond before my guts are on the floor and my head is crunching in its mouth. It's that fast.

But I react faster.

My right arm swings out in a hard punch, with all my strength behind it. The silver necklace is wrapped around my fingers like a knuckleduster. There's a crunch as my fist buries in its chest, cracking the sternum to fragments. The monster needs a massive heart to fuel that massive engine of a body. My fist fits inside it. I can feel it pumping for a moment before it stops dead.

Silver in the heart.

I let go of time, and it crashes back around me like an angry tide.

The air fills with screams, alarms, the sound of shattering glass. I feel horrified eyes on me and know that my life has changed.

The monster twitches, jerking and shuddering like a palsy victim, the foam from its jaws flowing with ever-multiplying flecks of red. The glowing red coals of its eyes burn brighter for a second before they roll back into the head. The wound I've made in its chest bubbles and festers, green pus flowing. It's not going to heal from this.

I let go of the necklace and the beast tumbles backward, pulling off my hand like a wet sock. I watch it thrash and twitch on the ground, blood and pus spreading over the floor, the muscles eaten away before my eyes, the flesh falling from the face and jaw in clumps, the suppurating chest hole actually smoking with the force of the reaction.

It's so fascinating, I don't notice the sniper who's been crouched at the other end of the arcade. The gunman who's actually used a werewolf rampage as a distraction, as a goad to get me to go where he wants me. Who programmed the monster to keep me running right where he wanted me.

All I hear is the *phut* of a silenced weapon and then a long needle embedding in the back of my skull.

Thunk.

I don't have time to blink before whatever he's shot into me comes to life. It burns and buzzes and hums, and my hands are shaking too badly to reach up and pull it out, and the buzzing intensifies, building and building, harsher and shriller until

it reaches a pitch

so harsh and shrill that it is

inconceivable

And the last thought that runs through my mind before I feel the flesh of my brain shredding in my skull is:

Whodunnit?

CHAPTER FOUR

Nemesis

First comes smell

Old, wet stone. Age. Cobwebs and dust. Something like rotted food. Metal, some wet, some rusted, some brand new. Ancient wood.

I knot my brow – the same brow I felt shredding like confetti when that whatever-it-was went off at the back of my skull. I reach up to feel what's left of my face, but something stops me – cold metal chains at my wrists, taking my weight.

Second, then, comes feeling.

Sound is third. The drip, drip, drip of water filtering through stone. Soft well-made shoes gently tapping against the cold stone floor. Pacing and scuffing. A filter tip burning as he inhales. The rattle of the chains.

I decide to go for the grand prize and open my eyes.

I'm in a dungeon.

An actual dungeon. Cold water dripping down ancient stonework, wooden benches, torture implements lined up on the wall... there's even a skeleton dangling from a set of rusted chains on the opposite wall. A spider crawls slowly in one eye socket and out the other. I don't think anyone picked that up from a doctor's surgery.

And right in the centre of the room, we have the person responsible. Not too tall – about five-eight – but stocky. Lots of muscle there, and by the way he's carrying himself he knows how to use it. Stands like a boxer – cauliflower ear on the left side of his head, broken nose... I'd lay money whoever's running this operation picked him out of a gym somewhere. It's been a while since he's been in the ring, though – he's put on a little weight, and I can't remember a boxer with a Tom Selleck like that. Black hair, steel-grey eyes, all the wrinkles around his face say he spends most of his time pulling intimidating expressions.

Armani suit. Three-piece, very fancy. He might not be the man at the top, but he's certainly high up.

The Boxer's noticed me looking at him, and he looks back. There's something sardonic in his eyes – a sense that this is business as usual. That all of this – the werewolf, the sniper, the whole complicated plan to get me out of hiding and into a dungeon – that it's all another day at the office.

I'm not sure I like him.

"Back in the land of the living, Mr Doe? Or is it the land of the dead?"

He doesn't smile at his joke. I decide not to either, or dignify it with a pithy comment of my own. Instead I start yanking my left hand against the cuff of the chains, hoping to pop the stitches. See how many jokes this bastard feels like making with his guts coiled around my fingers. But the stitches refuse to pop. It feels different, somehow.

I look up to my hand, and the wrist is whole – completely healed. My skin even looks slightly pinker, although I may be imagining it.

I tug experimentally against the manacle. How did that happen?

The Boxer snorts derisively. He's got a throaty voice – a slightly upmarket Ray Winstone. His teeth are yellowing, nicotine-stained, with a gold molar at the back of his mouth.

"An unfortunate side-effect of the weapon we used to take you down. The dart puts out a localised electromagnetic pulse – simulates your body's own reset system to shut you down for long enough to get you here."

What the hell is he talking about?

Stall for time. I try to sound like this is all as mundane for me as it is for him, but I can feel the quaver in my voice.

"So where's here?"

The Boxer snorts again. I'm starting to hate the sound of that – if you could buy pure contempt in spray form, that's the sound it'd make coming out – but I'm not in a position to tear the top off his skull yet.

There's probably not enough there for a decent meal anyway.

"You're underneath the Tower Of London, it might interest you to know. There's a lot of history here, Doe. Both official and otherwise. We've had quite a number of your sort down here." He walks over to the wall, making a show of lifting down some ancient cast-iron pair of pincers, most likely used to tear the extremities off enemies of the crown. I almost smile.

"You're not going to get much out of me with that..."

He snorts again. I'm really getting the impression he doesn't like me. "We have our ways and means, Sonny Jim. We've been dealing with people like you for some considerable time and let me inform you that when it comes to kicking your undead knackers in, we're the experts."

"People like me?"

"Zombies. The walking dead. Those that have snuffed it but refuse to shuffle off this vale of tears until they've made my life a total bleeding misery. We've known about you lot for centuries, but only in recent times have we got a better idea of exactly what you were and developed the means to study you, give you the kicking you filthy bastards clearly deserve and finish you off for good. Previously, we made do with the latter. Set the Wulves on you."

I don't like where this is heading.

"Wolves?"

"Generally spelled with a U. Werewolves to the general public. We breed 'em." He shoots me a look, a little evaluation. "Shat yourself, did you?"

There's no point in lying.

"You would too if one of those things was trying to tear you to pieces."

He snorts. This time it's laughter.

"Too bloody right I would. But as luck would have it, they're bred to hunt and kill disgusting abominations like you and not god-fearing Londoners like me."

"I'm a Londoner..." I regret it as soon as it slips out – it sounds weak and defensive and all it does it make him look at me like I'm the last piece of crap in the doggy bin.

"You're the furthest thing from a Londoner there is, sunshine. Whereabouts were you when you woke up for the first time? Place and date."

I remember exactly where I was. A Travelodge in Muswell Hill.

"London. Muswell Hill. Ten years ago today."

He snorts again, like I've just told him the Earth was flat, or Lee Harvey Oswald acted alone, or Ann Coulter is a beacon of truth in the murky world of the liberal media. This isn't going well. I keep looking at the skeleton. The spider's built a web over one of the eye sockets.

"Bollocks it was. What's happened here, Sonny Jim, is your defence mechanism went into overdrive after what you did to Emmett Roscoe. The tossers in the lab coats call it 'chameleon syndrome', but I personally call it being a cunt."

I get a sinking feeling. I've never met an Emmett Roscoe. I don't think I've ever even shot an Emmett Roscoe.

Have I?

"What did I do to Emmett Roscoe?" I don't bother hiding my curiosity, but all I get in response is a grunt. At least he didn't snort.

"What didn't you do, you filthy little bastard. I'll give you this, you're a holy terror when you're roused."

I blink, not sure if I've heard him right.

"Are you sure you've got the right man?"

"The right festering bloody corpse, you mean? I don't know, let's have a look at my bloody scorecard! You don't breathe, check, your heart doesn't beat, check, you can move severed body parts by remote control in a way that personally repulses me, checkity fucking check, you eat brains, big fat tick in that box – what a shock! You are John Rigor Mortis Doe and I claim my five pounds!"

I nod. I'm trying to think my way out of this one, but nothing's coming. The chains are too strong for me to break, and with my wrist inexplicably healed up I can't work my hand off and set it going. I'm out of options.

He leans in, eyes locking. He's more than a little bit too intense for my liking.

"Let's start again from the beginning since you're acting like you never went to school. Point one – how would you feel, Sonny Jim, if I told you there'd been others like you? Other zombies?"

How would I feel? Shocked and curious. Wanting to know more. Off-balance – I woke up five minutes ago in the company of a skeleton and the Marquis de Sade's toolbox, and now I'm having a surreal conversation filled with rhetorical questions with a man who has a chip on his shoulder the size of Stonehenge and more knowledge about me than anyone I know, including me. How would *you* feel?

"I don't know."

"There's a shock. Point two. How would you feel if I told you – again – that we'd been hunting them down for centuries?"

I didn't take it in when he said it before. He's making sure I get the message. He's got me.

The skeleton catches my eyes again. There's a fly struggling in one of the eye-socket webs, and I know how it feels. The spider crawls casually across the dome of the skull, taking its time, in no hurry... I wince, racking my brains. This must be what it's like to have a headache. I hear myself stumbling around in the dark.

"You said. You hunt... people like me. You bred that werewolf."

"Werewolves, plural." He chuckles again, almost a snigger this time. "We've got five pure-blood werewolves down in the cells. We had as many as fifty thoroughbreds back in the seventeenth century, but demand has fallen. There's just you now. The last remaining zombie as far as we're aware. Numero Uno on the endangered species list. Point being, right now your pasty rotting arse belongs to me."

He can read the expression on my face – the instinctive shock and fear, to know that there are *five* of them, and *in the building* – like five ticking bombs, or five deadly tarantulas, or five flesh-eating viruses in the air – five of those *things* just a cell door away, when even one would be enough to finish everything...

He reads my expression. I read his. It says I'm pond scum as far as he's concerned.

"I thought that might make you shit a brick. I'm pretty sure that's not the first time you've had a run-in with one of our little pets, although since you're a cunt as I mentioned earlier, you won't remember it. Still, that's probably why you left a brown trail all the way down Oxford Street. You knew Fido could kill you. You're ready to piss your knickers right now because you know, for a certainty, that there is one thing on this planet that can end your miserable attempt at a life, and we've got five of them waiting downstairs, waiting for us to cut you into meaty chunks and serve you up like Winalot – *bloody settle down!*"

I didn't even realise I wasn't settled, but he's right. I'm tugging against the cuffs without thinking, thrashing, trying to break out – all it's doing is getting this sadistic bastard's gander up even further... I force myself to stop. This isn't getting me anywhere. "Why don't you stop being a smart-arse?" I snarl, trying to sound threatening.

It just sounds pathetic. He knows it.

The spider reaches the fly.

I swallow, and then shake my head. Resigned. "You said you know what I am. That's more than I do."

The Boxer snorts again – *if he does that again*, I think, and feel impotent – and says nothing at all. I sigh like a petulant child.

"Go on, spill it. You're going to feed me to those hairy bastards downstairs, you can tell me now. I want to know." I'm wheedling. He just glowers. His voice, when it comes, is cold as stone.

"I just bloody bet you do."

He gives a smile that isn't a smile, just a twitch at the corners of his mouth. It looks like nothing so much as a dog about to tear apart a piece of meat put in front of it. He reaches into the pocket of his suit, pulling out a mobile phone, or something like it.

"As long as one of you is still functioning, the plan

goes ahead, doesn't it? Did you honestly think I'd forget what I was talking to, you filthy rotting git? Roscoe forgot. We know what happened to him. Roscoe told you what you were. In bloody meticulous detail. Poor bastard. Apparently he was some sort of genius, although if you ask me his judgement was more than a little faulty. He actually thought you gave a toss if he lived or died." The Boxer scowls, eyes like stone. There's nothing in them but hate. "The poor stupid bastard. He thought you were friends."

I've never met an Emmett Roscoe.

Never.

"You've got the wrong man." You can hear the desperation in my voice, the cold knowledge of just how bad this is going to get. He grits his teeth, that gold tooth flashing under the cold fluorescent light...

"If you keep on bloody whining I'll give you something to whine about. We are past the stage when I talk to you like you're a human being. You're a bleeding monstrosity and you're not getting out of this building alive, just so we understand each other. But before we feed you to the dogs I'm going to ask you some simple questions, if you think you can concentrate on something other than being a tosser for two minutes. I'll tell you right now, this can be easy or hard, but I am definitely leaning towards hard."

"You do know I don't –"

He lunges, and the thing in his hand sparks blue light.

The pain is gigantic.

It's like a capacitor, but much more powerful, and it doesn't even touch me – it just gets close to my ribcage, and the bone flexes, then flows like melting wax, bending like a magnetic field. Is this what it would be like for muscle and bone and flesh to shift, to stretch, to melt?

I don't know, but I can feel it right through me, right in my head, like he's pushing that thing into my mind and making my thoughts come to pieces...

...and for the first hundred thousand years it seems like the worst thing in the world, but then it gets worse...

...and by the time he pulls the device back and my flesh and bone and spirit begins to work back into the rightful place I've invented new cosmologies and pantheons to describe the pain and the agony and the horror of having your body and soul warped like clay...

...and I don't even believe it when it ends.

I can't speak.

I suck back drool and swallow the bile rising in my throat. My cheeks are wet.

The Boxer growls. His gold tooth glints.

"That was a starter. Give me any more shit and we're onto the main course."

I want to die, or stop existing, or whatever it takes to remove the memory of that pain. I hurl myself against the chains, beyond speech, beyond anything but a desire to get away, to escape, looking and feeling like an animal caught in a trap. The Boxer waits.

Eventually, I stop struggling. He waits until I've stopped even twitching, until I'm hanging limp in the shackles. Until we both know where we stand.

I never want to go through that again.

The Boxer clears his throat.

"Now that you've finished your interpretive dance, I've got your starter for ten. Think carefully."

He goes silent. In the eye socket of the skeleton, the fly struggles and thrashes as the spider liquefies its insides. It's a minute before he breaks that silence, and by that time I'm willing to tell him anything. Give up anyone I've ever cared about, sell out my neighbours, plant bombs in crowded places, anything, anything to stop him doing that again –

And then the bastard clears his throat and waits a little longer.

Finally, he speaks. I strain my ears.

"When is the time?"

When is the what?

"I'm sorry?"

He reaches out again. This time pushing the thing at my mouth.

There's a blue spark.

It lasts hundreds of thousands of millennia, infinite gulfs of galactic time. Civilisations rise and fall. Planets coalesce out of dust. The quantum throws up new universes, billions and billions of years long, one after another. And all through that, my face and skull is melting and warping, distorting and dripping off my skull, which softens and collapses in on itself like wax... and all my preconceived notions of self burn and blacken and fall to ash and despair... for ever and ever, world without end.

There's a part of my mind that tells me all this only lasts for four or five seconds. But it's like a mouse chirping in a thunderstorm. The agony is eternal and endless.

But it does end.

I make a bubbling noise, like melting fat, as my face begins to reform. I think I might go insane if he did that again.

He waits.

"What..." It's all I can manage.

He snorts again.

"Since you ask, it's the same kind of technology that put you down earlier. A microscopic electromagnetic pulse – disrupts your cellular cohesion and generally fucks up your day something rotten. Also has an interesting effect on your temporal senses and your cover personality, or so the lads in the white coats tell me. Personally I couldn't give a toss. Just so long as it hurts."

"Cellular...?" I'm barely coherent, but I don't think he'd make sense even if I could focus. Something's seriously wrong with this guy. I'm dead. That's all. Just your average walking dead man.

I'm not that... complex.

Am I?

"Don't bother your little head, Sonny Jim. Your cover personality won't let you understand it even if I told you, so you might as well lie back and think of England." He looks up at me. "You may have forgotten what you are, Doe, but I bloody haven't and you're not pulling your shit here. Now it's time for round two. Lets see if you can win the set of steak knives."

He clears his throat. *Oh God. Oh God, oh God-that-would-make-me, please...*

"When is the time?"

I don't know. I don't know what he means. I don't know anything. Jesus, just tell him something, tell him a time, any time –

"Fuh. Four o'clock. Tuesday. Tuesday four o'clock PM."

He scowls. His eyes are like ice. Grey ice.

"Are you sure?"

"I swear. Please. Tuesday afternoon, four o'clock. That's the time."

He shakes his head.

"Do you think I rode into work this morning on a chocolate fucking digestive, you lying little bastard?"

I start crying.

"*Stop bloody bawling!*" He bellows it, genuinely aggrieved. "Jesus fucking Christ! I didn't expect you to tell me the truth, and I don't expect you to act like a human bloody being but you could act like a *fucking adult!*"

I look up at him, shaking my head, unable to speak. I don't want to act like an adult. I want to beg. I want to fall onto my knees and plead. I want to lick his boots. I want to say and do anything I need to say and do to end this.

Is he *enjoying* it?

His voice is like a block of ice.

"Now listen here, you filthy little bastard. You can stop pretending to yourself that you're the hero in this little adventure story because, believe me, you are anything but. What you are is an inhuman undead piece of shit pretending to be a human being. You eat human beings brain-first and you want to kill every living thing on this bloody planet! And by the time I am finished with you you are going to tell me every one of your horrible plans for the human species so we can finally grind you up and serve you for dinner with a fucking Waldorf Salad! Capeesh?"

I shake my head. I'm not like that. I'm not some monster.

I'm just like you.

I try so hard.

I swear.

Please.

"Tough shit. Ding ding, round three, question fucking one. Either take off that fucking mask you've superglued onto yourself or take your fucking medicine."

Please.

Please.

"And at least take it like a man. Come on, spit it out, you little toerag."

Please.

"Fuck it! Time's up."

This time, he goes for my groin.

I scream so loud and so hard I think my throat is going to explode, and the scream lasts one hundred, thousand, million, billion... imagine someone driving a cricket bat layered with razor-wire into your most sensitive parts at one thousand miles per hour, while making you believe that you are worthless and ugly and pathetic and unloved, down to the very lowest core of your being. Imagine physical and existential nausea and agony flowing through every single cell of your body.

Imagine your dick melting like wax and running onto the floor.

And imagine that lasting until the end of time.

Imagine being trapped in Hell.

Just because he can, he keeps the button pressed. Ten seconds. Twenty. Twenty lifetimes. He draws it slowly up the front of my torso, and my guts and organs and heart melt and twist and distort, like a plastic model of a man left on a radiator. Like a melting snowman.

I see the look of pure hatred on his face as he lifts the tool up to my face, and my face is gone, and all my notions of self and identity and all of my illusions. My eyes run down my face and burst on the floor and keep seeing despite that, and my face is a screaming bloody ruin, screaming and screaming for a judgement day that never comes...

And then he switches it off.

And I tumble into blackness.

Interlude The First
Japan, 1578 AD

But the tale of the dungeon and the Boxer and the question with no answer was yet to occur on that day in the middle of winter, when Oda Nobunaga and his retinue trudged up the cold hill to take tea with the Cold Ronin, O Best Beloved.

It was spring, when the cold heart of the world thaws and the beautiful blossoms grow upon the branches, but there was no spring upon the cold hill. Had it been the middle of winter, in that early part of the year when a carpet of frost covers and smothers all that grows, it would still have been so cold as to invite comment. Not the cold of a snowflake falling on a bamboo leaf, nor yet the cold of a clear icy stream running through the mountains, but the cold that is seldom found anywhere but in the forgotten resting-place of one who died without honour, in a locked stone tomb where there is no company save the dead and no comfort save death. A chill experienced only in a place of deepest death and horror.

The noble retinue of Oda Nobunaga wrapped their coats tighter around themselves and shivered, yet made no sound of dissent. It was their Master's will that they take themselves up that cold hill in that chill wind, and as such it was to be obeyed without question, even as they looked around them at the stunted trees and the stony patches of ground upon which nothing grew, and prayed to their ancestors that they would live to see the morning.

Oda Nobunaga did not pray. He did not shiver. He did not look left, or right, or up, or down. He simply walked, facing into the bitter wind, one foot in front of the other, his ceremonial cloak wrapped about him, his sword at his side, showing no sign of fear or danger or even discomfort. He was Oyabun – it was not a part of his nature or his station to give in to fear.

And yet, deep in the hidden core of Oda Nobunaga, locked away from all human sight, there was a sense of foreboding. This was not the simple hiring of a mercenary, or a pack of samurai; to seek the Cold Ronin who lived on the cold hill was to seek something less than human. Men spoke in whispers of his cold, pale corpse-flesh, his way of staring at you, head cocked, as though he was a bird and you were a tasty worm ready to be plucked from the frozen ground. Occasionally, it was said that if he did not like what you had come to offer him, he would cut the top of your head off with his sharp katana and feast on your living brain – but these were, of course, only stories, and it would not do for Oda Nobunaga to show even the slightest tremor as his feet shuffled in the cold snow.

They had almost reached the top of the hill when Oda Nobunaga lifted his head and spied the Cold Ronin six feet in front of him, barefoot, dressed in a white robe, his flesh like marble in the high sun, his sword sheathed at his side. Oda Nobunaga swallowed, once, then spoke in a clear voice betraying not the subtlest quiver. "Nanashi No."

He bowed, and his retinue bowed also, almost comic in their efforts to out-scrape one another, noses almost touching the snow.

Nanashi No nodded almost imperceptibly.

"Oda Nobunaga. What leads you to disturb my solitude on these cold hills?"

Oda Nobunaga hesitated a moment. But it would be a mistake to lie to the Cold Ronin.

"Anger and hatred, Nanashi No, and the desire to defend my lands against those who would try to conquer them. You are aware, of course, of the warlord Uesugi Kenshin."

Nanashi No nodded once. "He attacked you recently, driving you back into Omi Province. There is doubt in some circles that you are still the strongest warlord in Japan after Uesugi Kenshin out-manoeuvred you so cunningly. In the last few months, Uesugi Kenshin has put together a grand army, which appears capable of driving you even further back and claiming still more land–"

Oda Nobunaga coloured, eyes narrowing in fury. "Enough!"

The chill on the cold hill deepened, and a single leaf blew between the two men. Oda Nobunaga felt his throat close and his stomach churn. "Th-that is... I did not mean to insult you, Cold Ronin. It was an unworthy outburst. Forgive me."

There was another pause that seemed to last an age before the Cold Ronin nodded.

"The price of doing business with me has increased, Oda Nobunaga. Explain what it is you wish of me, and please do so quickly. My patience is not infinite, and your unseemly behaviour has strained it to the breaking point." Nanashi No's voice was soft, but infinitely cold. Oda Nobunaga bowed again, deeply, and his retinue followed, each attempting to bow lower than the other, trembling despite their warm clothing.

"Forgive me, Cold Ronin. I wish you to assassinate Uesugi Kenshin as soon as is convenient. He is the heart and the brain of his army – without him, all of his plans will fall to chaos."

Nanashi No nodded again. "You have heard, I trust, that Uesugi Kenshin is in poor health and is not expected to last another year? Tell me, Oda Nobunaga, what profit is there for you if I strike my keen blade through a heart already dying?"

Oda Nobunaga looked into the cold eyes of the Cold Ronin and chose his words with care. To turn around and leave after such a journey would be intolerable, and to offend Nanashi No further would be actively dangerous. "Every beat of Uesugi Kenshin's heart is a danger to me, Cold Ronin. I find stilling it worth more than any price you name."

Nanashi No smiled, and the smile was without warmth. "Any price?"

Oda Nobunaga turned to look at his retinue, and the shuffling, shuddering men hauled two large chests filled with treasures – magnificent jade pieces, ornate vases, gold and glittering jewels.

The Cold Ronin stared at the wealth before him. "I am no collector of fine jade, Oda Nobunaga, and as such I have no need of this. I'm sure you see some prize to be fought for in this, but all I see is nothing at all."

Oda Nobunaga opened his mouth to speak, but Nanashi No simply shook his head. "A fat pouch of yen, Oda Nobunaga, will serve. Bring it to me by sunset. And one thing more. When you leave here, take only those members of your retinue needed to lift those twin chests of nothing, so that you can bear them far away from my cold hill. Leave the rest with me."

Oda Nobunaga opened his mouth again, but the eyes of the Cold Ronin forced his silence. He turned and nodded to the four best men in his retinue. They, too, were wordless as they picked up the crates.

The five men did not look back as they took their leave of the cold hill. Not when they heard the unsheathing of the sword, nor when they heard the noise of fine-tempered metal slicing through flesh and bone, nor when the screams and gurgles of those left behind reached their ears.

And when they heard the sound of teeth gnawing at the meat of the skull, a ravenous tearing, a gulping, a feasting, the sounds of an unholy communion taking place not twenty metres from where their boots shuffled in the snow... then, most of all, they did not look back, O Best Beloved.

Not once.

Imagine the finest of the Shogun's horses, O Best Beloved! Imagine the thunder of its hooves as it gallops through the orchards of the Shogun, the shifting of the muscles of its flanks. Imagine the magnificence of the beast, the life force emanating from every pore, the shifting of the black mane in the breeze.

Imagine it has no eyes.

The wet, red sockets gape, droplets of gore seeping from them, trailing back from the head of the noble steed as it runs blindly, hurtling forward. The life force is subverted, the magnificence of the animal broken by this one detail, transformed to horror and madness.

This is what it was to see Nanashi No running across the plain.

At first glance, he might seem a paragon of humanity, but even a brief glimpse would confer a sense of dismay upon the observer, a sickly feeling creeping down the spine and into the belly, a terrible understanding that something was unaccountably, irredeemably wrong. Nanashi No felt no pain and did not tire. He was the strongest and the fastest man from ocean to ocean. To watch such a man sprint, covering miles by sun and moon, never slowing, never stopping... to watch such a feat might impress at first, until you notice the sickly, clammy pallor of the flesh, the fixed intensity of the eyes, the bare feet never stumbling or tripping even on sharp stones or deep snow. Admiration was often the first emotion when faced with the Cold Ronin – an admiration that quickly curdled to unease and then to horror. For a man who never sleeps, never tires, never stops is not truly a man, particularly when there is still a dark stain tracing from the corner of his lips, from a grotesque appetite fulfilled.

In such a manner, Nanashi No crossed the gap between Oda Nobunaga's territory in the Omi Province and Uesugi Kenshin's camp in the Kaga Province in a matter of days, stopping only to evade confrontation with military forces. When he stopped running, there was no catching of breath, no panting – he simply became as still and silent as the corpse he appeared to be. It was in this state of stillness and silence that he approached the boundary of Uesugi Kenshin's camp.

The Cold Ronin stood on the thin branch of a tree, perfectly balanced and unseen, hidden from sight by a curtain of fragrant blossom, and simply watched. He watched the patterns of the guards – as they walked and waited and crisscrossed one another, when they came on and off their duties, where their gazes fell – for a full day and a full night. Then he left his perch to move and walk through them as though they did not exist, without sound or trace of his passing – his sharp mind and sharper wits allowing him to snake between the watchful gazes of thirty men charged to guard their camp on pain of shame and suicide as though he had no more substance than a ghost.

Once inside the camp, he moved from shadow to shadow, never in the light for more than an instant. He went unnoticed and unremarked upon, although he was a legend throughout the provinces – even those who

He listened to the sounds of grief, the thunder of similar footsteps as other lieutenants and familiars came to gaze on their dead lord, and especially to the pronouncements that Uesugi Kenshin's heart had simply given out, that there were no signs of violence, that he had simply died of old age there in the outhouse.

Nanashi No resisted the urge to sigh. As though one as strong as Uesugi Kenshin would submit so readily to the bony finger of death without completing the task he had set himself! It was clear that Uesugi Kenshin's plans for conquest lay as dead as he, that his heirs and second-in-commands would be unable to perform the duties set them if they so easily clung to comforting fables instead of looking at the truth directly in front of their eyes. Oda Nobunaga had been correct. He would become the supreme power within Japan.

The Cold Ronin waited as the hours passed, until the hour of midnight. Uesugi Kenshin lay in state in one of the nearby tents, and the heart had vanished from the camp. Where Nanashi No had needed to watch the patterns of the guards for a day and a night to gain entrance to the camp, he barely had to muster the smallest effort to escape unnoticed, and was soon in the trees beyond the camp's furthest edge with none the wiser.

But Nanashi No knew, and the knowledge was bitter as poison to him. He had cravenly murdered a strong man in order to help a weaker one rise to power. He had slaughtered a man in the most ignoble circumstances possible. Moreover, he knew that the story would spread – if not from the lips of Uesugi Kenshin's forces, then from his opponent, Oda Nobunaga, who would allow the legend of the Cold Ronin to bolster his own.

Almost unconsciously, Nanashi No set off to the east.

Better for the Cold Ronin to remain a legend, rather

than for more power-hungry men to break the blissful solitude of Nanashi No. And better that Nanashi No should himself disappear – board a boat and cast himself into the arms of the wide Pacific, with only his sword as a reminder of what he had once been. The Japan he knew was ending, and Nanashi No would end with it. When his storm-tossed boat finally reached whatever land lay on the other side of the great ocean, another man would disembark, more suited to the new world he found himself in, armed with a sharp sword from a far-off land to keep his blessed solitude.

Nanashi No, who would soon be no one at all, smiled a peaceful smile as he watched the blossom float from the trees. And then he walked towards the sea, O Best Beloved, and out of all stories forever.

CHAPTER FIVE

The Killing Man

...but that was long ago, and far away.

The man with the broken nose was named Albert Gregory Morse, and he was indeed a boxer – he'd been a boxer since he was nine, after a childhood spent scrapping in the streets and generally getting in the kind of trouble that would slowly wend its way down to the prison gates as the years went by. He was a social worker's poster-boy, grown up in a house with an alcoholic father and a sickly, underweight mother, and three other kids younger than him who needed feeding and clothing. But he never saw a social worker, of course – in those days slipping through the cracks was even easier than it is now, and besides, he didn't need some fey twat from the council to set him right. Albert Morse had the gym, the circle of tough men who lived by coded violence, who would ritually try to kill each other through the morning and then go to the pub on the corner for lunch and stand each other pints, all malice forgotten, who would let him watch the fights and punch at the heavy bag and keep the place clean for cash-in-hand. Who provided the path to his salvation. Who allowed Albert Gregory Morse into the Ring.

The Ring was a way to keep his family going, and to have a little pride as well. He was a practical lad, and sweeping up was as good a way of making money as any, but with a dustpan in his hand he was nobody. On

Saturday night, slamming his gloved fist into the face of some local tough who thought he was tough enough, breaking his nose and his jaw and sending him crashing down to the mat like a fallen tree, the numbers echoing like prayers in a cathedral as the crowd cheered for Albert Morse, he was somebody. He had a name. And even when it was his turn to tumble down, struggle to rise and finally collapse through pain and exhaustion and the ringing of his head as the number ten sounded around the hall – well, he'd given a good fight. The crowd knew he was a tough man to beat, and there was another fight in a couple of nights. Albert Morse felt no shame at being beaten in the Ring.

Albert Morse was often beaten. He was a good fighter, unskilled but with a rough, merciless enthusiasm for despatching weaker opponents, but a stronger fighter who could stand his sledgehammer right long enough would see the obvious holes in his defence and soon Albert would be eating the mat again. Albert accepted this. Every fight won was another purse, another week of meat, school, new shoes, kitchen appliances and a little whisky to keep the old man quiet, but even losing a fight brought money in. Being knocked half to death in the Ring was a lot better than working in a factory, he figured, and he could still sweep up in the gym for extra money during the week when he wasn't training, and with six mouths to keep fed and clothed, that was a mercy.

Like all teenagers, he was untouchable, unstoppable, unbeatable – but even at an amateur level, boxing is all about being touched, stopped and beaten. When he was not quite twenty-two, a doctor told him that if he took another six months of punches to the head, he'd be a vegetable for the rest of his life. Doctor Sengupta was not a man known for his tact, so when he took Albert's dreams away from him with a brutal frankness usually only encountered in hanging judges, it's perhaps not surprising that Albert reacted with his fists. Doctor Sengupta's nose and jaw were broken, along with two of Albert's knuckles, and when the bandages came off he was no longer welcome at the gym.

He made the local papers – the front page, this time, not the sport – with an editorial tying the incident into supposedly spiralling waves of Mod versus Rocker violence, a personal grievance of the editors that was already six or seven years out of date. The race angle was mercifully unexplored, although in Albert's neighbourhood that might well have won him as many friends as enemies.

So Albert Morse was rewritten as a tearaway, a hoodlum, a violent young offender, and in this capacity he was splashed all over the local press. He was vicious, and violent, and he did solve his problems by inflicting pain, all this is true – but he was bound by the Ring, by rituals and codes, his violence channelled for so long into a structure that, if not quite moral, at least followed recognisable rules of engagement. Of course, left alone, it was only a matter of time before this ingrained code degraded and his brutal personality led him into the path of an old lady out too late at night with too much money, to the courts, and to Wormwood Scrubs, in that order.

But he was not left alone.

His violence, his code, his need for money and most of all his need to appear a hero, if only to himself – all of these drew the attentions of the organisation known as Military Intelligence 23.

The first time the grey-suited man arrived at the Morse household, Albert assumed he was another reporter and told him to piss off. The grey-suited man was an ex-drill-sergeant promoted to MI-23 recruiter named Selwyn Hughes, and he knew how to deal with the likes of Albert Morse. Without blinking, he reached into his pocket, pulled out a short iron truncheon, and swiftly broke two of Albert's ribs, before kicking the lad in the teeth hard enough to knock out a molar and telling him to shut his horrible trap and listen. After that, Albert thought he must be a copper, but he did listen, and what he heard interested him enough that when he came out of the hospital he made his way to the Tower with the other tourists and asked the old lady selling the souvenirs if she'd seen his Uncle Dee nosing about. This was a contact protocol that new recruits were encouraged to follow.

It will surprise nobody to learn that 'Uncle Dee' was a reference to Dr John Dee, who had first attempted to study 'the dead who walk' in the reign of Queen Bess, although it was not until late in the reign of King James that the organisation that would become MI-23 was set into motion. Albert Morse knew none of this, and made little attempt to learn in later life; what interested him was the job as it stood in 1973, a means of getting his fists dirty for Queen and Country against things that go bump in the night, a career straight out of a Hammer horror flick, and one that'd pay enough to keep his whole family fed, clothed and schooled. It sounded too good to be true, and to begin with there was no indication that it wasn't. Who believed in monsters in this day and age, after all?

Despite his scepticism, Albert Morse settled in quickly, spending most of his time performing small tasks such as breaking the legs of journalists who'd got a little too close to something they shouldn't have, or putting the frighteners on old ladies who were talking too loudly about things they should've kept to themselves. It was nasty work, but Albert Morse found himself surprisingly untroubled by conscience. He didn't enjoy it – not exactly – but it was work that had to be done for the sake of the Crown, and Morse was a practical man. He knew that he had to get his hands dirty one way or another. He was out of the Ring, banished from its clear structure, its rituals, its codes of honour and law, and now he had to use his fists where he could. MI-23 was not the Ring. But it would have to do.

By his twenty-fifth birthday, Albert Morse had become very practical, and very tough. He was almost happy – as happy as he could be out of the Ring – and secure in his routine, in his duties, in what was expected of him.

He did not believe in anything that he had not seen with his own two eyes.

On his twenty-fifth birthday, Albert Morse had his clearance level upgraded from code green to code yellow, and he was taken down to the dungeons underneath the Tower Of London, in the lower levels.

It was there that he saw his first werewolf.

Ten feet of muscle, growling in a cage, sniffing the air. Albert Morse moved his hand through the bars, laid it on fur that was rough and soft, the beast standing, growling, acknowledging one of its masters. Albert could have run then – run, screaming, bolting through the doors as others had done, desperately running and hiding in some dingy rented room, curling up in the corner and sobbing, retching up their guts until the men in the grey suits padded silently up their stairs with their silenced guns at the ready, silence their code and the punishment for those whose nerve broke. *Kneel and face the window. I'm sorry it had to come to this – no, don't look, don't look. It'll all be over in a minute, son. You just close your eyes.*

Albert could have run. But he didn't run.

Albert did not see a thing to fear, there in the cage.

He saw a wonder.

The werewolf looked at him, eyes burning, glowing a brilliant blue, cocking its head. Under the coarse fur, muscles shifted. This was what Albert Morse had been chasing his whole life, without knowing it. This was power – vicious, violent, trammelled and restrained in flesh and muscle, coiled and waiting in the service of men. He took a deep breath, inhaling wolf, inhaling strength and fury.

The wolf growled, a long, rumbling bass note, and Albert felt it pass through the pit of his belly.

Behind him, Selwyn Hughes, code orange, smiled paternally. Albert turned, looked at him, eyes shining. He was breathless.

"What does it eat?" He swallowed, shaking his head. "What does it hunt, Mister Hughes?"

Mister Hughes told him, and after that there were no more thoughts of the Ring and the happy days of rules and boundaried violence. If the werewolf was everything Morse had always wanted to see in the world, then the zombies were everything Morse wanted to take out of it. Cold, dead men, dead physically, dead emotionally, hollow men walking amidst those who had life in them... and with their secret. The terrible secret of what animated them, what set them walking the world like clockwork toys, integrating with society, killing and feeding, the secret, forgotten program that instructed the dead-who-walk in their every action and reaction. The secret, sinister clockwork of the dead.

The clockwork that would end the world, if it was allowed to.

These secrets and others Albert Morse learned, his

savage boxer's brain turned to something greater, his ugly talents shaped and honed. Selwyn Hughes had seen something special in the boy that day he'd smashed his face in and sent him away in an ambulance. Something in those hollow eyes that said – I can replace you. Let me.

Hughes was old, past his prime – he'd had one heart attack already, and his world was not a restful place. He knew that Morse had what it took to be code orange, the one man at the centre of the web of strangeness and charm that held civilisation back from an unimaginable abyss, so it might have the liberty of choking to death on poison or going to war for fresh water or any one of a million vastly preferable ends. He knew that Morse could stand where he stood, at the gates that separated humanity from the final end that passeth beyond all understanding, of which the legions of the dead-who-walk were only the part visible to us.

Most importantly, Hughes knew that Morse's reaction to the werewolf meant that he could work with the man designated code red.

In a few years, when Morse was old enough and more steeped in the lore and learning of MI-23, it would be time for him to have an audience with code red... with the man named Mister Smith.

But that was long ago, and far away.

If the wolves come out of the walls, it's all over, thought Albert Morse, and his mouth gave that little twitch that wasn't quite a smile. But there are wolves and wolves, and it was nearly over now. Morse rubbed his scarred knuckles, as he often did while he sat with his coffee and waited for the door to the Red Room to open.

The clock on the wall ticked, dry and dusty like a beetle in a long-lost tomb. *Not long now*, thought Morse. *Nearly over.*

Twenty years it had taken him after Selwyn died. Twenty years of hunting the bastards in their hundreds, then their dozens, then one by one, and finally – John Bloody Doe. The last of the zombies, the last night-horror. They'd feed him to the wolves in the morning and then MI-23 was all done.

Morse was almost sad at that. He was his job now, he ate, slept and breathed it – and when it was done, what would be left of him? He thought of all the things he'd never done. He had a potting shed full of old dead geranium bulbs, bought at the garden centre – this year he'd get round to planting the fucking things, he always thought, and never did. Never any fucking time. He thought of Romper, poor bloody Romper who beat his tail against the floor and whined because he wasn't walked enough. He should never have bought a bloody dog anyway.

Sorry, Romper. You were the only friend I ever had after Selwyn went. Should have tried harder. Look how I fucking treated you. And Hilda at the Prospect, showing me a little kindness for the first time since I took this bloody job. Never showed her any in return. Just buried myself in fucking work. Never called, never wrote... you're a piece of work, Morse. You never even went to your Mum's funeral, did you? Useless bastard. And all the people I bloody did it for – Tom and Steph and Nancy – they're all grown and out of my life and they don't want anything to do with me. You're a real hero, Albert

Morse. A knight of the fucking realm.

Morse sighed and swallowed coffee, black with no sugar, feeling as bitter as what went down his throat. *Bollocks to it anyway. It had to be done. No sense whining.*

He realised it was probably the last time he'd see Smith for any length of time.

He realised he was happy about that.

I did it, Mum. I saved the world, me and my men. Me and the wolves in the walls. Could be a lot fucking worse.

Beats Tommy and his poncy bloody art college, anyway.

Morse scowled, and set the empty mug on the little table next to his chair.

What kind of world lets a bloody dog die of cancer anyway?

Not one worth saving.

Morse sighed, leaning forward. At that moment, the speaker above the door crackled into life.

"Albert Morse, code orange clearance. Please proceed to the inner lock."

Morse stood slowly, stretching.

"About bloody time."

One door closed, another opened. In between, there was the inner-lock – security system, black-panelled room of flashing lights and lines, sweeping beams, scans and soft artificial voices, carefully programmed for the absolute minimum humanity.

Morse stood, bored, listless, fingers itching, eager for the process to end. The thought that the room could fill with cyanide gas at any moment never occurred to him. Once, it might have – when the novelty of the procedure was still fresh, when he was thirty, the thought of a malfunction or mechanical failure had been enough to wake him up in the watches of the night, sweating and shaking, the tang of almonds in his nostrils until he drowned them out with a swig of Glenfiddich – but those days were gone. Now all it was was a procedure that had to be endured in order to come face to face with his Lord and Master.

Neither did he look left or right at the automated machine-guns in their brackets on the wall, or down at the floor, which could have slid away at any moment, toppling him into an acid so pure and potent that it would have reduced him to a molecular soup in seconds.

To Albert Morse, the threat of death had become as ordinary as crossing the street.

He spoke his name, once, in a bored tone of voice.

Aside from the whirring computations of the room, there was silence for seven seconds before the door swung slowly open.

A moment of contemplation in the hour before the beginning of the end of the world.

Once, Albert Morse would have been shitting himself, but time has a habit of making the bizarre seem almost mundane.

And Mister Smith was bizarre.

The room was ordinary enough – a circular chamber, lined with oak-panelled bookshelves, with a desk in the middle, similarly styled, and a door at the back, leading to the system of antechambers that were home to Mister Smith. There were no windows, or mirrors, but the lighting was designed to be warm and cosy, and often the only light came from a fireplace set off to the side. There was an armchair in front of the fire, and an office chair near the desk – for guests.

Mister Smith did not need chairs.

The first time Albert Morse had met him, he had vomited into the waste-paper basket, then desperately begged forgiveness. Mister Smith was used to such reactions. He was barely four feet in height, his body wizened, shrivelled up like a toy balloon at a birthday party for a stillborn child, the Saville Row suit, sized for a ventriloquist's dummy, hanging grotesquely on his frame, a doll's shrunken corpse dangling horrifically from the vast, inflated head. Mister Smith's skull was a three-foot-wide balloon, bald, with blue veins pulsing in the corpse-white, almost green flesh. The face was small, in the same proportion as the shrivelled body, although the eyes were enlarged, vast, milky orbs with livid green irises that seemed to glow with a strange inner radiation. Mister Smith was simply a vast, pulsing brain, which had retained those scraps of flesh necessary for speech and the five senses – the rest was vestigial, the functions of the vital organs provided by the brain itself, the lungs used only to provide a wheezing gasp of air past the lips, so Mister Smith might spare his guests the rudeness of telepathy.

Mister Smith floated slowly towards Morse. The wrinkled mouth made an approximation of a smile.

"The nights are drawing in, Mr Morse. You must be cold."

He shot a glance at the logs in the grate, and they instantly ignited into a roaring blaze. The lights dimmed accordingly. "Please, sit. I should offer you a brandy."

Morse blinked, and frowned. "Brandy, sir? Are you

sure?"

"The work is over, is it not? We have the last of them. Sit, sit."

Morse moved the armchair, taking only the edge of it, not allowing himself to get too comfortable. Something in Mister Smith's easy manner made him tense – not through fear of the abomination that floated in front of him, but fear of the very confidence he himself had felt in the corridor, fear of contemplating the end of the work before that end was in sight.

"He's still alive, sir. Begging your pardon, but it's not over until we feed the little bastard to the wolves and have a poke through what comes out the other end."

Mister Smith's not-quite-smile grew wider.

"John Doe is not going to give us any trouble. The only reason the creature stayed hidden as long as it did is because of its heightened chameleon response – and that was triggered by the death of Professor Roscoe in New York. It's much weaker than the others – remember Mustermann? Mengano? Doe's even weaker than Janez Novak and you didn't even need the wolves to finish that one. In fact, the more I think about it, the more I think this might be an ideal opportunity to study one of them."

Morse choked, standing suddenly. "You have got to be fucking joking!"

Mister Smith looked at him. Morse realised he'd spoken very far out of turn.

"Pardon my French, sir. But... I mean, you can't be serious. We have been trying to exterminate these little bastards since the Middle Ages. They're dangerous. You were the one who told me what Whiteside Parsons found out about them. You know what they're here to achieve –"

"End the world, yes, yes. You can stop there, Morse. I can tell what all of your arguments are going to be just by looking at you, and I appreciate everything you were about to say. But remember what these things are."

Morse shook his head. "The Dead Who Walk, Sir. Fucking zombies. The very things, if I can *remind* you, *Sir*, that we have been trying to wipe right off the face of the planet like a bloody Cillit Bang advert since the reign of—"

"Since Elizabethan times, yes, yes, good Queen Bess and John Dee and all that. But the current Queen Bess is not in full control of operations, is she? I am. We may be answerable to Her Majesty, but Victoria handed the duty of organisation and administration over to me, and it's a duty I take very seriously, very seriously... sit down, Mr Morse."

"Sir, please—"

"Sit down. I insist."

Morse felt himself sitting, leaning back in the chair, felt himself relaxing. Inwardly he seethed. He hadn't been treated like this in years, and it was an unpleasant reminder that while he did most of the legwork for the organisation, he was still the number two – both in terms of command and in the evolutionary chain. Morse was humanity as it stood now, and Mister Smith was the future – humanity several links up the chain of being, a product of Darwin's genius and Victorian eugenics. Almost from spite, he allowed himself to wonder whether humanity had simply exchanged one monster for another, knowing Mister Smith would catch the thought.

Mister Smith looked almost hurt, but carried on.

"The Dead Who Walk... it's a misnomer, isn't it? You've evidently swallowed our own propaganda on the issue – all those zombie movies we bankrolled to make the public react correctly to the mind-eaters in their midst... do you realise that before the wonderful Mrs Shelley wrote her novel, people would bring zombies into their homes? It was assumed they were suffering from the cold..."

"I'm well aware of that, *sir* –"

"Let me finish, let me finish..."

Suddenly Morse could no longer speak. He slumped back in his chair, fuming in silence and swearing loudly in his mind.

Mister Smith paused a moment until Morse finished. "There is no such thing as a zombie – not in the way we have allowed the public to construe it. The thing in that cell is not dead, is he, Morse? He was never dead at all. He has always been that way. He always *will* be that way. John Doe, Hans Mustermann, Jose Lopez... they have human names, but they were never human. They have the appearance of dead men, but it would be truer to say that their disguise as living men is incomplete – but perfect enough that we think of them as men, as individuals, as thinking creatures. Perhaps they even fool themselves. But, of course, they are neither human nor individuals in the way that you and I are."

He paused, running a dry tongue over dry lips.

"These creatures... these Dead Who Walk... they are collections of cells, much as we are. You could describe yourself as a collection of single cells banded together to form one being, but in your case that would be facetious. Separate your heart from your body, your brain from your head, and both parts would die. This is not the case with the being we're keeping downstairs. Mr Doe is a gestalt entity – millions of cells that form together to create a reasonable approximation of a human being. Even after centuries, it is not entirely accurate in its internal workings, but from the outside it appears human

– even to itself."

Morse looked incredulous. Christ! He'd thought the bastard was acting.

"Oh yes, oh yes... I monitored your interrogation of the creature. According to its surface thoughts, it had no idea what you were talking about. I've noticed before that there is a dichotomy inherent within these zombies – on one level, a constant running chatter of thoughts, an imitation of human brain patterns, and on the other... the programming they follow. But let's return to their physical structure..."

Morse rolled his eyes. How many times had he heard this lecture? And all they had to do was throw the monster to the wolves and it was over.

"Please, Albert. I am getting to the point. These cell collectives cannot be damaged by normal means. Splitting them into smaller clusters won't help – even once the small parts have been brought out of communication range, they will act on their own. I understand Mr Doe has experimented with this property by using his own hand as a remote combat unit. However, his surface mind is still attempting to put it in terms he feels a human being could understand. Which brings us to the chameleon syndrome – the cell-clusters imitate the dominant culture in their immediate area as a camouflage mechanism. However, Doe murdered Professor Roscoe because Roscoe found something, and in response to that Doe effectively murdered himself – shutting his surface memory down to ten years, moving to a different country, boosting his chameleon reflex by several hundred per cent, and hiding his true nature even from himself – under a belief system that seems to be composed equally of our own 'zombie' propaganda exercises and old private eye films. The hitman with a heart of gold, as it were."

Morse furrowed his brow. There was something in this.

Mister Smith's lips twitched.

"You can speak again if you'd like, Albert."

Morse scowled. "I thought after twenty-odd years of working together we were beyond that little stunt."

"Albert –"

"Never mind, I'm starting to see where you're going with this. I'll have that brandy, though. I've a feeling I'm going to fucking need it once this is over." He leant back as a decanter floated across the room, pouring itself into a nearby glass.

Mister Smith set the decanter down with his mind and continued.

"These cell-clusters also possess full-spectrum time-sense – a control over their own temporal perception, allowing their minds to view the passing of time much faster than the one-second-per-second standard ordinary humans enjoy. However, since we've been able to create a workable version of this time-sense in our werewolves since the late fifties, it's ceased to be too much of an issue. But you know all that. Tell me, Albert, where do you think I'm headed with this?"

Morse smiled humourlessly. "Emmett Roscoe. Or rather, what Emmett Roscoe found out about John Doe. And making use of that secondary thought-stream."

"Good, good... I'm glad we're on the same page here, Albert. Thanks to Dee, and later Parsons, we know that if the zombies were to be left unchecked they would end the world – but we don't know how, or why... or when."

"When is the time. Your specially selected starter for ten."

"A question that would only have meaning to the secondary thought-stream, bypassing the primary.

However, you were working under the assumption that the creature could not hide its true nature from itself. So when it refused to break..."

"It was already broken, but it didn't actually know what it was hiding. Christ, that little bastard even manages to stab itself in the back."

"Quite, quite... If it is the last of its kind, there's not much it can do. But if its not – or if it was put into motion by other hands – we need to know. We need to break it – that is to say, strip away the surface thought-stream so that all that is left of the monster is the basic id, the part that will tell us what we want to know."

"In other words, a nice spot of garden variety torture."

"I thought you'd like that part."

Morse took a sip of his brandy, then stood. "Nothing would give me greater pleasure than to electrocute that decomposing bastard in his dead nuts until he dances us a polka. But excess pain just seems to make the bastard pass out – shut down, whatever – presumably to protect itself from exactly what I'm trying to do to said testicles. So! Let's try another tack. Let's push that... 'primary thought-stream'... that bloody split personality it's got until it takes more of the fucker's energy to keep up the bullshit than it does to drop the mask like a hot fucking turd. Then we can have a nice cosy chat with the gestalt entity formerly known as John Doe. I'll do the talking and the arse-kicking, you monitor from here. Dig right into that dead head of his until we've got everything we need to know."

Mister Smith raised one grotesque eyebrow. "What do you suggest?"

"Let's take a lesson from the Yanks. A spot of Torture Lite. Diet Bastardry. Sirens. Klaxons. Bright lights. Nothing's going to work on the little shit unless it's mostly in the mind. It doesn't need to breathe, so waterboarding's out. What about water torture?"

"Water torture?"

"Drip drip drip, little April showers. Rig up a tap or something so it's constantly dripping on the forehead of some poor bugger who you've conveniently strapped down so he can't move a fucking muscle. Very effective when it comes to making people go completely bloody doolally in a very short space of time. Also, it's well known. I saw it on the bloody *Avengers* once. Part of the culture. It'll work on John Doe because John Doe always tries to fit in because he thinks that's going to make him a human being instead of the fucking apocalypse waiting to happen. And because he's got such a bee in his bloody bonnet about trying to be human, he has to react to a torture that – according to us humans – *breaks* humans. Therefore, he's going to be helping us every step of the way." Morse paused. "Well? Am I talking out of my bloody backside or what?"

"Hmm." Mister Smith frowned. "It's worth a try. Do you want to be the one to set things in motion, Mr Morse?"

Morse looked at the wizened head of Mister Smith, eyes like storm clouds.

"I should fucking cocoa, sir."

CHAPTER SIX

The Body Lovers

I wake up to the squeaking of wheels, like a supermarket trolley. Then the feeling of movement, the bump-bump-bump of a metal cart with no suspension being wheeled over rough slabs of centuries-old stone, bump, bump, bump. Electric light passing overhead like UFOs. The smell of cobwebs. Metal bands strapped over wrists, ankles, waist, throat, and a pair of heavy pads on each side of my head, keeping it in place.

I'm on the move.

They've got me chained down to some sort of gurney, wheeling me through the old stone corridors to the next destination. I don't think this is part of a prisoner release program – whatever the Boxer was yammering about while he was taking me to pieces, it didn't sound like the kind of thing they'd change their minds about. Which means that whatever they're wheeling me towards, it's worse than a torture that feels like a billion years of indescribable agony.

But hey, no sense panicking.

Bump, bump, bump.

I flex, trying to break the bonds, but no go. Whatever they're made out of, it's stronger than I am. These people know everything about me – my powers, my limits, how to break me, how to fix me. And that worries me a lot, and not just because they're wheeling me to Room 101 for a taste of who-knows-what.

It worries me because they think I'm going to end the world.

What did the Boxer say? Something about times and

plans. Something about a guy named Emmett Roscoe.

Much as I hate to say it, that name is starting to seem familiar.

Bump, bump, bump.

Wheels hitting stone slabs with the rhythm of a nightclub somewhere. Emmett Roscoe...

Nothing. It's gone. And I've got more important things to worry about.

Such as what they're going to do to me now. It occurs to me that if they have done their worst and not found out what they were looking for – and God knows I don't know what the hell they're looking for – this might be it. The big finish. Cement overshoes. A swim with the fishes.

Thrown to the wolves.

This might not be a hospital gurney. It might be a dessert cart.

But hey – no sense panicking.

Bump, bump, bump.

Whoever's pushing this thing knows I'm awake now, but he's not saying a word. A good soldier. Or maybe he's seen a lot of these before. Maybe he's pushed so many struggling bodies to the wolf pen that I'm just meat to him. He's thinking about dinner tonight, or whether he remembered to set his TiVo to record that documentary on The World's Most Dangerous Shoplifters starring Sheriff John Bunnell, or maybe looking forward to the match on Saturday. Chelsea versus Everton, should be a good one... Face it. He doesn't give a damn.

Or she. We live in enlightened times.

Bump, bump, bump.

Crash.

The gurney slams through a set of steel doors, and we're there. I can't turn my head or crane my neck, so

I have no idea what's going on, but I'm not hearing anything but footsteps. No snarls, no growls, no howls. So I can breathe easy on that score. On the other hand, those footsteps are padding around the room. He's doing something. Scrape of metal on stone... something being set up, checked.

I really wish I could turn my head.

I get a glimpse of whoever-it-is as he steps back this way – not a face I've seen before, just a technician, and by the look of it he doesn't particularly care who I am either. He just grabs hold of the gurney and pushes it towards whatever he's been tinkering with. Some sort of copper piping...

Huh.

I'm staring up at a tap.

That's new.

I've got to admit, I'm waiting for the other shoe to drop here. A while ago, I was screaming in agony as a high-tech science-fiction capacitor remoulded my cells like Play-Doh, and now they've decided to upgrade to plumbing. What are they going to do, wash me to death?

He's setting it all up very carefully. Marking position exactly. Something's up here.

And then he turns the handle.

There's some kind of washer in place in the tap, because water doesn't come out immediately. It trickles out, just a drop at a time. Hitting right in the centre of my forehead. *Drip. Drip. Drip.* Annoying. What are they trying to do here? Annoy me into submission?

Drip. Drip. Drip.

Oh, wait.

Drip.

I know what this is.

Drip.

I saw this in *The Avengers* once.

Drip.

This is that water torture – the one where they hold the victim under it until they go mad. It was on telly.

Drip.

Actually this *is* pretty annoying.

Drip.

Make that really annoying. I can't move. I can't move and it just keeps dripping away.

Drip.

Turn it off.

Drip.

I can't move. I want to scratch my nose. Rub my forehead. Massage my temples. I want to scratch that itch in the small of my back.

Drip.

Suddenly I've forgotten how bad the torture earlier was. This is torture – right here.

Drip.

This is the worst torture in the world. I can't move a muscle and this water is just dripping on me, *drip-drip-drip.* And I can feel what it's doing. I can feel myself starting to go crazy. This is actually going to work. It worked on the telly. Why am I surprised that they'd use it in real life?

Drip.

It always works on the telly. They're going to drive me mad with this.

Drip.

Drip.

Drip.

Dr–

Fuck it.

I grab time hard and squeeze it like I'm gripping the

balls of some tosser in a bar room brawl. The water-drop slows, then stops, hanging in the air.

Right.

We've established that this is going to work. Maybe it's psychosomatic, but it's going to work. Just like on the telly. So. How do I get out of this one?

The straps are made of something I can't break. So that's out. I'm stuck here for as long as they leave me, and they're probably going to leave me here a while.

I keep time held in my mind. The droplet hangs in space above my head, unmoving – like a sputnik floating in space.

I can't stay like this. In subjective time, it could take years for them to come back to me. I'll have gone crazy with boredom by then.

So. I can't break out, and I can't keep holding onto time forever. What other options are there?

Think.

The ball of water drifts downwards. I relax, letting it tumble through the air, then clench time tight in my grip again, bringing it to a halt. Relax... and grip. The ball inching downwards in little jerks until it splashes against my wet forehead. Above, another grows from the tap, ready to take its place.

I can't reverse those droplets, but I can control how fast they fall.

So.

Let's try something I've never tried before.

Let's turn time up to eleven.

I let go. Time washes over me like a cold shower... and then I grab hold again, and twist... and time keeps moving... falling... thundering down...

Faster.

And faster.

The drips become a trickle, the trickle a flood, a constant pressure that settles on my face. I can handle this for ten minutes or so before I have to slow time down again. And for me it's only going to be ten minutes.

I start hearing sounds – little blips and clicks. For a moment I see a pink and white blur in the air above me – a doctor? A technician? Feel a trace of something cold against my chest, probably a stethoscope, some kind of instrument... how long would it take them to check me? An hour? Eight hours? A day?

There it goes again.

Grab time. Twist.

Faster. Faster.

How fast am I going? Eight hours for every second? A day? Two?

I'm thinking how I probably look from the outside. I'm doing the best I can not to twitch or move too much, just holding still with what seems like a wet gel pack resting on my forehead. I'm probably frozen solid, eyes open, expression unchanging... looking like a real dead body, in other words.

I'm hoping that's the effect they're after.

Faster and faster.

More blurs. So fast now – there's a constant pink and white mist in the air. How many days have gone by now? How many weeks? How many weeks are passing even while I think that? I'm getting more blips and clicks in the air, like a forest of crickets. Talking to each other, firing off questions. Maybe questioning me. Lights are flashing in my eyes. Interrogation. All the activity is building to some kind of—

Jesus!

It takes everything I can not to jerk. It felt like someone slashed open my leg and poured battery acid in it – I actually slowed down for a moment and caught a glimpse of a room full of freaks in lab coats, the Boxer standing around looking grim... that was the capacitor. The pulse generator they were using on me before.

I must be going too fast for it.

I wait, tensed, for another, but nothing. They must have held it on me for a while, hoping for some kind of reaction.

It occurs to me that, for the first time, I am acting like a real corpse.

I am normal.

I am just like you.

When you're dead, that is.

More buzzing, flashing, bleeping and clicking. What's it been? One minute? Two? I'm probably in trouble here. I need to slow things back to normal as soon as they take me out of this room, because otherwise – if I look like an ordinary corpse – what's stopping them from feeding me to the –

Wait, what –

Everything's changed –

Hands inside me –

Let go –

– and time slows and groans back into place like a bullet train pulling into the station. Everything went wild there for a moment, blurred, racing past me. They took me somewhere else. It'd barely registered before I felt something – in me.

Hands. Blades. Like having a food processor grinding into me.

I feel... empty. Literally.

And there's an old, balding man with little round glasses standing above me with a scalpel, dictating into some sort of microphone.

I'm being dissected.

"Holy shit!"

I suppose I should have stayed quiet. Well, you try staying quiet when someone cuts you open and takes out your internal organs. Go on, I'll wait.

Dr Glasses stumbles back, opening his mouth to scream. Without thinking, I grip time, slow it, and then reach up and grab him by the throat, crushing his windpipe in my hand and then snapping his neck. I smash the microphone for good measure. No sense taking chances.

I let go – time wrapping around me like a cheap overcoat – and he staggers back, eyes bulging, head lolling obscenely, trying to sputter something, his tongue protruding through his lips. Then he tumbles down like a sack of potatoes.

It's not until he falls that I realise I'm not tied down any longer.

Why didn't I notice that?

And there's nobody else in the room. No guards, no cameras. No sign of any surveillance at all.

How long would it take them to decide I was no longer a threat?

Maybe I'm not a threat. I feel thin. Washed out. Light-headed. Maybe it's from time running without me for so long.

Maybe it's because half of me's been carefully removed by Dr Glasses.

How long was I lying in that room?

There are pages and pages of typewritten notes here – file cabinets on the walls, drawers dated September through to October. That split-second flurry of activity took nearly two months. I'm lucky they didn't decide to feed me to those monsters – if they had, I'd never even know it'd happened. Just lights out.

I'm not sure I want to think about how long I've been under here. Long enough for them to stop seeing me as dangerous. And I don't think the Boxer was going to stop thinking that any time soon. Maybe he's dead.

Maybe he died of old age.

I swing myself up off the table for a closer look at the notes.

First incision: September 5, 2010.

Three years.

They kept me on that table for three years. Kept the water running for three years. Monitored reactions for three years. And then they figured I was just another body and schlepped me over here to cut me open and chop me up.

I don't know if you've ever been in that situation, but it's pretty strange, let me tell you. It disconnects you. I feel like I've been taken out of reality and put down somewhere else, somewhere without any rules.

2010.

Jesus Christ, I'm in the future.

I wonder if we've got flying cars yet?

The words on the page are typed neatly, laid out perfectly, but I can't read them. They're swimming in front of my eyes and all the *di-oxy-rybo-nucleics* and *gestalt* units and *seratonin detection* sitting on the page pretending to mean something just won't connect together into anything that makes sense. They float around, chopping and changing. Somewhere in here, there's a key to all the mysteries, but I can't find it. I read *New Scientist* – I'm not stupid. But this is something else.

I've woken up in the future. What the hell did I

expect?

And then there's the sound of glass clinking against glass, and I stop caring what year it is. The paper tumbles to the floor.

Chink.

I'm suddenly very aware of the gaping, yawning emptiness under my ribcage, the tent-flap of skin and muscle yawning open. I was wondering where all of that went. Now I know.

Big glass jars line the back of the room, stretching away from me on a single, long shelf. Each of them is marked and filled with something soft, wet and red.

One of my organs.

Clink.

One of my kidneys is looking back at me. Literally. There's an eye in the middle of the purplish-brown mass. It closes, then opens, like a sick parody of a come-on.

Next to it, I can see a lung, pulsing slowly in and out, breathing on its own. Embedded in the surface is a single, pulsing vein.

The further away from me the organs are, the weirder it gets.

Chink. Chink.

My stomach, lying at the bottom of a jar with a set of vestigial fingers poking from the lining. The fingers wiggling and twitching.

A length of intestine, reared up and swaying like a cobra. Like a centipede.

At the back of the room, my heart. There are... legs growing out of it. Like spider's legs. Little hairs poking out of red flesh. My heart, scrabbling as it pumps, scuttling behind the glass, a pair of mandibles extended from the left ventricle, snapping and clacking.

My heart is an insect.

With every thrash of its legs, the jar rattles against its neighbour, my pancreas pushing back against the wall of the jar like a slug.

Chink. Chink. Clink.

My heart is at war with my pancreas.

Chink. Clink.

Mandibles clash against glass. The jar is rocking now.

I take a step towards it, and it turns.

It's looking at me.

Another step.

I can feel it now. The spider-heart. I can feel it in my mind, and it's so... alien.

An insect intelligence communicating with mine.

What is it?

What am I?

What sort of person was I?

Another step. It calms, slowly stopping movement. The intelligence... recedes.

No, that's wrong.

It merges. Blends.

Fits in.

The jar stops moving.

I take another step.

Another. I'm close enough to reach out and take the jar in my hands, turn it around slowly, eyes looking over what's inside.

Just a lump of meat.

A human heart, sitting in a jar. No legs, no jaws... nothing that couldn't have come out of a human being.

I look at the other jars.

Nothing.

Just organs.

I think I'm going to be sick, but there's nothing to be sick with. I've got nothing down there. Then I want to laugh, but I've got nothing to laugh with either. Then I want to be sick again.

I crack the lid of the jar, reaching in and grabbing my heart. Inert muscle.

I shake it a little.

Probe it with my mind.

Nothing.

I'm trying to remember how things were ten minutes ago. Ten minutes ago when my biggest problem was water dripping on my forehead.

Three years ago.

Without thinking, I raise the still heart to my lips. Teeth bite into the muscle, tearing off a strip, swallowing. Then bite again.

I'm in shock.

I'm barely aware I'm doing this.

Bite by bite, like tearing into a rich, red pepper. A meaty, juicy heart.

I finish it and pop open the next jar, reaching in and gripping a pancreas that slid up the side of the jar like a slug. And I bite. And bite. And bite.

There's nothing below my ribcage, but I can feel myself getting stronger. Full of all the good things a body needs.

I bite into a lung, chewing and swallowing. Letting myself go. Letting myself drift away for a while.

Letting myself heal.

The worst part isn't the taste. It isn't the meat and formaldehyde on my tongue, or the heavy feel of the raw meat as it slides down my throat.

It's that it feels so natural.

So terribly, wonderfully natural.

CHAPTER SEVEN

Cat Among The Pigeons

Three years is a long time in politics, but the Boxer had not retired.

He could not retire, as long as the thing on the dissection slab remained. It anchored him to the job, to the life, an inert lump of matter that kept him getting up in the morning and taking the bus to the Tower. Once upon a time, Albert Morse had felt angry at the situation, filing endless petitions with Mister Smith to have the thing on the slab destroyed – he knew better now. It was inert. It hadn't moved or even twitched in months – years, even. John Doe was a broken doll, a puppet without any strings, and the murderous drive that had once possessed Albert Morse had mellowed a little every day that he hadn't moved, spoken or thought, the icy resolve thawing into simple habit.

After a year, he'd relaxed enough to get another dog, a one-eyed hound from an animal rescue organisation, and while walking the beast on the common he'd met Shirley, who worked with traumatised children in a clinic in Battersea. They'd married at the end of 2009 and were in the process of adopting.

He'd slowed down. Gained a few pounds here and there, some more grey in the temples. Stopped waking with the dawn, now relying on the shrill shriek of the alarm clock to wake them both at seven. He was never earlier than nine, and never stayed longer than five. Nobody complained – he was an anachronism now, and he had the feeling Mister Smith insisted on their regular chats out of a need for companionship more than a need for information.

Still, some things never changed, thought Albert Morse, as he stood in the airlock and waited for the sweep of the scanners over his body. He was getting more and more conscious these days of the fact that a malfunction would riddle him with bullets and drop his body into an acid pit. In fact, he wondered why he'd never considered the possibility before.

He must have cared, surely.

He breathed an audible sigh of relief as the door to the inner office opened. Time had changed him.

Time had not changed Mister Smith.

"Good morning, good morning..." he murmured, floating upside down, his withered body held in the lotus position. His eyes were fixed on Morse, but he gave the impression of looking at something else that required the bulk of his concentration. "If you take a seat, I'll bring you a cup of tea in a moment."

"I can pour myself one if it'd save you the trouble, Sir." Morse answered, moving to pour one for each of them. If Mister Smith was scanning the creature in the dissecting lab, he wouldn't have energy to spare for parlour tricks.

Mister Smith did not respond for five minutes, as Morse took his seat and sipped his tea, watching closely. He'd been through this before, and the result was the same – eventually, Mister Smith drifted over to the chairs by the fire and apologised for being distracted.

"Think nothing of it, Sir." said Morse, and smiled – a real smile. "Any changes?"

"No, no... another of the removed organs has developed the beginnings of a rudimentary consciousness, but I expected that. The main corpus itself is still completely dead – inert. Not a single thought structure running through its mind. I'm almost astonished that it's holding

"I understand that you're full of fucking shit! I'm not going to leave my wife to fend for herself in whatever shitstorm you've called down on us! And if you think—"

He didn't get any further before he was swept off his feet and across the room, slamming into the wall behind him, hard.

"If *you* think I'm going to jeopardise the continued survival of the human face for some bleeding heart you happen to be screwing, you're very wrong, Morse. You know what I can do. I tell you now that if you do go to your wife instead of the agreed location then you will find her dead of a massive brain haemorrhage." The eyes in the huge head glowed a terrible, fiery red. "But do please test me. I haven't killed anyone to prove a point in decades."

Morse hurled himself forward, fingers clawing for the homunculus. He got halfway before he was slammed back against the wall and held there, feet dangling off the floor.

"I said *forget* her! There's a back way out of here, Morse. I'm opening it for you now – the security will be disabled for the next thirty seconds. So run. *Run!*" The command was a snarl at the base of Mister Smith's throat, and it echoed in Albert Morse's mind and soul. Then Mister Smith let him go, and he dropped to the ground.

"I'll be back for you. *Sir*." he snarled.

And then he ran.

Mister Smith turned slowly in the air, and waited, marshalling his strength.

"Die, John Doe. Die. For the sake of everyone on this planet, die quickly... and for your own sake, die before you face me."

CHAPTER EIGHT

The Big Kill

I'm lost.

This place is a maze – endless corridors of grey stone and dripping water, endless twists and turns and stairways that always seem to be leading down, never up. I've just been walking, looking for someone to tell me the way out of here, but it's no go. There must be guards in a place like this. Maybe they're being kept out of my way.

After all, it's not like I'm going to ask nicely if I find them.

I'm trying not to think about swallowing my own heart back there, not to mention my lungs, kidneys, small intestine and the rest. There isn't even a scar on my belly now, and it feels like everything's back in place. Frankly, I didn't know I could do that, and I don't know if I could do it again – I never even considered the possibility that I could heal from a simple gunshot wound, never mind being taken apart like a cheap watch and stored in a neat line of jam jars.

It was like I was in a trance.

Like an emergency subroutine on a computer made of flesh and bone.

A catastrophic damage protocol for a meat robot.

Well, I've got better things to do than think about that, right?

It's not all damp corridors and wet stone down here – occasionally there are rooms coming off from the main complex, cold stone chambers like cells, dormitories with rows of empty wooden beds, long since fallen into disuse, crowded with cobwebs... I'm getting the impression that this place has been running on fumes for a while.

Maybe I was the last thing left to study.

The Boxer mentioned something like that – that I was the last of my kind. In a way, it makes me wish I could have figured out those notes. Or maybe it doesn't.

Some truths you just don't want to know.

My head's killing me. I'm going to have to get out into the fresh air before too long. I'm just taking corners at random right now – anything that feels right. That's probably making me even more lost than I was, but what the hell. Eventually I'm bound to come across somebody, surely.

I push open a heavy oak door and find myself in some kind of mess hall, presumably used by soldiers back when the Tower was more of a going concern than it is now. Or maybe used by whatever secret agents have been running it lately.

Make that definitely. Someone's been here.

There are two silver candelabras on each of the oak tables in the room, each one with three candles burning brightly, making the shadows flicker and dance across the walls – none of which makes this place any friendlier. Whoever did the decoration had a strange sense of feng shui.

Portraits of stern-looking men dressed in everything from doublet and hose to sharp business suits. I can see the Boxer in one of these pictures – 'Albert Morse'. I'll be sure to call him by name when I'm ramming his teeth down his throat.

Occult runes on some kind of ancient parchment I don't recognise, in temperature-controlled glass cases. Actually, I'm not even sure that is ink on parchment. I think it's a tattoo.

Some kind of... I'm not even sure what's in this picture,

some sort of balloon-headed freak in a three-piece suit that wouldn't look out of place on a ventriloquist's dummy...

But it's the tapestries that send my blood cold. Great big hanging monstrosities, embroidered with Latin words, occult symbols and God knows what else... and great pictures of snarling wolves tearing into the dead. Everywhere I turn, I can see intricate pictures of wolves, digging at graves, slashing at hanged men, gnawing on skulls.

All my aggression dissipates. It's like eight pints of ice-cold water's been injected directly into my veins.

I don't know what the hell I'm doing here. I need to get out. This whole situation is terrifying.

I'm so scared all of a sudden.

When was the last time I was this scared?

Oh, no... it wasn't...

It was at Sweeney's place.

When the werewolf was there.

Suddenly I'm backing away, wanting to run, whatever it was that took me here not enough to keep me from scrambling right out the door and running as far as I can through this goddamn maze until I hit the fresh air.

But I just freeze in place, looking at those runes, those embroidered red eyes blazing in fur.

All of a sudden, I can't seem to look anywhere but at those tapestries, and my heart is climbing up into the roof of my mouth and something's going to happen –

– and then there's a tearing noise and a hairy, clawed hand slashes right through the cloth and suddenly the air is full of howling.

Oh my God.

There are tunnels behind the tapestries and they lead right to the wolf pit.

I don't have time to think of anything else before three more of the tapestries explode into ribbons, the alcoves behind them filled with pulsing, snarling fur and teeth, with cold yellow and blazing red eyes. Four of them. All around me.

I turn, wanting to run, to get out of there like a hare out of hell, but there's one at the door.

That's five.

I'm so afraid.

They snarl, saliva dripping down onto the wood of the tables. I'm right in the middle of the room. Four of the wolves are circling around the tables, claws clicking on the old cold stone.

I turn to the one at the door and, Jesus Christ, it's so fast, it's leaping – grab time, grab time and squeeze it like you'd like to squeeze the Boxer's throat, squeeze it tight –

It's still so fast. My legs give out from under me and I go down and I can feel razor claws raking through my hair, a millimetre from my scalp, one nanosecond away from tearing off the top of my skull like popping a can of mixed nuts. Searing green eyes meeting mine, green as unripe acid apples. Thick, lustrous fur.

It's young. Untrained. Or that would have finished me. Razor teeth snapping and clacking and chewing me to pieces in quick gulps. Ego and identity breaking down into chunks. Everything I am chewed and swallowed and shot into the abyss of a wolf's stomach. I'm so afraid.

I'm looking at the other wolves out of the corner of my eye; fur matted, eyes glowing in red and yellow. Older and more experienced. Easily capable of rending me to pieces. But they're standing there, shifting impotently as this young upstart sails over my head.

Why aren't they attacking?

They're shifting around the table, coming at me from around the sides. They're going to get in each other's way like that. Why don't they just jump onto the table and leap from there, catching me between four sets of sharp, savage claws in a slow-motion death scene that I will make last forever, an endless hell of total terror, a fear so deep and terrible that it becomes an agony that never ends, but better than nothing at all, so I'll force myself to feel everything as they —

Stop it. This is getting me nowhere.

You were a detective when you got up this morning.

And that's a clue.

So why don't they leap over the tables?

Oh.

Of course.

Silver candelabras.

I break left. Fingers wrap around the handles of the candelabras. It's all so slow.

I swing the candelabras around, candles flying, flames flickering. The werewolf's already leaping – right for me this time. Great foaming jaws open towards me...

...and then the silver sticks smash into them with the kind of force I'd use to knock down a good-size wall with a sledgehammer.

Stitch that.

These bastards might be tough as nails but silver is the great equaliser. Sonny-boy's jaw flies apart like a cheap plastic toy from a chocolate egg. The look of fear in those green burning eyes is so goddamned gorgeous I almost don't realise I've left a big hole for the two on my left to come through. They're up on the tables and leaping for my head, claws outstretched...

Against ordinary enemies this would be a slow-motion ballet, but it's taking everything I've got to keep up with these animals. Candelabras block outstretched claws, smacking them away, breaking the bones of the hands as I jink right, letting them miss me by inches, barrelling into the tables on the other side of the room, burned by the silver.

I wheel around, aiming a kick to the half-face of Kid Werewolf, then lunge, driving the candlestick up through the roof of its mouth and into the brain – then ducking down as the claws swipe the air where I was. My heart's pounding. The adrenaline's flowing. The fear is... not gone, but changed. The situation is almost impossible but not hopeless. I feel stronger, faster than I've been in years. I've got silver on my side.

There's a dark joy flowing through me. Like I'm close to the threshold of something, and if I just survive this, I can find it.

I've never felt this alive.

I vault back, describing a lazy arc through the air as claws rake above and below, listening to the sound of flesh falling off bone as the Beautiful Boy shrivels and falls into a thousand slippery pieces out of my field of vision.

Something's changed. Maybe it's the reset button they pushed in me, or the long rest my body's had.

Maybe it's that I'm the last of my kind. Maybe, on some deep, buried level, far underneath the surface of my head, I know I'm playing for all the marbles.

Whatever it is – I've never been this good. *Never.*

They can't touch me. The four wolves have sores and boils on their hands from where I've smacked them with the candelabras. Without even thinking about it, I reach out and grab hold of another to replace the one that's buried in the skull of Scrappy-Doo. One of the remaining wolves lunges – a big red-eyed, scraggy-haired sonovabitch – and I swipe the candelabras together at neck height, crushing his windpipe. Just before his neck disintegrates and sends his head tumbling, I lift my foot and kick it into his face, sending myself backwards into a somersault. At the top of the arc, I flick the big heavy silver antiques like sai swords, watching as they bury in two hairy chests and yellow eyes flicker out like streetlamps...

It's beautiful.

It's poetry.

The stench of rotting wolfmeat is heavy in the air, and it's just me and the last of the wolves. He's dripping saliva, snarling with his red eyes blazing like searchlights, and I've got no silver to hand. But I don't care.

I feel strong. Strong and hungry. I could eat for hours. I could tear through that wolf in a second.

I feel like... like Satan on the day of the Apocalypse.

Does that make me a bad person?

Does that make me a monster?

Come on, you little bastard.

Make the first move.

I dare you.

There's a long moment of silence before it leaps. This is the same kind of nightmare I ran until my muscles ached to get away from. The same beast that was making me piss myself in fear less than a minute ago. And I'm grabbing its paws and swinging it around, using its momentum against it while it snaps and snarls.

What is this? An emergency boost? Some dormant skill kicking in?

What's in the saddle here?

The wolf goes flying, slow-motion into the skeleton of one of its brothers. There's a candelabra still lodged in the eye socket of the grinning wolf-skull, and the wolf's shoulder comes down on it hard. Impaled on silver.

Thank you, long-dead interior decorator. Thank you for being so stupid.

As the wolf howls, I let go of time and let it flow about me like the cloak of some mighty warrior. Then I grab another of the silver sticks and walk over, nice and slow, taking my time.

It thrashes, snarls and spits. It must be in agony.

I feel dark and terrible. I feel sadistic. I feel like a scorpion in the jungle, like some terrifying killer insect. I feel evil and damned.

I feel more like a monster than I ever have before.

And it feels good.

That's right, you Universal reject. You've met your match now.

I grin, staring him down, taking a good long look into those pain-wracked red eyes, that snapping muzzle.

Then I smash its brains in.

That should be the end of it. That should be me out the door and racing towards the sunlight, but I stay, breathing in rotting wolf-flesh, just feeling stronger and stronger.

I read once in a book somewhere that the Bocor, the voodoo priest, the maker of zombies, could get the Loa, the god who'd given him patronage, to wear him like a coat, ride him like an animal, control him. That's what it feels like now. Like I'm being ridden.

Like something much stronger and older and more powerful than I am is whispering in my ear, an insect Loa telling me that wolves need to be controlled if they're going to all attack at once like that. Controlled by a superior mind. A superior brain.

Did I deduce that?

Or did I just smell it?

I feel like I'm devolving, like I'm reducing to my basic essence, my core, like this terrible, wonderful machine that I am is moving into some kind of overdrive and my carefully nurtured consciousness cannot keep up. Like I'm sliding slowly into avatism.

I feel like there's something primal hatching in the centre of my mind, some awful desire to kill and eat and feed on my prey. I feel like an insect. I feel like a killer. I feel like a monster.

I am a hungry monster in a dark castle and somewhere there is food...

Somewhere...

brains

...I'm walking. Running. Lurching forward, ridden by my personal Loa, by the wonderful, terrible Insect Intelligence buried in the heart of me and, oh God, I'm so hungry, and this was where I was being led all along, this was what it was always about, the door smashing and splintering, thick oak but breaking against my dead fists, a terrifying red light burning into my eyes and then I'm through, inside some sort of airlock, some sort of trap-box, electronic voices screaming and wailing in my ears – *intruder detected* – and I can't even remember how I got here but I can't focus on anything except the

brains

and I must have blacked out for a second because the trap is sprung and the floor's swung out from underneath me and I can feel my feet splashing in acid, burning and melting and reforming as soon as they do. I'm wading forward like I'm wading through a swamp, dissolving and reforming. I didn't even know I could do something like that, but I don't care, I'm so close to the goal now that my mouth is watering. So close to that one thing I was put here for. I can smell it. My thoughts feel strange. Alien. Insectile. Nothing seems to matter, not the machine guns opening up, not the bullets tearing into flesh that heals as soon as they pass through, not the thick steel door to the room beyond. Nothing's going to stop me. Nothing's going to stop me from getting at the

brains

I'm barely conscious. Hands smashing at the second door. Denting the steel. Punching through. Grabbing. Tearing. So close. Can't think about anything

except

BRAAAAINNNNNSSS

And suddenly I'm inside the room. I'm trying to keep my thoughts clear. Trying not to think about that thing floating there with his big beach ball head, with the tender brain inside. I'm trying not to let that dark, sadistic insect part of me get any more of a hold on me, because I'm afraid of what it's doing to me. I'm afraid that this might be my last chance to get away, to get clear of this beach-ball-head man before something terrible happens, that this might be my last to chance to leave without grabbing hold of him and tearing his skull open and eating his delicious, succulent, moist—

It's not going to happen, John.

Oh God. Oh God that never made a thing like me.

He's in my head.

Yes, John. I'm inside your mind. I commissioned a lot of research on you, and I do believe it's paid off. I really do think I can affect you, John. In fact, I think I can kill you.

He's in my head. He's got me right where he wants me. Did he lead me here?

I need to think –

I'll do your thinking for you, John. Don't worry. I'll try not to make this hurt too much.

No, no, get out, get out, get out –

Don't struggle, John. This is for the best.

Get out! Get out of my head!

What the hell are you?

I'm Mister Smith, John.

Prepare for psychic annihilation.

CHAPTER NINE

Playback

There's a little man sitting in my head.

A little man ripping and tearing and biting at the walls of my mind, plunging hooks into my sense of self and yanking out pieces, flaying my preconceived notions with barbed wire, slashing and tearing, damaging, killing me from the outside in, boring his way into me like an oilman drilling for a big strike.

And deep down inside there's an opposite force, something down deep at the bottom of my brain, some terrible insect monster that's wearing me like a coat, controlling me, moving my limbs and sending me crashing forward, raging, attacking, hungry for the unspeakable.

And everything I always thought I was is stuck in the middle.

I don't know how much more of this I can take.

It's all going to be over soon, John. Don't worry.

I can hear him in my head.

He's reaching into my head and yanking out wires. I can feel lights going off on the switchboard of my self, a dark void starting to open up. I've heard the word 'soul-destroying' a number of times, but I never really thought about what it meant before. Now I know.

Listen: six years ago I went to the park.

It was a beautiful autumn day, and the leaves on the trees were a riot of burning red, orange and gold. There were couples picnicking with hampers straight out of a picture-book, kids throwing balls and sticks for healthy dogs to catch and bring back, tails wagging. There was just enough cloud to keep the sun from being oppressive, and just enough wind to let you appreciate what a warm September day it was.

I stood on a hill, looking out at the people smiling and laughing and holding each other, and I felt like I belonged in the world. I felt like there was a place for me. I sat on the grass and stayed there for hours, just people-watching, seeing the world go by. That was when I decided I didn't want to be a killer anymore.

How long ago was that? Eight years? Four?

I went to... I think it was a fairground... in the summer...

Gone. Destroyed. Nothing left now, John Doe. Nothing left to do but die.

Let go, John, let yourself end and fall into pieces.

You are the enemy of all that is, John Doe. End and die.

That was the happiest day of my life...

What was I saying?

No, it's gone. Got to concentrate. I'm fighting a war on three fronts here. Every chunk this freak takes out of me opens me up to that yawning hunger at the core of me. I don't want to give in to that. I don't want to become nothing but hunger.

You are nothing but hunger, John. Don't fool yourself. All I'm doing is stripping away your illusions so I can crush the real you and end your threat forever.

Die, John. Roll over and die.

Jesus Christ, will you shut up for a second?

There's him yammering in my head, almost but not quite masking the alien insect thoughts down deep in the centre of my psyche, the ones that want me to tear and eat and feed... and then on top of all that, there are the chairs.

The ones flying at my face.

It's really hard to deal with total evisceration on the psychic plane when there's a massive leather armchair flying directly into your sternum. Slowing time doesn't help – no, John, none of your little time-tricks now. I can control my perception of time as well as you can, so no matter what speed you're seeing things at, I'll be right there seeing them with you. You can't escape me, John.

He's right.

The heavy armchair slams into me, sending me crashing across the room and into the wall, pinned like a bug under somebody's thumb. That giant head turns to look at me, eyes glowing, not showing the slightest strain. Telekinesis – he can crush me like a cockroach without lifting a finger.

As if I didn't have enough on my mind.

The chair catches light, along with the floor beneath my feet and my hair and skin. Pyrokinesis – telekinetic acceleration of molecules to make things ignite. It hits me – he's not heating the desk. He's heating me, and everything I touch is going up as a result – my skin's got to be three hundred degrees right now. And I'm taking it. And deep down underneath, in the dark part of myself I don't want to acknowledge...

...I'm loving it.

Does that make me a bad person?

Does that make me a monster?

What kind of person am I?

Whatever I am, I'm a little too resilient to go up in flames just yet, but it's a matter of time – he's going to keep turning up the heat until I melt. Now I know how a lobster in a pot feels.

All this on top of the sharp claws scrabbling inside my head, tearing and scratching at my thoughts and memories. I can't just lie here and die – pinned to a wall by an animated armchair and roasted like chicken. It's too stupid a way to go.

I ball my fists and slam them against the blazing wood, smashing and battering at it like a madman. My hands rise and fall, rise and fall, thrashing like one of the wolves, letting the hunger underneath take control, letting it turn me into an animal. Into a biting insect. Into what it wants. The chair creaks and splinters – the combined pressure from the telekinesis, the fire and this little workout splitting the wood, great cracks that slowly travel through the structure until the whole thing bursts apart into component parts. I fight my way free of a drowning sea of wood, leather, foam stuffing, fire and fume – and I'm right back where I started, with a slight difference in temperature of about five hundred degrees. The whole room's going up.

How very aggressive of you, John. Well, there's more where that came from.

That's when the desk levitates up from the floor and starts a suicide run towards me.

This isn't funny. That thing's got to be solid mahogany – it's not going to burn easy and if it hits, it's goodnight Vienna, or as close as I can get anyway. I can feel him tugging and tearing at all the little pieces of me like he's yanking out clumps of my hair, but I can't worry about that now. I need to let go of all conscious thought – do this on pure instinct –

The desk flies towards me, one ton of mahogany that could crush me like a beetle under a boot –

– and then I step –

– jump –

– what –

– vault over the desk as it passes noiselessly underneath

me –

– wait –

– and then as it smashes into the wall, I'm reaching out and grabbing hold of that big-headed little bastard by one half-shrunken ear and drawing my fist back and then –

– AAAAAHHH!

I can hear him inside my mind, and for once it feels good. That poke in the face seems to have broken his concentration – the dome-headed freak can't be used to direct physical pain if he's squirrelled away in here, especially not having his nose pulped by a solid right cross...

That... makes two of us.

Let's see how you like it.

I stagger backwards. Something just smashed into my face and smashed my nose down like a pancake.

Then something does it again.

And again.

And again.

A constant cracking of bone, like the beat of a drum, the pain fresh and alive every time – *crack, crack, crack* – and the worst part is, it's not even my nose.

That's right, John. But every blow you give me, I'm going to give you back a thousand times – that's if you ever reach me again. It's not only tables and chairs I can move, John.

I feel something grabbing hold of me – like a giant hand with a hundred fingers, squeezing from all directions, then hurling me towards the wood-panelled wall. He's got me in the grip of his mind – tearing my thoughts, delivering the sensation of a broken nose a thousand times a second, and slamming me around the room like a kid smashing his sister's favourite doll.

I'm pinballing off the walls... the ceiling... the floor... I can't get my bearings –

And now you're out of reach, let's show you just how hot I can make things for you...

There's something that feels like a rush of air, and suddenly everything gets very hot, very quickly. He was only testing before – now he really means business. I can smell flesh – my own flesh – cooking like bacon, charring and burning... flames start to spring from my arms and legs. I can feel my face burning, my eyeballs bursting and running down my cheeks...

Die, John. Die! DIE!

Don't listen to him. Don't panic. I can get through this. Whatever I am is stopping me from burning up completely, and I can still... see, somehow. I know where he is in the room. I can smell him, even above the burning flesh and the melting fat of my own blazing body.

It's his brain. It's like a beacon.

What *is* he?

Would you really like to know, John?

Don't listen to him – just break free of his grip –

Yes, I think I will tell you. I think drowning in my memories will probably stop you struggling free while I burn you to ooze... yes, yes, I think you should know my story intimately.

And suddenly I'm somewhere else. Somewhere warm and safe, protected by darkness and fluids. Sensations come to me, muffled, from beyond the soft organic walls of where I am.

The year is 1839.

The year is 1839. The biophysicist Herr Doktor Emil Klugefleisher has made his home in London after being forced to flee his native Germany due to circumstances unknown. He is the toast of the scientific community for his theories on the development of the human brain, taking Galvani's theories of bioelectricity in bold new directions and experimenting to alter the mental capabilities of rats and apes in utero, albeit with little practical success. There is even talk of his being accepted into the Royal Society.

All of his work threatens to crumble into dust when his maid, Eliza Smith, reveals to him that she is pregnant and that he is the father. In an instant Herr Doktor foresees his whole reputation wiped out at a stroke by the scandal. The answer is obvious – the girl must vanish. Klugefleisher considers simply strangling her and dropping her body into the Thames, but the action seems rash. He reconsiders. His basement laboratory is soundproofed, and he is in need of a human test subject, after all. Why not kill two birds with one stone?

The fledgeling police force in London take little notice of Eliza Smith's disappearance, not suspecting so well-regarded a citizen as Herr Doktor Klugefleisher. In reality, the girl is now little more than a mindless shell, the regimen of chemicals and electricity that is designed to affect the foetus in her belly having rotted her own brain tissue to the point where she cannot speak or feed herself, or even think.

Awareness first comes to you as you grow in her womb. The garbled snatches of private thoughts reach, not your ears, but your growing frontal lobes. Slowly, you begin to understand. The womb is commonly regarded as the paradise to which many seek to regress, but for you it is a horror beyond description. The amniotic fluid you float in bubbles with foul, noxious chemicals. Electricity sizzles through nerve endings, causing intense pain even as it acts on your nerves and cells, warping and mutating your body. The accelerated growth of your head is constant, unending agony, and all the while you can feel the cold, frozen evil of your father and the babbling insanity of your mother. This is your earliest memory.

Not mine...

You wanted to know my story, John Doe. Allow me to tell it in my own way, as a weapon to destroy you completely. Feel my life happening to you, every nightmare, every agony, every spirit-crushing second of torment compressed into the telling of it. Listen to my story and die...

After four months, your mother finally dies, and Herr Doktor Klugefleisher is forced to cut you out of her womb. It is hard to say whether it is the chemicals and the electricity that kill the poor woman, or whether it is you – your immense, lolling head is already much larger than a normal baby would grow and the womb now presses against you, stretched beyond endurance, your mother's agony constantly battering against your mental defences to merge with their own, one more horror in a sea of horrors. Her death comes as a relief.

Your first sight when the knife carves through flesh to release you is the grinning face of Herr Doktor, staring down at his prize. As he lifts you in his arms... his hands gripping the sides of your head as your body dangles, shrivelled and almost lifeless... and then there is a knock at the door above. As well as receiving thoughts, you have been broadcasting your own – thoughts of pain, fear, misery! The good Doktor is inured against such, but his neighbours are terrified at the sensations that crawl across their souls – which their limited minds can only translate as the sound of purest murder echoing from the house of Herr Doktor Klugefleisher. And so the police have arrived to enquire as to the nature of the disturbance.

Klugefleisher turns his head – and you lash out, using telekinesis for the first time as a small child might flex infant fingers. You catch his head within your mind, and his head continues to turn... turn... turn! He pleads! Begs! His screams for mercy become shriller as his vertebrae begin to tear apart one by one, but there is no mercy in you... only a cold desire for revenge!

A sickening crack of separating cartilage and the devil doctor lies dead – a fitting punishment for his crimes against humanity!

You float in the air, contemplating the dead man, as the police break down the door, motivated as much by the emanations of rage and grief that spill from your warped brain as by the ominous silence... only to fall back, screaming in terror, as they break open the soundproofed room to find you floating above the corpse... your distended head supporting your withered frame like a child's balloon supporting a string...your eyes, black and pitiless, glowing with the power afforded you by the madman's forbidden experiments!

I can't feel any part of me – all I'm aware of is old Victorian stone and the smell of blood and in front of my eyes there's an old German scientist with his head on backwards. I'm drowning in melodrama.

And I think he's doing something to me. Some essential part of me is starting to lose... integrity. Coherence.

That's right, John Doe. I'm taking you apart, brick by brick, cell by cell. There's going to be nothing left of you but single cells, isolated, unconnected, a thin soup of living, mindless sludge on the floor.

You can't win, John. Herr Doktor Klugefleisher created me as the ultimate development of the human mind. Had Darwin's theory been in common usage at the time, he might have thought of me as the product of millennia of human evolution... come, don't you want to see how I was studied? How I became a curiosity for Victoria until she saw my true value and assigned me to aid in the work begun by John Dee? Perhaps you'd like to see first-hand how I came to take over MI-23, how I began the work of eradicating your kind, one by one...

Or perhaps it's enough to know that all of you from the waist down is a thin, liquid ooze. Your body cells don't respond well to the kind of heat I'm putting out, John. You were never the strongest of your kind, and now that I've learned how to pry your cells apart from one another it's going to be very easy to turn you into nothing but a thin, lifeless gruel.

Goodbye, John.

He's got me.

I can feel my mind simplifying as I burn and melt on the floor. Feel that terrible alien hunger creeping up to take over, that part of me that was in control all along, playing me for a fool all my days, the nasty little inner demon that's made me the bad guy in the story of my life. Hell with it, anyway – I should relax and let balloon-head take care of it. God knows, after seeing what this body's capable of, I wouldn't trust myself with it. And these people are allegedly the good guys, even if they do make Jack Bauer look like a liberal bleeding heart.

Why not let them save the day?

I try and relax and let it happen. I'd close my eyes if I still had them. But it's no good.

I'm selfish. I'm evil. I'm an insect who only cares about survival.

And I want to live.

He's inside my head, drowning me in his memories while he dismantles me piece by piece. All right, then. All right. If he's such a fan of memories... I'll give him what he wants.

What are you doing, John?

Just let go and let that drive to live take over... stop

suppressing that animal part of me, that weird insect part that's wanted to rise to the surface ever since I got within sniffing distance of this guy. I can't see what that part of me wants – what's been making me act so crazy this past hour – but I'll bet he can.

Let's let the dog see the rabbit.

John? What are you thinking... you can't escape, John...

What are you...?

Oh God... oh God, I didn't realise... I didn't... *get away from me...*

GET AWAY! GET AWAY!

And then it's just screaming. Screaming in my brain. And whatever he saw made him lose his cool enough to let me out of his grip. I wonder what it was?

I'm not burning anymore. I can move. It's too late, though.

I'm moving already.

I'm a passenger in my own body. I can feel it – oozing liquid half sliding and slopping, arms moving with inhuman strength, propelling the top half of me across the burning floor, padding and lapping against the hot wood, fingers flexing and uncoiling with enough force to send this melting, distorted flesh prison that used to look like a human being up into the air...

...arms wrapping around the gigantic screaming head that's still broadcasting terror and madness into my mind... but not a terror for his own safety.

For the safety of the planet.

I wish I could stop this happening. I wish I could do something, anything apart from just watching it happen. But I'm not in control anymore. I'm a fading voice, an unreal personality, a cheap disguise torn away in the final scene.

I wish I'd let myself die.

But it's too late now.

The arms tighten enough to crack open the huge skull like an eggshell and I can smell the grey matter slopping out –

– *the BRAINS* –

It's so hard to stay coherent –

My teeth chewing and gnawing and swallowing down the stringy grey matter and suddenly a light switch goes off in my head and I

I

I

Understand

Everything

And then the world ends.

Interlude The Second
New York, 1976

– and in that last moment of self-awareness memory floods in and Johnny hears the twinks chatting under the strobe lights of '76 –

"I don't care about sex, I just want somebody to hold, I'm *such* a pervert –"

"Oh *God*, don't tell me you've been talking to Texas Barry, *please*, Texas Barry spins that exact line *all* the time, Stevie went home with him once, the man's got no cock to speak of –"

"Oh, don't, don't tell me that, I'm on downs, why would you tell me *that* –"

"Oh please, he wants to marry every boy he meets, oh, oh *God*, this is my song, this is my new song, come on I want to dance –"

– and they jump up from the sofa and move onto the floor and dance and instantly their places are taken, one man this time, older and watching the lean tanned boys twirl and flex and move around the floor and toss their heads back in something like ecstasy and look so good and sing in time with the music, 'make me believe in you, tell me that love can be true', old but newly discovered to them, a sweet reminder to Roscoe that old things come good sometimes –

– and Roscoe's cruising for twinks at the Tenth Floor and feeling alone and out of place because the New York scene is mutating so quickly now, new joints springing up every week but the white straight polyester crowd is edging out the blacks and the gays and the both and the men are fat and permed these days and their teeth are bad and they don't like to dance, why would they want to dance like fags anyway, they're here for one reason and that's to get drunk and get laid and what the hell, maybe that's cool despite everything because God knows it'd be nice to get some dick action in New York at thirty-eight years old –

– and seven months, nearly thirty-nine if you think about it and Roscoe's thinking old man's sour dour thoughts tonight as the speed kicks in and rewires his brain and the twinks dance like it's just for him, erection like a stone at the bottom of a lake in his pants, hard but drowned deep in cold water and soon to be eroded into sand and nothing and he's thirty-eight and lonely and lost in New York and something's going cold inside him and it's been four months since he did anything and there's grey in his moustache and his belly's starting to nudge over his belt and oh God what if nobody ever wants to fuck him again –

– and oh God that kid looks so damn good in that vest, what is he, eighteen, seventeen, it's like he stepped off a beach in California and through the doors of the club and all Roscoe wants to do is gently lead him into the toilet and unbutton his tight jeans slowly and with the reverence that should be accorded to the risen Christ or a reclining Buddha and blow him just as an act of religious devotion more than anything –

– and Roscoe doesn't do a damn thing as per usual except mutter like a crazy bastard and drink coffee and maybe he should get up and dance but he doesn't have the rhythm in him anymore, it'd be like those goddamn white straight polyester assholes that are gonna be the face of disco music for 1977 and until the end of time maybe and maybe that shitty little punk asshole on Fifth

Street was right, Jesus, he should have beaten hell out of that little bastard but what if he was telling the truth –

– and Roscoe can't handle these thoughts any longer, he can feel the drugs taking him into some down deep dark place so he latches onto the twinks again, so warm and healthy and just glowing with life and sex and strength and that's what it's all about and Roscoe listens in because whatever they're talking about is better than this shit in his head –

"Oh God, I forgot, guess who I ran into on the street, just try to guess –"

"What? I can't hear you –"

"Johnny Doe! He was panhandling down on thirty-eighth, letting tourists touch him for a buck –"

"Oh my God, is Johnny Doe coming, I'm totally in love with that man, he's like Bowie meets Bogart –"

"He's decadent, he's just *totally* decadent, have you touched his skin ever, it's ice-cold –"

"That's what it must be like to fuck Bowie –"

– and that's a weird thing to hear because it was four months ago with Johnny Doe in that alley and Roscoe taking him into his mouth and running his tongue slowly up and it wasn't ice-cold but it was cold and so weird that he nearly stopped but Johnny does look a lot like Bogart or some kind of outer space Ziggy Stardust cool dream Bogart anyhow and it'd been a couple months since Jason left him because his goddamn shrink told him to, never trust a fucking Jungian, and Roscoe had him in his mouth and couldn't smell him and it was like Johnny didn't have a scent and that was so weird and so hot at the same time –

– and his cum was *black* –

– and afterwards Johnny asked his name, looking down and kind of smirking like the cold bastard god of decadence he was, and Roscoe got defensive and told him the PhD part even though he usually kept that quiet because this asshole was a freak not a rock star and Roscoe didn't need this dominant-submissive game-playing shit right now –

– and suddenly Johnny Doe dropped his cold-ass decadent pose and took Roscoe back to his place and they drank whiskey sours and Johnny gave him a handjob on the couch and that was the weirdest because all the time that cold hand was moving and stroking and teasing and touching and getting Roscoe harder than anything ever had in his life that soft cold Village voice was telling the craziest story Roscoe ever heard –

– and Johnny Doe was saying he wasn't a human being –

– and then he finished Roscoe off and left his head spinning from the intensity and the information that Johnny Doe was Ziggy Stardust and *The Man Who Fell To Earth* and *Dracula AD 1972* and whatever the hell else he was and that was why he had no scent and why you couldn't feel his pulse or hear his heartbeat and Johnny took him by the hand and led him into the bedroom and and and –

– and word spreads fast in a place like this and another young hot perfect guy was joining the first two and the newcomer's solid black muscle was the perfect counterpoint to the sleek white marble bodies dancing around him and this brand new 1976-model twink reminded Roscoe of that time he took Jimmy home –

– and the morning after Jimmy's dad was at the door with a shotgun ready to blow Roscoe's head off and Roscoe barricaded himself in the bathroom and called the cops and they never came and eventually Jimmy's dad blew a hole in Roscoe's Warhol print saying it was the path to degeneracy and took off and Jimmy wanted to get back together but by that time Roscoe was sleeping with Jason and they were going to move in together and this used to be a funny story Roscoe told at parties and now he wanted to cry thinking about it and what was so special about Jason anyway after Roscoe had fucked a spaceman –

– and he has to listen in on the twinks again just to block out that gnawing fucking hole right through him, the twinks turned right around like meerkats to stare at the entrance and the crowd making awestruck noises and celebrity noises and Jesus noises –

"Johnny –"

"Johnny, over here, Johnny –"

"Remember me from the Garage, Johnny –"

"Johnny – Johnny – *Johnny* –"

– and six foot of Bogart/Bowie pure pale blue-white flesh shock-white hair walking through the door and every inch of him cold and decadent and ignoring all the lust and need and the backlash bitching and milking that goddamn Bowie bullshit everyone expects of him these days and maybe that's why he does it –

– and Roscoe stands up slowly and heads to the office in the back that Gary said he could use whenever he was speeding and stressed and needed a place to be alone, thank God for Gary, and he closes the door on the music and the talk and the bullshit and just sits behind the desk in that little office and rests his head on his hands and waits and wants to cry –

– and Roscoe thinks back to him and Johnny Doe lying in bed listening to the couple in the apartment upstairs screaming at each other and how Johnny wanted to know who he was and what he was and everything and Roscoe with his head full of dope smoke saying anything that came into his head and still freaking out on that experience and on Johnny's cold space muscle and Bogie eyes and smile and making all kinds of promises –

– and he wishes now he'd never said a word –

– and Roscoe took all kinds of samples out of Johnny, like skin samples and blood samples and stool and hair and listened to the heartbeat Johnny didn't have and listened up over coffee to ten years of Johnny's life story, starting off in a cheap apartment on Haight-Ashbury, dealing acid and reds until Altamont shot down the hippie dream and he came east to the Village to lose himself and melt into the first culture he found and before that he hated hippies like poison and hunted Reds behind the cold dark whiskey sour desk of a private eye, Bogie not Bowie in those days and before that he fought in the war like everyone else and before that he ran hooch and hung out with Dorothy and before that well it doesn't matter but there's a lot of before that you can keep a secret right Emmett right –

– and Roscoe had heard some weird coming-out stories in his time but Johnny's was the oddest, coming on like he didn't care about nothing except fitting in to whatever scene would have him, so he asked all the right questions and a few crazy ones and heard things that made his blood run like ice and killed his hard lust dead as arctic tundra, things like Johnny saying he snuck into the morgue sometimes and ate brains –

– and Jesus Christ, Johnny admitted he ate brains and why the hell didn't Roscoe call the cops right then except maybe this was his last chance to do something right with his life and this was too big to let go of –

– and Roscoe nearly freaked out and called the cops or the FBI when the blood sample turned into a goddamn slug crawling around the tube and the hair turned to bone and the skin crawled off the microscope slide and he spent three days throwing up until he finally burned the goddamn samples in a furnace and even then he lay awake every night for weeks afterwards –

– and it was one of those sleepless alone nights that all the jigsaw pieces came together and he realised what Johnny was –

– and he'd been avoiding Johnny ever since and he figured Johnny never came to the Tenth Floor, he was always in the Paradise Garage if he was anywhere, but somehow Johnny picked the one night Roscoe figured he was safe and now he'd have to tell him or maybe he could just hide in this little back office forever or until the dawn when everyone went home and slept it off –

– and the door opens with a creak like an old tomb –

– and Roscoe's skin nearly crawls right off his back with the fear like Johnny's skin crawling around on his desk then sprouting tiny little insect legs and Roscoe turns and nearly vomits and babbles a hello oh hello Johnny I didn't know it was you I didn't know you were in here Johnny how are you Johnny oh God oh Christ –

"Hey, Emmett."

– and Roscoe chokes and goes quiet because his voice is so cold and alien and dead like the ultimate Ziggy Stardust Sam Spade fusion the kids all want to fuck only it's flat granite stony as a grave marker –

"I was looking for you."

– and he smiles and that's the scariest thing of all because that's the smile of the Johnny Doe who made Roscoe bacon and eggs in the morning, the sexy sweet guy who's okay in spite of it all and that makes it so much worse because underneath there's something looking out at him like a snake waiting to strike –
– and Roscoe feels something cold and wrong and bone-hard clutching at his heart –

"What you got?"

– and maybe it's the speed and maybe it's the raw fear crackling up and down Roscoe's nerves like neon but he opens his mouth and out it spills like poison –
– and first it's all just crazy stuff about how Johnny's like a commune of individual cells who get together to

be a collective and imitate a human being right down to the personality and how the further away from him offcuts like all the samples get, the more they show a life of their own –

– and how the cellular imitation isn't a true duplicate because it's cold and dead and deliciously decadent here and now but there and then just freaky and the reason why Johnny wants to fit in all the time with any new scene he comes across is because he's got to lay low and not draw attention and whoever's really calling the shots in that cell collective, the alien intelligence buried deep inside his sweet human soul, keeps him in situations where being a little weird isn't going to be enough to get noticed –

– and that's why he's mister Ziggy Decadent right here right now in 1976 and he was a hipster dealer back before that scene fell apart and the cops got wise to him and who knows maybe in the past he was in even stranger places than Bicentennial America like Monocentennial or Nocentennial America maybe if you can dig that who knows he isn't talking –

– and maybe in the future things will get so crazy strange and information rich that he can just be normal –

– and Johnny's looking like he figured most of that out already and that's not what he's here for, like maybe he's doped out every little nuance of what he is and he just needs to know why, or maybe he just wants to know what Roscoe knows –

– and his eyes are like little lethal grey bullets –

"That's it?"

– and Roscoe knows he has to keep his mouth shut now –

– and he opens it anyway because those eyes won't let him do anything else –

– and in the end it's all about the brains –

– and the reason Johnny breaks into the morgue and eats brains and maybe takes them fresh from heads too isn't any kind of crazy vampire bloodlust or serial killer compulsion because it's a lot smarter than that –

– and it wasn't until Roscoe wondered why an alien gestalt entity would need to eat brains that it came to him that the collective absorbs brains to analyse the tissue, the synapses, the cortical development and all that jazz like it's a walking talking spectrometer or *Star Trek* scanner taking samples forever –

– and suddenly Roscoe's flashing back to that late night double feature he caught when he couldn't sleep for the speed, some dumb Elliot Gould flick with a cat and a gun and a murder or something but following up with *2001: A Space Odyssey* and Jesus Christ if that isn't what's happening now because Johnny's the monolith and the sentinel and all of that stuff rolled into one, an alarm system waiting to signal somebody out there in the dark –

– and instead of waiting for us all to take that trip to the moon, Johnny's sampling brains, analysing the chemistry and power of all those little grey cells up there, waiting for that one special brain that'll tell him we've got to that stage of evolution where we're worth harvesting like crops, because if you want slaves, you don't want them too smart and you don't want them too dumb either –

– and if you want to eat a good steak you take it from a cow, not some dinosaur due to evolve into a cow in a billion years –

– and that means that whatever's out there is going to make future man look like a dumb animal –

– and Johnny's eyes are like two chips of black ice on a road Roscoe's skidding down with no control, steering wheel slick and slippery in his hands –

– and Johnny walks towards Roscoe and oh-so-gently takes hold of his face like he might lean in and kiss him one last time –

– and the sound of Roscoe's neck snapping is like the click of a door locking something away for all time –

– and Johnny doesn't even seem to be aware Roscoe ever existed as he walks out of that room and out of the club and out of New York, heading for the airport, whatever inner voice driving him now to forget, start over, find a new country and blend in deeper, deeper, deeper as he moves towards starting his new London life as straight and normal as anyone has ever been or ever could be –

– and Emmett Roscoe isn't found until four o'clock in the morning –

– and nobody makes it to the funeral except his mother –

– and the next year the club is gone and they're burning records in stadiums because it's faggot music and the good days are pretty much over and there's disease and death and hate coming hard on the new decade and word on the street is no future for you –

– and thirty-three years after that Johnny Doe is opening one giant red death eyeball slick with alien oils and juices and shrieking in the insect language of the death angels because he finally got that one perfect special brain he wanted and the signal is travelling out in a faster than light stream of information calling the Elder Gods the Insect Nation living in no-space no-time to fold down into this dimension to burn the world to harvest the human race –

– and that's that.

CHAPTER TEN

The Twisted Thing

There was no sound in the room.

The walls were gutted by fire and the furniture had either been smashed or incinerated in the war between the two monsters. The floor was a mass of burnt carpet and mangled timber, in the centre of which lay what looked like a twisted, leathery doll, the massive head torn open, cracked like an eggshell and emptied, the eye sockets hollow and staring.

This was what remained of Mister Smith.

Next to the mutated, mutilated corpse, there lay the thing that once called itself John Doe. That name no longer fit. No human name could. The corpse was barely a torso, torn, partially melted and almost unrecognisable, strips of brain matter still hanging from what was left of its teeth. It was inert.

But not inactive.

Deep inside the charred and ruined lump of flesh, alien cells pulsed and chattered, communicating, analysing. Processes that had been primed millennia ago stuttered into motion. The command was simple.

Analyse the brain tissue, then heal to the required form. To the soldier form.

To the signaller.

The cells broke down the grey matter, swarming over it like tiny ants, deconstructing and exploring each strand of DNA. Mister Smith was not like ordinary men – his strange creator had seen to that. He was man as he would perhaps be in one thousand or one million years, a skull packed with the future.

The swarming cells of the thing that was once John Doe crawled across the torn, tattered scraps of Mister Smith's mind, reading and devouring. This was what they had been waiting for. This was a mind advanced enough to serve the collective.

The Insect Nation.

The cell-collective read the DNA strands carefully. The humans had indeed evolved to a stage where they could make slaves for the Insect Nation. Or was this an anomaly? There were no other functioning cell-collectives on the planet to communicate with. The chameleon personality, used to gather information about planetary culture, was inert and offline.

The cell-collective swarmed and chattered, turning the data over. Until further evidence presented itself, the collective had to assume that Mister Smith's brain was the normal configuration... that the Earth had matured enough to provide a slave race.

It was time to send the signal.

It was time to end the civilisation of this planet.

The flesh of the charred corpse that was once John Doe shifted.

Slowly, the pores began to ooze – a thick, white pus that slowly dripped... *slithered*... over the destroyed flesh, coating it in an opaque layer. The white coating thickened as the minutes passed, oozing, congealing, hardening.

Forming a cocoon.

The minutes ticked by.

Gradually, the cocoon lost its shape, the humanity inside melting, flowing, until the thick white skin resembled nothing so much as a large, circular blob of wax, or a lump of slimy dough, flat at the bottom.

In truth, it was an egg, and from it would hatch the final end of man.

Inside the cocoon, there was nothing resembling a human being – nothing but a soup of alien cells, floating, multiplying, small bolts of strange electricity sparking from one to another. This was the next phase of the program. It was time for the simulacrum to be cast off, the disguise discarded.

Now was the hour of The Sentinel.

Gradually the cells began to coalesce, flowing together, hardening, strengthening, forming structures. Outwardly the cocoon seemed to expand and vibrate, the membrane shuddering as though hundreds of tiny fish were conducting a war inside it, fighting each other for dominance. The primal soup inside bubbled and strained against the shivering white skin.

Gradually, a skeletal structure began to form. Alien organs grew like planets coming together from cosmic dust. The bubbling, boiling spew inside the thick white membrane thickened and began to solidify.

The cell-collective had previously taken a shape necessary for collecting data on the genetics and brain structure of the prospective slave race. That phase was complete. It needed a new form.

A form that would serve the interests of the Insect Nation.

A form that could call them across the void of space.

A form that could do their bidding when they arrived.

A form that – if it became necessary – could kill the human beings in their thousands.

Slowly, the thick white membrane of the egg-sac began to tear, a clear pus leaking out and pooling on the charred wooden floor.

Something unfolded from within, rearing up to full height. A mass of thin, hard white flesh and bone, fully nine feet in height, stooping in the confines of the room.

It was shaped almost like a man. The resemblance was slight, but close enough to lend it an additional air of terrifying inhumanity. There was nothing that we would recognise as a face on the thin, swaying head that bobbed slowly on the long neck. The creature had only one single eye, a vicious red orb with a milk-white centre like some grotesque cataract, and below that a mouth – a circular hole studded with hundreds of small teeth, tiny needles designed to shred and tear. The limbs were stretched and elongated, with cruel spikes of some bone-like substance extruding through the skin, and on each hand there were ten long, bony fingers, each ending in a slashing, raking claw, alongside thumbs that were little more than sharp hooks made to slash and tear. Instead of feet, the creature had a pair of large stone-like hooves. They stepped nimbly from the withering remains of the egg-sac with a gentle grace that belied their killing power.

There was strength in those spindly limbs – strength to defend itself against attack, strength to kill without mercy or hesitation if the order came, and strength to break free of the prison it found itself in. Without another look at the mess on the ground that had once been Mister Smith, The Sentinel clattered forward on its hooves, sinking its fingers into the stone of the wall. The claws easily penetrated the brickwork, acid secretions drilling into the rock, before the fingers flexed, the muscles straining for only a moment before the stone cracked, a chunk of wall tearing away with a noise like buried thunder.

Without hesitating or wondering at its own abilities, the creature tore another chunk out of the wall, slowly boring its way up towards the surface.

It took one hour and forty minutes of continuous digging to reach the open air, but this did not concern the Sentinel. It had waited millions of years for this moment already, and the signal had to be clear and unobstructed as far as possible.

It was night when it finally crawled from a hole in the shattered pavement, like a worm erupting from graveyard soil. The street outside the Tower was deserted, and there was nobody to see the hideous bone-white creature clambering up through the shattered concrete, and perhaps that was for the best.

Nobody wants to see the end of the world when it comes.

The Sentinel stretched to its full height in the moonlight, the single pulsing eye gazing up into the night sky, looking up and beyond. On the other side of that sky, outside of all space and all time – in the realms of un-space, of no-time – there was the terrible, endless chittering of Those Outside. The endless writhing and crawling and biting and buzzing and howling of the Insect Nation, the Un-Reality, the terrible light beside which our own reality is no more than a guttering candle. The Insect Nation waited, out beyond the borders of all that is or ever was. They waited, and they sent forth probes, lesser life forms that would fold down through space and time to impact against some forming ball of lava and primal muck. A place that would one day support life.

Sentinels.

Sentinels that would mimic that life, moving alongside it, growing and evolving with it, living in its shadow, taking regular samples of the seat of its intelligence. Sentinels that would wait for centuries, for millennia, waiting against the day that that humble form of life would evolve into something capable of total planetary efficiency, capable of spreading and ruling galaxies or universes.

Something that would be worthy to serve as slaves or foodstuffs for the Insect Nation.

That day had arrived.

An indefinable trembling shot through the body of The Sentinel as the circular mouth widened, the needle teeth clattering against each other. The terrible mouth widened impossibly, sickeningly, the jaws stretching as no human jaws could, distorting as the first echoes of sound came from the structures inside the throat.

It began as a scream.

An inhuman scream – a keening wail of torment, the kind of sound human beings dread in the depths of their darkest nightmares, a hideous, bone-jarring shriek that went on and on and on into the night. Dogs howled alongside, then sank down and huddled into their paws as the scream rose in pitch and intensity, spiralling up towards some terrible note beyond human hearing. Eventually, the dogs died, blood leaking from ears, eyes and noses.

The air was filled with the shattering of glass and for a moment Central London was engulfed in thousands of shards, falling through the air like sharp slashing rain, beautiful and deadly. The scream rose in pitch, the pulsing eye of The Sentinel rolling back as the inhuman vocal chords pierced all barriers of sound, moving into uncharted frequencies beyond all knowledge. It could not be heard with the ear now, but deep in the clenching gut of all those within reach there was a feeling of terror, of infinite, indescribable panic. Men and women cried in their sleep, then vomited, choking on their own terrified bile as the sound moved further and further out of human comprehension.

This was the sound of the Outer Realms, the awful music of those spheres that revolved like floating, bloated cysts in the qlippoth-universe, the anti-place where the Insect Nation gathered and flexed.

The summoning-sound.

The pressure in London seemed to drop as the scream passed into that Other World that lay beyond and behind and beside our own, and those who were walking the neighbouring streets began to bleed – first from the nostrils, then from the ears and eyes, collapsing as their insides hemorrhaged and began to leak slowly out of them.

In response, the sound of a billion feeding insects began to grow, the noise rising in volume – the terrible echo of feasting creatures, monsters living and writhing in climates no human mind could possibly conceive. Then came a sound never heard before – the cracking, grinding thunder of things unimaginable to mankind folding themselves down through higher planes of geometry to come into existence in our reality.

What must it have been like to hear that sound – to know that here and now, after all those centuries of human striving, the end had finally come?

The first craft appeared over Hyde Park. Descriptions of it vary – to some it was a crackling, sizzling engine made of massive oiled parts, grinding against one another, lightning arcing from them. To others it resembled nothing so much as the carapace of a massive, hungry beetle, jaws clacking open and closed in a sickening rhythm. To a few – those whose minds did not instinctively protect them from the sight of something not meant to be seen – it was a grotesque, impossible construction of terrifying angles, both machine and monster, feeding tubes and tentacles dangling from the underside, pulsing with oil and slime, dribbling acid and bile on the ground below that killed whatever it touched.

Those who saw the invasion vessels as they truly were did not last long. They screamed their own throats raw, rupturing vocal cords and choking on their own blood and vomit long before the first of the devourers stripped their bodies for food and fuel.

As similar floating engines materialised over London, tiny black ovoids, like the eggs of nits or lice, dropped down from the underside of the first invasion craft, impacting in the soil, and quickly doused with the fluids spraying from above – the same fluids that reduced plant and animal life to smoking, toxic husks, black and skeletal remains. The reaction was almost instantaneous – the black shells cracked, split and disgorged writhing white maggots of various sizes, ranging from the size of a thumbnail to the size of a watermelon, that burrowed quickly into the toxic ooze surrounding them. Within a matter of minutes, they would be capable of scuttling vast distances at speed, finding their prey still shaking in terror in nearby streets and houses, burrowing into flesh and bone, working up into the skull. There they would tear into the cerebral cortex, chewing and ripping, nesting in the skull to shelter. For a few hours, the victim would stagger, eyes rolled back into the skull, drooling, moaning, sobbing, occasionally attacking his fellow men as the nesting maggot spurred him on.

For a few short hours, the zombies would rule London.

Finally the maggot would be nourished enough from draining the fluids and meat of the brain and the body would have reached the limit of its development, and the bones of the staggering man would shatter, spraying blood, the skin splitting as the creature inside flexed obscene muscles, a newly-formed black carapace covering it completely as it stepped out of its host and went to continue its terrible mission.

This was the first wave.

Other ships began to materialise over the wide-open spaces of London, disgorging their terraforming ooze and their legions of mind-eating worms, plague-ships carrying the ultimate obscenity in their holds. But already the pattern was changing. The maggots were transmitting back to the main intelligence, the hive-mind of the Insect Nation, as they chewed through the skulls of their victims, pronouncing the matter inside inferior and unserviceable. This species – this 'human race' – was not sufficiently evolved. It was useless as slave labour, for the most part possessing not even rudimentary telekinesis. As a source of nutrition, it was substandard. A War Wyrm, grown to maturity on the brain matter on offer on this world, would be barely thirty feet long and hardly even capable of chewing through steel and concrete.

The Sentinel had been deceived somehow. This species was not yet ready.

The Insect Nation had been called too soon.

There was a great chittering, like a tide of strange otherworldly static, that emanated from the hovering ships, washing over London, crashing against the terrified ears of those who'd watched fathers, sisters, infant children scream and haemorrhage, who'd seen friends and neighbours with great holes torn in chests and faces, eyes rolled back as they tore and smashed blindly at everything around them while maggots writhed in their minds. It was the noise of debate and decision.

Planet Earth was useless.

But it could still serve a function of sorts.

If all animal and human life was erased from the planet – if every vestige of humanity was torn down to leave a thick mulch of protein, a soup for larval forms to grow in – then this spinning ball of mud, filled with its backward, hobbling creatures, might have some use after all. A breeding ground. A place of experiment, to find new and more powerful forms that could live and grow on less.

They were here now, and it would be a shame to waste the journey.

The chittering static ceased, and silence rolled over the doomed city. It was decided. Organic life on this world would be broken apart, slowly and with care, their molecules and atoms split into nutritious mulch. From the burned and tortured cradle that remained, new forms would grow, forms capable of surviving more efficiently in this cramped, enclosed space of four dimensions with its buffeting wind of seconds and moments.

One of the floating motherships broke from the rest, turning slowly through the air and drifting towards Buckingham Palace.

London held its breath.

CHAPTER ELEVEN

Survival, Zero

Listen:

The doctor had told Megan Hollister she was too old for children at forty, but she and Neil had made the decision to try anyway. They'd each spent years telling themselves they didn't want a child – didn't want to be tied down, didn't want the financial hardship or just the basic, total, complete responsibility of having a life in their hands – but the truth was that they hadn't wanted a child with the people they'd been with. Within a month of Meg's first meeting with Neil – that ridiculous blind date at that ridiculous jazz-theme restaurant that her sister had set up – she'd found herself brooding. She had looked at babies being brought into the theatre in front of her and thought about how sweet they looked and how nice it was that their parents were exposing them to culture at such a young age, instead of thinking about how horrific it was going to be when the little brat started bawling at the top of its lungs halfway through the second act, obliterating the performance and ruining the whole evening for everybody else. She'd looked around her apartment, already measured up for when Neil moved in – his lease was almost up, and he was making commitment noises – and she found herself looking at the spare bedroom and measuring it for a cot or a playpen.

On their wedding night, they'd finally broached the subject, and he'd been going through exactly the same thing. It was time for children. It was probably too late for children – Dr Mears thought so when she'd broached the subject at a check-up – but they could try, and there was always IVF, or adoption. It was the commitment that was important. Knowing that they both wanted the same thing. That was enough. That had been enough – a month later, she was pregnant, and Dr Mears was fussing around her again, telling her how bloody irresponsible they'd both been and how difficult this was all going to be. Meg had only smiled – she had faith in herself and her child. Faith in the future she was building.

The delivery had gone as painlessly as deliveries do, and little Evan was as perfect a baby as anyone could wish for. She'd cried, seeing Neil holding the little boy, only looking, unable to come out with any of the usual half-sarcastic little jokes and put-downs he used to take the weight out of moments of emotion. This was too big, and he had no words. She'd reached to him, gently brushing her fingers against his arm, and he'd given her a glance and a shy little smile, as though meeting her for the first time. Then he'd gone back to looking at his son's brown eyes. His own eyes. The silence between them was like a warm blanket, and she buried herself in it, feeling complete in a way she hadn't understood people could. She remembered all the times she'd rolled her eyes at baby conversations and smiled. She'd have to watch herself – she still had childless friends.

But she hadn't been able to contain herself, and her childless friends had rolled their eyes and made her blush, and smile, and carry on anyway because it was so good to tell it.

Her wonderful little boy.

Her little Evan.

In the end, they'd left the apartment and found a nice

terraced house out in Zone 5, left the centre. She'd even left her job. *When you're tired of London, you're tired of life*, they said, and they were right. She was tired of that life. This was what she wanted now – a little peace, a little solitude in the days when Neil was out at work and it was just her and the baby. And the nights, with him sleeping by her side and the cot by the bed, the whole family – and that word still had a wonderful resonance in her thoughts and on the tip of her tongue – all together, Mummy and Daddy taking turns to get up and grouch and get the bottle.

It was three in the morning, and the family wasn't together. And Megan couldn't sleep.

Neil was away for the weekend – a business meeting in Tokyo, one he couldn't get out of. His paternity leave had been criminally short and it was long over. His bosses had forgotten what it was like to be a new father, or they just didn't care. He moaned to her whenever she let him, but he knew the cold truth, that they couldn't afford for him to switch jobs right now or look for something less intensive. So Neil was gone, and the bed was cold, and Megan couldn't do anything but look forward to when he came back to them both.

She certainly couldn't sleep.

Little Evan was being an angel, sleeping peacefully in his powder-blue cot, and Megan knew she should just drift off and let herself sleep until he woke her, but she couldn't. There had been strange noises in the distance – a scream, like an animal, and then some kind of static noise, like hundreds of crickets. She'd thought about turning on the television to see if anything was happening, but she'd told herself not to be silly. She'd find out what it was in the morning. Probably it was one of those night-noises, those sounds in the early hours that are never explained.

A bump in the night.

It was enough to put her on edge.

She decided to fetch herself a glass of warm milk and then go back and watch the baby for a while. Maybe that would help her to relax, seeing that little face that meant the most to her in all the world, sleeping peacefully. She wondered if all mothers felt so strongly about their children – certainly they did, but little Evan wasn't only flesh of her flesh, but a tiny little miracle, eased safely from the impossibility of late conception, grown in perfect health despite Dr Mears' endless worry and fuss, delivered without a scratch, against such terrible odds, odds she hadn't even allowed herself to consider.

He was everything to her.

Megan sighed, and lifted herself off the bed, the nightgown rustling against her thighs as she padded to the kitchen. The light of the fridge illuminated her tired face and the bags under her eyes as she reached for the milk carton.

There was a sound.

Nothing she could quantify. The sound of something breaking, or bursting. A crunching, cracking sound, as though something was being pushed with great force through brick and wood. She turned and listened.

Silence.

Seconds ticked by, the cold of the carton in her hand matching the chill in her spine. Then she put the carton down on the counter, feet padding back towards the bedroom.

She would just check on the baby and then she'd go back and pour her glass and put the carton back into the fridge.

Just a quick check.

Just to be on the safe side.

The door to the bedroom whispered open slowly, and Megan gently padded into the room, trying to pretend that her heart wasn't trying to pound its way out of her chest. She remembered the stories in the newspapers years before – missing babies, missing children. A big blank shape formed in her mind, words she never allowed herself to think, to admit even existed, but only felt the edges of occasionally, in moments of terror: cot death. She looked at the cot, trying to deny the terror that was flooding through her.

Little Evan was there. And he was breathing. The tiny baby chest rose and fell, tiny little movements as the child lay curled up under the blankets, facing away from her.

Megan breathed out a soft sigh of relief. She shuffled over towards the cot, not noticing the hole in the wall of the bedroom, down at skirting board level. Gently, she reached a fingertip down to trail lightly over the soft, smooth head of her wonderful, miracle child.

And then little Evan turned over in his sleep.

He had no face.

The face had been eaten away, chewed through, leaving nothing but a gaping hole tinged with torn, red flesh, and inside that hole there was only pulsing white maggot-flesh, inhabiting the baby's hollowed out corpse, pulsing in and out in a manner that seemed almost like breathing.

Megan stared.

And then she began to scream...

And scream...

And scream...

Listen:

Jimmy Foley was thinking about strike action in the hour before he died. The government were experimenting with extending the hours the tubes ran into the early morning – the Central Line ran until past three a.m. – and that was all fine and dandy, but the bloody bastard idiots seemed to think that late-shift drivers like Jim Foley could just carry on into the watches of the night without any kind of remuneration, not even overtime pay. So Muggins Foley gets stuck in a bloody metal box at three in the morning on a Saturday for no extra money and he has to bloody lump it – *not likely, mate. Not bloody likely. See how your bloody three in the morning metal box runs with nobody driving the bastard...*

And on and on in that vein. Jim Foley's knuckles were white with anger as he gripped the tube control, turning it away when the train was stopped, turning it back and pushing the lever forward when it was time to send the train west along the line.

They called that a 'dead man's handle'.

Jim Foley was not a young man. He was fifty-seven years old with a sagging paunch and the grey straggly ruins of what had once been a Kevin Keegan perm nestling above his ears. He thought everything since Pink Floyd had been a load of rubbish and had a particular hatred for Orchestral Manoeuvres In The Dark, ever since his son brought a seven-inch single back from the shops that sounded like a robot having it off with a Clanger in the gents toilets on the bloody space shuttle. He'd snapped the bloody thing across his knee and the boy had told him he was a fascist and got a clip round the ear for his trouble. Danny worked in a bloody merchant bank in the city now and Jimmy went round his house every second Sunday for dinner and a lecture on how UKIP were the only way forward for Britain. Jim frankly preferred his son as a member of the red brigade – there'd be less rows about unions for a start – but at least he wasn't listening to Orchestral Bloody Manoeuvres In The Bloody Dark any more, which was a blessing.

Pull the dead man's handle back and twist away – "mind the doors please, please mind the doors" – wait for the signal – turn and push forward and that was Holborn. Nobody got on. Nobody got off. The place was empty as a tomb.

Jim shook his head. They were all using the bloody night buses. He was just wasting his bloody time without even any bloody overtime to show for it. By the look of it there was no point even striking – nobody was using the bloody Tube anyway so they'd all be stuck out in the pissing rain like spare pricks at a bloody wedding...

The train thundered on.

Tottenham Court Road.

Jim shuddered.

This was a hell of a place to be in the small hours. He remembered – was it three years ago? He'd heard about what had happened. They'd called it a terrorist attack.

Some... thing... running amok down the pavement, tearing heads off bodies, turning people into red mist. There were people who said it was a monster, a will-o'-the-wisp that moved too quick to see and unravelled people where they stood. Apparently there were stills of CCTV footage floating around the Internet that showed something covered in hair and a mouth full of teeth ripping passers-by to shreds. But they could do anything with computers these days and Jim knew better than to believe what he saw on the bloody Internet.

But he knew what had happened on the platform that day. Hundreds of people running for their lives, trampling each other, stampeding down the stairs into the station and crushing against the barriers, clambering over the dying to get down to the platform. Dozens – hundreds – panic-stricken, crowding and shoving on the narrow space of the platform...

They counted forty-two people who went over the edge. The lucky ones died instantly, fried like bacon on the third rail. The unlucky ones lived long enough for poor Dave Patton to come down the tunnel and slam into them, smashing them like pumpkins and dragging them under the wheels to slice and maim the corpses. Dave hadn't come back to work. The word on the grapevine was that he was shut up in some bloody home drooling on his straightjacket. Jim supposed the sight of that toddler's arm smashing his front window did that to him, the poor bastard.

Jim must have taken the train through Tottenham Court Road a thousand times since then, but he still felt a split-second of chill as the train pulled in and he saw the plaque on the wall. He'd seen the pictures of the clear up – the men in the white suits hosing the blood off and picking up the severed bits in bags. It gave him the horrors and then some.

Nobody got on, nobody got off.

The horrors were one thing, but Tottenham Court Road shouldn't be empty, even at three in the morning. There was only one bloke on the platform and he looked like he was pissed as a fart. Jim watched as the little hoodie bastard weaved, staggering along the platform, bumping against one of the Cadbury machines and then lashing out at it with a fist, bashing at it again and again. Bloody disgraceful. Bloody thugs getting pissed and smashing up the bloody platform.

Bloody sickening.

Still, not his problem. The platform attendant would deal with that little thug soon enough. Probably listening to that 'emo' music. A clip round the ear wouldn't do him any harm. He'd had many a clip round the ear from his old dad, and it hadn't done Danny any harm either. Look at him now – pulling in eighty grand a year and all because he took a clip round the ear from his dad. Jim didn't agree with Danny about some of his politics, but he knew that if he'd let them loony liberals have their way, Danny would have grown up a little tearaway like that bloody yob on the platform...

The train moved towards Bond Street.

...trouble with them bloody liberals is they didn't like how things were in the real world. If Jim hadn't been firm with Danny, he'd probably be in prison right now with a bloody glue habit. Jim had taught him to work hard and play hard, and now he was on eighty grand a bloody year. Eighty grand! And he'd come from humble origins like his father, not like half of those posh public-school tossers in the city. Working hard and playing hard, that was the secret. Danny was probably out right now in one of the city bars, having the time of his life. Because he'd earned it. That was what those liberals didn't understand –

There was someone on the line.

Jim slammed on the brakes and the whole train juddered and screeched, slowing itself but not nearly enough. It was a man – about twenty – with a fancy suit and designer stubble. A city boy.

There was a hole in his chest about the diameter of an economy size can of beans. Jim caught a glimpse of the inside of the man's lungs. He was... that wasn't bloody right... he was standing on the bloody third rail. Right on the third rail. Just swaying and trying to keep his balance with his eyes rolled back in his head... moaning...

...and then he was a smear on the windshield.

"Ah, Jesus Christ!" Jim tried to close his eyes, but he couldn't.

The platform was crowded.

Men in suits and good shirts, with little bean-can-size holes in them, their eyes rolled back in their heads and something white and pulsing visible in their open, yawning mouths. Blood running from nostrils and ears. Lashing out at each other, at themselves, moaning and mewling. Like a crowd of...

...of bloody zombies.

Oh, Christ.

Jim Foley's eyes widened.

Danny was in the middle of the crowd, short, gelled hair glistening in the lights, the side of his neck gaping and flapping, his eyes white orbs in their sockets.

The inside of his mouth was black.

His body was swollen. Grotesquely so. Jim wanted to call out. He wanted to say something, then shout something. To bring his son back.

And then his son burst.

Two wiggling chitin-covered legs burst through the skin and flesh, waving hideously as they shredded the meat of Danny. His ribcage swung open like double doors and something... *something bloody stepped out of him...*

An insect man. A chitin-skinned horror shaped almost like a human being, with a mask of featureless black, leaving the ruined flesh of Danny to slump down with his shattered skull and empty face.

Jim looked at what was left of his son, and rammed the lever forward as far as it would go. The train shot into the darkness of the tunnel, leaving his stomach behind, his ears ringing with the moaning and howling of the lost souls. He couldn't process what he'd seen. The human mind can only witness so much before it cracks open like an egg.

When Jim saw the massive slime-coated worm blocking the tunnel ahead, a circle of razor teeth gnashing and clattering together in anticipation, he didn't blink, didn't even flinch. He didn't think at all.

The train ploughed on, into oblivion.

Listen:

Callsign Magnet had been woken up by the screaming.

He'd tumbled out of bed and yanked the door open to a scene out of a bally nightmare. Footmen staggering around like stroke victims, moaning and smashing their fists against the wall hangings, shattering the antique vases. For a minute he thought they'd gone off their collective rocker, but then he'd noticed the holes – torn, ragged holes punched through bellies and sides, about the size of espresso saucers – and the way the eyes rolled back in the head.

Magnet had done tours of duty in Afghanistan and Iran. The papers still had the idea that he was some sort of cosseted nancy-boy who never thought past his next line of coke, even after that, but he'd seen things in his time that would turn the average civilian white and make him void his guts into the nearest lavatory.

But never anything like this.

"If you could move back into your room, Your Highness."

One of his security detail, white and sweating, holding a Walther level on the shambling footmen. Callsign Magnet had known George Hayes for four years now. He didn't generally sweat.

"George, what–"

"Please, Your Highness, we need to concentrate on... on the incursion. If you could move back to your room now." He swallowed, taking a step to the left, crabwise. "Put your hands behind your heads and lie down on the floor! Now!"

Magnet hesitated a moment, and George shot him a look. "*Please*, Your Highness."

If he'd been anyone else – or if he'd been with his unit in Iran – it would have been "get to cover, you silly bastard", but the Palace staff were used to observing the proper form at all times. And George was right – all of his training put the family's safety at the top of the agenda. Magnet wouldn't be helping him by staying, just keeping him distracted. He backed towards his room.

"Be ready to evacuate when I give the all-clear, Your Highness." George said, then turned back to the rioting footmen. "I said put your hands behind your heads and lie down on the floor or I will be required to use lethal force! I will not tell you again!"

Magnet nodded and closed the door.

Moving quickly, he pulled on a T-shirt and a pair of khaki trousers, and laced up his boots. George was doing the right thing by following the protocol, but it was a reminder to Magnet that he wasn't a normal soldier on leave. He wasn't normal at all. He was a tourist attraction – a living monument. He couldn't go out for an honest drink without the bloody tabloids breathing down his neck, couldn't go to a party without it ending up on the front page and – what really stuck in his throat –

abandon his duty – not for anyone, and certainly not for a man claiming to be from an obscure department, telling him a fairy story about aliens and spacemen and goodness knows what. George Hayes was not that kind of man. They'd had a professional and personal relationship very few people could have understood, a strong friendship that could only have been made possible by that particular mix of personality and circumstance. And now he was dead. And maybe the world with him.

Callsign Magnet was very aware of what MI-23 was asked for.

There was silence on the other end of the line.

"How far are you from that fire exit, Magnet?"

"Five hundred yards or thereabouts."

"I'm going to give you a choice. You can make a run for it and try to survive on the streets if you want. I don't think you'll live, even with your training, but maybe you will. If you do, I've got a group holed up in Centrepoint. we're forced to move... well, you'll be dead. But you'll have a chance to survive, for all that's worth. But I want you to understand that the country you knew – the civilisation you knew – is over as of roughly two o'clock this morning. There is no longer a reason why your life is more important than anyone else's."

"I didn't mean—" His cheeks stung. He felt the feelings pride and anger swell up like bile.

I know what you meant. That's why I'm giving you other option. I wouldn't give you this job if I didn't think you were capable of it."

Magnet swallowed. "Job?"

We need intel. They've taken the Palace, which means 've probably got Her Majesty. That tells us several gs to start with, but we need more if we're going know what we're up against. I need you to confirm

he couldn't serve in a unit without those same damned tabloids getting wind of it and splashing it everywhere, putting him and his men in danger. Presumably they thought they were 'rehabilitating' him... he shook his head. Now wasn't the time to go over the old frustrations. This was obviously some sort of biological attack and he needed to follow procedure and get out fast before he put anybody else at risk.

Get out before he put anyone at risk. He smiled at the irony. What made his life so special that it had to be protected at the expense of others? He'd had to learn to even ask himself that question and the answer was painful to grope for. It was the idea of him that was important. Not even that – the idea of him was the drinker, the clubber, the tit-squeezing playboy sponging off the nation. That was what sold. What people needed to protect was the idea of the idea. The idea of a tradition that went beyond the reality. A tradition more insubstantial than smoke, but still wrapped around him like swaddling bands...

There were gunshots in the corridor, and then the sound of George screaming.

Magnet tore out of his room and took the situation in with a glace. George was dead. A footman had torn open his throat. Magnet delivered a kick to the face of the footman stood over George, then grabbed George's gun and radio and sprinted in the direction of the nearest fire exit. Priority one was to get out of the building. He didn't think further than that. He simply didn't have time to let himself.

The radio crackled into life.

"Hayes! What's the word?"

Magnet ducked into a doorway and lifted the radio to his ear.

"George is dead. Over."

"Shit!" The voice on the other end of the radio was rough – working to lower-middle class. Deep and booming. "Who's this?"

"This is Callsign Magnet. I'm armed with a P99 –" He checked the ammunition. "– nine shots and one in the chamber. That's it. I'm heading for the fire exit next to the library on the east wing. Over."

There was a moment of silence.

"Callsign Magnet. Jesus Christ... right. What do you know about the Meggido Protocol?"

"Repeat that? Over."

"Meggido Protocol. Mike... Echo... Golf... Golf... sod this bollocks, have you heard of it?"

Magnet looked out from the doorway. The corridor was clear. He made a dash for another doorway down the hall, checking the room for enemies and then lifting the radio to his ear again. In some part of his mind, Callsign Magnet was amazed at how easy this was – how numb he felt. His ancestral home had been attacked from within – attacked by what looked like a biological agent that caused haemorrhage and madness – and he'd seen a man he'd known for years, a man he'd trusted his life and his secrets to, a man he felt he could honestly call a friend, killed outside his door. His father and brother were in the highlands, but Grandmother and Grandfather were here and he had no idea what had happened to them. He wouldn't know unless he could get himself outside and get the full situation from someone in charge. They might be dead.

He shook his head. Now wasn't the time. As if to confirm it, the radio sparked into life again.

"Magnet! Get your head out of your arse and respond!"

Magnet frowned. For a second, the old prejudices

sparked into life. *Who does he think* – he bit them I

"I was changing position. Give me your name rank. Over."

There was a dry chuckle from the radio. A without mirth.

"My name's Morse, boy. Military Intelligen Confirmation code Tango Niner Alpha Hotel password Metatron."

Magnet felt a chill run down his spine.

"I've... I... I read you. Over."

"Good lad. Now, you were given the basic brief know the codes and you know that when I say ask what colour. I'm answerable only to Her Maj only Her Majesty gets the in-depth version of so I'll have to ask you again and see if we're sin the same hymn sheet. The. Meggido. Protocol know what it is?"

There was silence. Magnet swallowed hard, his memory.

"No. Never heard of it. Look here, are you tr me..."

"You've had the brief, Magnet. You know wh tasked to do. What you're seeing is a sympto being arsed up at the very highest level. Arma arrived in the shape of a massive xenobiolc and you're in the middle of it."

"You can't be serious –"

"Dead serious. Now, this'll sound harsh, bu to convince your man Hayes to abandon yc

"Abandon me? Good God, man, are you winced even as he said it. It sounded like h into his own hype, as it were – thinking o valuable piece of porcelain that could neve damaged. But the idea was insane. Georg

a suspicion of mine. This is a one-way ticket, Magnet. Your chances of coming out of it are slim to none, but everything you can tell me gives our end a chance to beat this."

Magnet hefted the gun in his hand, testing the weight. "I'm not generally asked to do suicide missions, Mr Morse."

"Does that mean you won't?"

Magnet fell silent for a moment. When he spoke, his voice was without emotion. "I'll do it. Give me the gen. Over."

"How far are you from the throne room?"

"Conservative estimate, two minutes."

"Get over there and tell me everything you see."

Ten seconds later, Callsign Magnet was moving back up the corridor, walking crabwise against the wall, gun up, ready to shoot. He knew he should be terrified. By all rights, he should be in a corner, puking up his guts and wetting himself, tears streaking down his cheeks. If he were a civilian, he probably would be. But he felt calm, in control. The adrenaline was pumping through his veins, but it didn't rule him. He had a job to do. People were relying on him. Those were the things that defined him in this moment – nothing else.

He was a soldier.

Three footmen reared out from around the corner, jaws working mindlessly, hands smashing out at anything within reach, their eyes rolled back in heads. Magnet could see white matter pulsing through their open mouths and he knew with a sick certainty that he was not looking at the men he'd known, but at their hollowed-out bodies, worked like puppets by the grubs sitting inside. This was the world of MI-23 – the world Morse had inducted him into over the tinny little radio.

He fired twice, planting shots directly between the eyes, then moved forward quickly to smash the third in the back of the head with the butt of the pistol, crushing what was left of the fragile brain matter. The three bodies stumbled and fell, shrieking noises coming from the mouths as the grubs within pulsed and shook in their agony. Magnet hoped they would die. He knew they wouldn't.

He continued along the corridor, moving towards the throne room. It was one thing to be slotting zombies, but another if he came across any of the security staff. Those would be zombies with guns. Would they be able to use them? Would those foul little beasts be able to plug into a lifetime of skills and learning and box him in? Probably a question for the boffins. Magnet would just have to take these things as they came. He had to keep alert – ready for literally anything.

It was that alertness that saved him when the gleaming black metallic claws shot out from around the corner at throat height.

Magnet threw himself back, snapping off a shot with the pistol that plowed through the thing's hand, bursting it into fragments of black chitin and white pus. He swallowed hard as the creature swung around the corner.

It was very much like a man.

Perhaps six feet in height, covered from head to toe in a black carapace that looked like some sort of futuristic armour, with sharp spikes at the elbows, knees and shoulders. The face was a featureless, blank, black mask, with twin mandibles clicking and clacking below the chin, as if communicating in some unknown form of Morse code. Instead of fingers, it had claws that looked sharp enough to cut through bone.

Callsign Magnet didn't hesitate. This wasn't the time

for niceties. He raised the pistol and squeezed the trigger twice, sending two bullets crashing through the centre of the featureless mask, painting the wall beyond with a splash of white. As the black-clad monster staggered and fell backwards, Magnet breathed a sigh of relief that it kept its brains in the same place as a human would – then choked, gagging on a mouthful of his own bile.

Wrapped around the monster's right leg was a length of torn skin, worn like a stocking. There was no rational reason why it should be there, unless...

...unless that damned horror had torn its way out of a human being.

"Morse? Magnet. I've identified a hostile. Black insect thing, like a six-foot walking beetle."

"Yeah, we've seen them around. We think they're the adult form of the larvae, or one of the adult forms, anyway. The zombies stumble around until they're eaten through, and then beetle boy tears his way out like he's removing a suit of clothes. Turns my bloody stomach."

Magnet nodded. "I thought that might be the case. *Christ*! I'm about twenty seconds from the throne room. I'm going to open the door a crack, try and have a peek inside without being seen. Over."

"Good luck." The line went dead.

Keeping the gun up, Magnet inched closer to the double doors of the throne room. They were opened a crack already – Magnet moved closer, then widened it with the toe of his boot before checking left and right – making sure he wouldn't be interrupted. Then he put his eye up against the chink between the doors.

His blood froze. He felt bile in his throat and tears in his eyes.

It couldn't be.

Surely this couldn't happen.

"Morse. Come in. Keep it low." He didn't recognise his own voice. This cracked whisper.

"What's the word, Magnet?"

Magnet swallowed hard. Everything that he was had folded up into a little gibbering ball of cold, taut fear and panic. It was only his training and his duty that let him speak at all. "There are six of them in the throne room. Six of the beetle-men. They're... it looks like they're... guarding..." He swallowed, squeezing his eyes tight shut, tears starting to crawl down his cheeks.

"Take it slow, Magnet. Talk to me."

Magnet lifted his head. If he fell apart now, people died. Morse needed to know the full horror of it all.

"There's something sitting on the throne... it's like a ball of stretched skin, with several... I don't know, tentacles, or flagella... pushing through it. Sort of waving around. There are long flaps of empty skin trailing down to the ground – I think they used to be the... the arms and legs. Morse... it..."

"Keep talking."

Magnet took a deep breath. "There's a face. Stretched over the ball of skin. It's. It's. It's my grandmother."

There was a sharp intake of breath on the other end of the line.

He felt his throat filling with saliva. "They've eaten her and... turned her into some thing. I can't take this, Morse."

"All right. It sounds like they've turned Her Majesty into... into their command centre. I'm sorry, lad." Morse sighed, a rush of crackling static. "Get your arse over to Centrepoint. We've got ways of fixing this, but I'm going to need you on site."

"Fix this? *Fix this?* That's my *fucking grandmother!*" Magnet hissed. The rage was boiling up inside him again, and this time he didn't bother to bite it back. "I'm going to 'fix this' myself, Morse, right now. Magnet out."

"For God's sake, Magnet—"

The radio clattered to the ground.

On the other end of the line, Morse heard three shots, and then the sound of something sharp cutting meat. A butcher's-shop sound, repeating again and again and again...

And then silence.

Listen:

Jean-Luc Ducard was a man of many pleasures, and he had worked for them all. He had worked for his home in Geneva – a three-storey building with a sumptuous wine cellar, in one of the most expensive and exclusive areas in the city. He had worked for his antique Georgian bookcase filled with expensive first editions that he never read. He had worked for the wine cellar that was so sumptuous, and for the musty, dusty vintages that sat in it, that he never drank although he was told by many that they were extremely rare and extremely fine. He had worked for the expensive dinners he picked at in many fine restaurants. He had worked for his beautiful trophy wife, who he ignored and who he suspected – but did not care enough to verify – was being regularly serviced by his gardener, who maintained the expensive garden that he had worked for but never set foot in.

Monsieur Ducard was a proud man. He was proud of his home, and his wines, and his books, and his garden.

He had worked for them all.

He sipped his coffee, studying the first rays of the morning sun, and prepared for his daily exercise regimen. Monsieur Ducard had turned one room of his house into a luxurious gym, filled with the latest and most advanced exercise machines. Each day he would dress himself in a royal blue tracksuit, seat himself on the comfortable cushions of the multigym, and read the paper, promising himself that he would begin his exercise routine before too long. In this way he would pass a quiet half hour before changing for breakfast, and tell himself that he had spent a profitable half-hour turning some of his sagging flab into muscle. In his mind, the sheer fact that he had unearthed himself at such an ungodly hour with the intention of exercising was as valid as the exercise itself.

In the same way, he told himself that his steady accumulation of wealth – through subtle manipulation of stocks, shares and the definitions of what constituted taxable income – was hard, difficult labour similar to toiling in a mine. He felt that the sweat of his brow had earned him his manifold luxuries, despite the fact that he employed several top-level accountants and lawyers to do the actual work of wealth creation while he himself lounged in a tastefully-appointed study, took the occasional call that informed him of how much he had earned that day, and read the morning papers. Occasionally, he left his opulent study to perform some small task, such as ringing for a pot of green tea or writing a cheque for the People's Party, and then paced languidly around his home, admiring his many possessions and occasionally checking for finger-marks or other signs that they had been touched or disturbed. He would occasionally ring for the maid and imperiously tell her to improve her work. He could not abide signs of use on the many objects he owned.

And why not? He had worked for them all.

Had he woken to the sound of the radio on that fateful day, he might have had some glimmer of what was about to happen to him. But each morning he was woken by the sun. The radio – a precision-engineered model with high-powered Bose speakers – was never switched on, lest the parts become worn out through overuse.

Monsieur Ducard finished the cup of coffee and set it down on the edge of the balcony, turning back towards the bedroom in order to change from his robe and pyjamas to the blue tracksuit he exercised in.

The cup rattled.

Monsieur Ducard turned, concerned. The cup was an antique, and very fine china.

The cup continued to rattle, jiggling in the little espresso saucer, and suddenly toppled off the balcony before Monsieur Ducard could catch it.

Monsieur Ducard cried out in horror. It was as though a beloved child had fallen from a high cliff.

The entire balcony began to rattle now, shuddering and clattering under his feet. In fact, the whole house was beginning to shake. Monsieur Ducard turned and raced down the stairs, thinking only of the cup – one of a set that had cost him tens of thousands of francs. Originally used by Il Duce himself! Perhaps it had only fallen into the bushes, in which case it could be sent by courier to a restorer of antiques – he had to make sure. It was vital.

On the walls, the paintings rattled, vases shuddered dangerously on their tables and the chandeliers swung crazily, glass and diamonds tinkling against one another. The whole house trembled like a living thing. Monsieur Ducard looked around in horror, scarcely able to take in what was happening, still driven forward by the ghost of the fallen cup. The tracksuit clung to his grotesque, flabby body as he hurried out of the front door.

The whole street shook, undulating like jelly underneath him, slates crashing around him as they slipped from his perfectly-maintained roof. Under his feet, the pavement was cracking, the surface of the road tearing like paper in the first rays of the dawn. Monsieur Ducard searched desperately. Where was the cup?

There!

It lay on the pavement, miraculously intact. The spirit of Il Duce must have been watching over it. Quickly, as another crack split the concrete inches from the precious porcelain, Monsieur Ducard darted forward, gently plucking the precious cup from danger and nestling it in his meaty hands. Despite the earthquake going on all around him, he breathed a deep sigh of relief. There wasn't a single scratch on it! Thank God, thank God, from whom all blessings flow... his precious cup was whole and safe again.

Smiling, Monsieur Ducard turned to look back at his wonderful house.

Behind it, miles high, there was a wall of blood.

No, not blood – a wall like one facet of a massive ruby, beautifully carved and polished. It was impossible to tell where it ended, or how fast it was moving, but Monsieur Ducard had a brief instant of understanding as the force field expanded through his home, sundering atomic and molecular bonds and reducing all of his precious commodities to a rain of elemental sludge. His eyes widened ion horror, and in a last desperate gesture, he held the precious cup out, away from his body and the oncoming wall of ruby light.

Then the ruby wall passed through him as well, and

Monsieur Ducard ceased to exist, leaving behind a precise mix of minerals and gases that could never be reassembled into human form.

The cup was the last to go.

Listen.
Listen.
Listen.
You can hear them dying.

CHAPTER TWELVE

The Secret Adversary

"Shit."

Morse switched off the radio and put his head in his hands for a moment. Then he stood up and breathed in deep, tasting the air – old and dusty, full of cobwebs. They hadn't been using this room long enough to imprint themselves on it – it was still heavy with the accumulated dirt of years of disuse, a hidden place squirrelled away in the middle of London. The walls were painted grey, the paint cracked and chipped. There was one steel door, camouflaged on the other side, and one window that nobody wanted to look out of. The only other furniture in the room was a table with an old radio set on it, which Morse had been using to contact his opposite numbers in Europe and America, a generator to power the radio, several filing cabinets filled with protocols and procedures, and a safe which contained food rations, fuel for the generator, two automatic pistols and spare ammunition.

The bolt-hole had been set up for if the worst came to the worst – if the world ended, the Tower was compromised and Mister Smith was killed in the line of duty. Three things that couldn't happen, shouldn't happen and nobody wanted to imagine happening. *Christ*, thought Morse, *no wonder they hadn't spent any bloody money on it. Just bought a room in a skyscraper, sealed it off and pretended it didn't exist.*

Welcome to bloody Centrepoint. Right in the guts of dead London.

Not as far in as poor Magnet, though.

"Bloody Christ!" He swore under his breath, and it echoed around the room like a shout.

The silence struck him. The group was waiting expectantly for him to speak, not daring to draw a breath. He'd have to tell them, then.

"Right."

He turned, not looking at any one pair of eyes.

"We've lost Callsign Magnet."

Tom Briscoe spoke first. A heavy-set man of about forty-one, with curly black hair. The day before, he'd been a lawyer working for an independent television company – now his grey suit was covered in dried blood. He wouldn't tell anyone where the blood had come from. He wouldn't take his suit off. He slept in it – his last link to a vanished world that he couldn't be made to believe was gone.

"That... that was Buckingham Palace?" he swallowed. "That surely wasn't..."

Morse forced himself to meet Tom's eyes, looking into the watery grey orbs coldly, clinically. He didn't feel like doing his bastard impression right now, but it was the only thing they'd understand. One crack in the foundation of his authority and everything would tumble down. "That surely was, Mr Briscoe. And I just sent him to his death. Feel free to speak up if you have some sort of problem with that."

Nobody said a word. Behind Tom, Charu Kapur looked at the ground, tracing the dust on the floor with the toe of her trainer, arms wrapped around herself. She hardly ever said anything, and when she did, it was in a whisper. She was barely fifteen and the day before, she'd been the youngest of a family of nine. Now she was an orphan. She'd seen four members of her family die in front of her eyes. Occasionally, she'd take a pink mobile from the pocket of her tracksuit and look at it, hoping for a text or a missed call. But there was never any text, or a missed call. There wasn't even any signal. But she kept looking anyway.

Someone might have left a message. Surely someone might have.

The soft chug of the generator was the only sound in the room.

"That's settled, then. We know where their base is – where they've set up their central intelligence – and thanks to radio contact with America and Europe, God rest them, we know what they're going to do. Any questions?"

Briscoe coughed, clearing his throat. In the corner of the room, Mickey Fallon tutted once, but didn't speak. He was another who didn't speak. He was seventy-one, but still in good shape – a welder, once, now retired and living in York. He'd been visiting his grandchildren when it had happened. He didn't have grandchildren now, and there wasn't any York either. He hadn't spoken since he'd told Morse his name. There was nothing to speak about.

Briscoe coughed again. His hand trembled for a moment, as though he was going to raise it and ask a question to the teacher. Then it fell back to his side.

"Mister Morse... um... you can't seriously expect us to believe all this nonsense..." he looked around him at the others. Great beads of sweat glinted on his brow, and there was something wild and lost in his wet, grey eyes. "Aliens, for goodness sake! It's... it's just silly, now. I'm sure the armed forced are dealing with... with the terrorists..." He swallowed. "Look, I have a meeting tomorrow! Nine o'clock sharp. An important meeting!"

He looked down at the floor, shaking his head. Then he looked back up and repeated it softly, as though dealing with a particularly difficult maître d'.

"Nine o'clock sharp."

He smiled, gently. There were tears in his eyes.

Silence.

Sharon Glasswell began to sob. She had turned nineteen only a week ago. Her Mam had made a cake and made her have two slices 'cause she was eating for two now. She must have conceived the week after the wedding, the doctor said. It was like her whole life had come together at once, everything she'd ever wanted. It was going to be a little girl, they said. Jase wanted to name her Lily after Lily Allen, but Sharon wanted to name her Agnes, for her gran who'd died. Jase had given her a slap and said who's ever called Agnes and they'd had a row, right then and there, in the street outside the McDonald's with all people staring, and then...

And then something had happened in the sky.

And it'd started.

Sharon couldn't seem to stop crying.

Jason Glasswell was twenty. He was six foot with sandy hair shaved to a grade one. He supported Chelsea. He knew what a Chelsea smile was. He'd done it once when he was sixteen, to a fat prick in the pub who told him he didn't have any respect for his elders. Took his eyes out an' all. Teach him for starting. He had a job packing boxes in Hackney but he was thinking of going into the army. He didn't know what was going on or what the fuck had happened but if this fat prick didn't shut up and stop bothering his wife he was going to fucking do him. He fucking would.

Thoughts like these helped Jason Glasswell deal with some of things he'd seen. He could deal with giving some fucking cunt some. He could deal with that. That'd be a pleasure. There were other things he couldn't deal with. So he sat back and thought about putting the blade of a box-cutter through the sides of Tim Briscoe's mouth.

Briscoe muttered softly. "Nine o'clock." It was no more than a whisper. Jason Glasswell grinned at him, one hand gripping his wife's shoulder, the other feeling the comforting shape in his pocket.

Morse looked at them all. Three years of complacency and his emergency strategy had been reduced to grabbing five random strangers off the street and getting them out of harm's way when the trouble hit. He'd sent the signal out immediately, but none of his actual team – his hand-picked, highly trained specialists – had made it to the rendezvous point. Maybe they'd died trying to make it. Maybe they'd just decided to die with their loved ones. They knew what was at stake.

The trouble with the end of the world is that you never know how people are going to take it until it happens.

So now he was stuck babysitting the handful of civilians he'd managed to save, and not a single one of them was worth much in a fight. Too old, too young, too fat – the boy could probably use his fists but not his head. Morse could smell the aggression coming off him like musk. Reminded him of himself as a lad and frankly he wouldn't have trusted his twenty-year-old self to piss in a bucket... and there was more than that. Maybe it was Morse's years – maybe he was just an old man who didn't much like the noise they called music, et cetera, et bloody cetera – but there was something off about the boy. He was a bit too ready to do some damage. He'd kicked up a right fuss when Morse had saved him and the pregnant girl – "don't you fakkin' touch my wife", all that nonsense. If Morse hadn't shown him the gun he might have gone for him. Still, the boy had calmed down since. He'd taken a good look out of the window at what was going on and then he'd shut right up.

Although Morse had a nasty feeling that may have been because the boy enjoyed watching.

Oh well. Too late now.

They were all he had, so he might as well use them. And that started with toughening them up a little bit. Starting with watery old Tom Briscoe, the fat lawyer and current weakest link. Right now, his fear was forming a tough little shell around him, stopping any of the truth getting in. Morse lowered his voice to a menacing growl, speaking deftly and purposefully, and began the process of cracking it.

"Mister Briscoe. Here is what we know for a fact. All of this has been confirmed by people with clearance a lot higher than mine – international agencies who have been waiting for this the same as we have. Now, this is not by any means pretty, and it isn't going to make you feel like giving me a hug and baking me a bloody cake, and to be brutally frank and frankly brutal I couldn't particularly give half a cup of dog piss whether you believe me or not. But I am telling you now that there is an alien intelligence – a semi-octopoid creature ruling an insect civilisation that comes, as best as we can determine, from somewhere outside the boundaries of what we conceive of as time and space – sitting on the throne of Her Majesty and directing a wave of what can only be described as zombies. Zombies, Mister Briscoe. Zombies. With a capital fucking Zed! And I'm sorry to inform you that that is only the larval stage, Mister Briscoe! Those are the fucking kids!"

Briscoe blanched. The man turned literally white. It would be wrong to say that Albert Morse got any kind of real pleasure from it, but he did feel a certain satisfaction in knowing his words were striking home.

The lips moved, and what came out was a squeak, like

a little mouse. "It-it's preposterous –"

"Zombies, Mister Briscoe! Zulu! Oscar! Mike! Bravo – fuck it, I'm not spelling it! Dead humans whose cortical centres are being driven by the larvae that are eating them from the inside out! Eventually those larvae hatch into... Christ, I doubt we've seen the half of it. But if you take a look out of that fucking window your eyes are so studiously avoiding, you will see exactly what's going on. In living bloody Technicolor!"

Briscoe swallowed, shaking his head. He didn't look out of the window.

The sun had not yet risen over Tottenham Court Road, and so the light that came into the dark room was firelight. Oxford Street was ablaze. Staggering human corpses tore at each other, at anything that moved, occasionally at things that didn't. All the windows of the stores had been smashed and the street was cracked and filthy with blood and the bodies of those who'd simply keeled over and bled out through their ears. There was a massive hole just underneath Freddie Mercury's plastic statue where something that looked almost like a black worm, with a mouth full of row upon row of razor-teeth, had bored out of the pavement and chewed into the crowd, before slithering down towards Soho, chewing through halted buses and taxis as it went. Occasionally, in the crowd, other things could be glimpsed – black, almost skeletal walkers, covered with a layer of chitin and slashing out with fingertips like knives. The Insect Nation was busily destroying London from within and without.

This is what Jason Glasswell had stared at in awful wonder. Tom Briscoe wouldn't look at it.

"Strangely, I didn't think you would. And believe it or not, it gets better." Morse paused for breath, wishing he had a cigarette. "According to my contacts overseas, they've set up a force field of some kind around London. Big glowing ruby jewel of a thing. Started off nice and snug around Morden or thereabouts, then it expanded. Evidently they're not that bothered about keeping anything they've found here because anything in the path of that field is broken down into elements. A nice, thick, red, bloody mulch. That's Manchester. Birmingham. York. Edinburgh. Aberdeen. Dublin. Calais. Earlier, when I was talking in French to that bloke on the radio, and then he screamed and the line went dead? That was Paris dying."

Briscoe shook his head, back and forth, back and forth, gritting his teeth, tears flowing down his cheeks. "No. No, you're lying. Please."

"You heard Paris die, Mister Briscoe. I hope you weren't planning on a holiday there anytime soon because I have to say that your travel plans are completely fucked. Don't visit Berlin either, unless you like wading. And you can forget Beckham playing for Madrid again – no Madrid to play for. Terrible shame, I understand he's got dazzling form now he's a rapacious half-insect killer with knives where his hands should be... do you want me to go on, Mister Briscoe? You look like you do."

Tom Briscoe didn't look anything like that. He was sobbing like a child, great fat tears rolling down his great fat face. The others were staring. He had them now. "You heard me talk to the Yanks. You know they tried to nuke it. The Russians will have as well, and the Chinese. But nobody's got anything that can get through and put us out of our bloody misery. Anything hitting that wall just gets turned into component sludge – bombs, planes, people, the lot. Even the nukes. All the radiation just goes into the shield and all that's left over slops onto the ground. There's no help coming. We're marooned."

He had them now.

Time to make some use out of these malingering bastards.

"So I suppose we're just going to have to help ourselves." Morse walked to the safe and twisted the dial – left, right, left, right... and then the safe swung open and Morse took out the guns. He passed the first one to Tom Briscoe, who was blubbering like a child. He gave the second one to Mickey Fallon. Then he handed them each three clips of ammunition, and slipped two into his own coat pocket. His gun was already loaded.

"Where's mine?"

Morse turned to look at Jason Glasswell, who'd let his wife go and was standing up. Sharon, with her big belly full of child, reached up her hand towards him. "Jase, don't –"

"Shut it!" he snapped his head to the side, full of venom, like a snake striking. Then he turned back to Morse, beady blue eyes staring out of his face. "Where's mine? Eh? Don't I get one? How come fatso there gets one and not me? Eh?" He was leaning in, breathing hard. The posture would have been the same if he was accusing Morse of looking at his bird.

Morse didn't say anything.

"I'm, ah, I'm really not sure I can use one of these –" Briscoe stumbled, and reached out with the gun in his shaking hands. Without turning or looking, Morse lifted one hand. Tom Briscoe drew the gun back to himself and looked away. He looked sick.

"See, he doesn't need one. Gimme one. Why not, eh?"

Mickey Fallon stared, an ammunition clip in one hand and the gun in the other. His weathered old face was expressionless, but he weighed both objects in his hands, as though judging when to put them together.

Charu shuffled backwards, slowly, unconsciously, her phone gripped tight in her hand. Her eyes flickered from the confrontation to the glowing screen. Someone might have left her a message. She had to check. She had to.

Morse looked bored.

"I want a gun. Gimme a gun. *Gimme one.*"

Jason Glasswell reached up to give Albert Morse a little push in the chest, a little starting push, a little are-you-looking-at-me push. A little prod with the index and middle fingers of each hand.

Without blinking, Morse reached up and took hold of both his middle fingers and broke them.

Then he kneed Jason Glasswell in the testicles.

Then he grabbed the collar of his jacket and slammed him face-first into the side of the safe, breaking his nose and knocking him out cold.

Then he tossed him onto the floor next to Sharon. Sharon opened her mouth to scream something and then caught the look in Morse's eye.

Albert Morse coughed. "My apologies, Mrs Glasswell, for that dreadful display of violence. Do me a favour and when he comes round tell him not to be such a cunt."

He turned back to the other three. And scowled.

"From now on, do what I fucking say shall be the whole of the law. Here endeth the lesson."

He looked at them all, one after the other, letting it sink in.

"Now. Let's pull out fingers out of our arses and save the fucking world."

CHAPTER THIRTEEN

And Then There Were None

On the map of the Underground, the Northern Line is black. A solid, funereal scar running from top to bottom, bifurcating briefly in a nod to a history long forgotten. Black as the depression of a commuter elbowing his way onto a Waterloo train at half-past-eight, knowing that the day is already sinking in grim black quicksand and there is no escape. Black as the filth and grime that clings to the black moving handgrip on the escalators that drag you down and down into the crushing press of the rush-hour crowd. Black as the fur of a rat skittering in the darkness, searching for food in the gaps under the shuddering rails and the rumbling trains. Black as the armbands on the relatives of the suicide who threw himself under the wheels of the 11:18 to Morden. Black as the crows flying over the grave. Black as mascara tears. Black as a night without hope.

A black line, going down.

Albert Morse stood on the platform of Tottenham Court Road and looked down at his bloodied shoes.

"Christ alive. I've heard of going to pieces, but..."

Nobody laughed.

The platform was covered with shredded bits of people. Burst faces and torn swatches of skin. Ribcages opened up like birdcages. Scraps of muscle still clinging to lumps of bone. Their torches made out bright circles of rotting skin in the blackness, and the odour of spoiled human meat clogged up their noses and mouths like thick black tar.

Behind him, Morse could hear his band of five stop

dead in their tracks, afraid to step, afraid to breathe in case they inhaled the stench of the dead. Sharon's breath hitched, a terrible gurgling noise as though she wanted to scream but couldn't force it out. Morse turned and saw that her eyes were bulging, almost ready to pop out of her head. Young Charu was luckier – Mickey had clapped a hand over her eyes at the first sight of it. His face was like ash.

Tom Briscoe vomited copiously, a torrent of bile pouring over the drying blood. It seemed like he'd never stop.

"What is it? What's going on?" mumbled Charu, a rising edge of hysteria creeping into her voice.

Mickey swallowed.

"Never you mind. Never you mind." He shook his head. "It's like... it's like one of them violent videos. That's all. Nothing you want to see. If you ask me, they should ban 'em." He swallowed. "You just hold on to me now and keep your eyes shut and we'll be getting out of here very soon." His eyes moved to meet Albert's. *Won't we?* They said. *For God's sake, don't make a liar of me. For God's sake, we have to go.*

Jason was the last onto the platform. He'd been lagging behind, stumbling through the dark following the bobbing torch beams, pissed about his broken fingers and his broken nose. He'd only gone along because Sharon had begged him to. "I can't stay here alone," she'd said. She was crying even though he'd told her he hated it when she cried. Stupid cow. If she did anything to put that baby at risk she was getting a black eye. And as for that old twat who'd broken his—

"Jesus Christ, what the fuck's happened here?"

Morse didn't turn around. He was helping Sharon down from the platform onto the line, trying to keep the light away from the blood and bones. "Just get yourself down here, Glasswell. It's a long walk through the tunnels and we need to get—"

"I'm not walking through this! And get your hands off my fucking wife!"

Morse turned around, counting heads – Mickey, Charu, Briscoe – all here. He debated whether he should just move off and leave the Glasswell boy where he was. But then he'd have to leave poor Sharon as well, and leaving her alone with him would be a death sentence. At least this way she had a chance. The same chance they all had.

Maybe he could be useful, anyway. Every pair of hands was useful.

Morse didn't want to have to shoot the boy.

"The larvae in them finished its metamorphosis. So it tore out of them like a chick hatching out of an egg. Take a look for yourself." Morse tossed him one of the torches so he could do just that. There was no point in sugarcoating it.

Jason caught the torch in scrabbling, sweat-wet hands, and took a good look. His voice was like tissue paper. "I'm not. Cuh-christ. I'm not. I'm not walking through that."

Shannon looked up at him, staring into the beam of his torch like a startled deer. "You've got to. You've got to come with us."

He shook his head.

Mickey broke the silence with his soft, deep Northern tones, old and sad. "They should bring back the National Service. That'd help with a situation like this." He nodded to Sharon. "Come on, love. He'll catch up."

I hope you're wrong, Mickey, thought Albert Morse as he shone the light down the dark black tunnel and led his random group of rebels into the darkness. *I hope he stays on that platform forever. Because he won't take a telling and very soon he's going to put me in a position where I have to kill him.*

Stay on the platform, Jason Glasswell. Stay with all the blood and the shit and the filth. Let me get your wife and kid somewhere safe. Somewhere where you're not.

Morse was almost praying.

He heard Jason picking his way through the meat behind them anyway. But then, God had been dead for a long time.

"Right," said Morse an hour earlier, "According to my notes, there's an armoury underneath Waterloo station – guns, ammunition, tinned food. Originally set up during the Cold War, decommissioned after the fall of the Berlin Wall. Except it wasn't completely decommissioned – we got it. It was to be used in the event of a situation just like this one."

"How come you're not there?" Charu said softly, toying with her phone. Behind her, Jason Glasswell was lying next to the safe, nose broken, eyes blackened, unconscious with his little fingers twisted just so. "How come you're here and not there?"

Morse smiled humourlessly. "I didn't know it was there, did I? All our eggs were in one basket. We all figured that when things went to the wall we'd have my head of division on our side, who happened to be a bit special even if he was a soulless fucking bastard, and we'd have all the equipment at the Tower as well, see? This here is what's known as the worst-case-scenario shelter. The one that never got funding, ready for the scenario we never bothered planning for."

"Christ." Mickey shook his head. Morse nodded.

"Well, we had God on our side, or something very close. And we were all fucking idiots. Anyway, when I got here, all the protocols were in the safe, and I spent a couple of hours following them. Lots of radioing people on top-secret frequencies, advising them that we were in a state of Infra-Red Alert. For all the good it did anybody. Most of the people I called will have been turned into a rich protein shake by now – the rest, well, they're not here. It's just me and the people I could drag off the street when everything hit the fan. And the worst case scenario that I cracked open a little while ago, after I talked to the Americans and they told me the fucking nukes didn't work."

He paused, breathing in deep for a moment. This was above Top Level clearance and he was about to share it with a bunch of muppets he'd dragged in off the street.

Old habits died hard.

"There are a number of what we call suitcase nukes," he heard himself saying, "in the armoury under the station. Hopefully more than one. I'll be taking at least one and heading down the line to Green Park. Once I'm there, I'll set it up on a dead man's switch and get as close to Buckingham Palace as I can. Big bang, I get to die a fucking hero and we're shot of those chitinous tossers in one fell bloody swoop, mission accomplished and we can all go home. Or in my case to the lake of fire."

"Won't..." Tom Briscoe stuttered out the words. His knuckles were white on the pistol he was holding. His thumb was pressed against the safety catch, keeping it pushed on as though it might switch over by itself. He'd been a good choice for the gun. "I mean... won't it..."

"You'll be fine. Obviously you'll have to stay down there for a few years, but there's food there, literature,

DVDs... It's set up to handle a battalion of one hundred for five years, so you're not going to run out of anything. I imagine it beats being left up here to be chopped into individual meat cutlets." Morse didn't have a clue whether this was true or not – the papers were frighteningly vague – but he knew for a fact they were going to die if they stayed here. Might as well give them some hope to keep them going.

"No..." Tom shook his head. "I, I meant the creatures. The tunnels will be full of them. Overrun. We'll be torn apart." He shook his head again mechanically. "We can't go down there. We just can't."

The tough-love approach hadn't worked. Neither had giving him a gun. He was still going to be slightly less use in this situation than a crisp iceberg lettuce. Morse looked at him carefully, then gently took hold of his shoulder. "Come over to the window, Tom."

Briscoe shook his head, feet dragging, eyes squeezed tight shut, but Morse was stronger. He spoke quietly, gently, as though talking to a man on a ledge. "Look down, Tom."

Briscoe shook his head, tears squeezing from the corners of closed eyes. Morse could feel him shaking. He continued to speak gently, softly, as if calling a kitten down from a high branch.

"They're not there, Tom. It's okay. You can look. The whole street's empty. Promise." Morse was telling the truth – the wrecked street was deserted. Occasionally a rat would scurry across the cracked and broken pavement, or a pigeon with bloodied feathers would alight on the remains of a roof. Nothing else.

"They've been moving down towards Leicester Square – heading for the Palace. I think they're massing there... waiting for instructions, maybe. No way of knowing." He patted Tom's shoulder. "But I know one thing. They're moving above ground, Tom. We've seen them coming out of the subways but they haven't gone back down, have they?"

Tom shook his head. He couldn't speak.

"It'll be all right, Tom. It'll be fine," lied Albert Morse. He could feel the eyes of the others burning into his back. He turned, bolstering his voice with all the authority he could muster. "We should get our arses moving, though, right fucking now. The sooner I can kick some alien arse, the better, and the sooner I get you lot to safety the sooner I can get on with the vital arse-kicking matters that are plaguing this nation. Come on."

"What about Jason?" Sharon's voice was confused, fearful.

"What about him?"

"We're not going to just leave him here, are we?"

Morse looked at her for a long moment, and in that moment he cursed her, and cursed her bloody baby, and especially cursed her bloody stupid husband. Jason Glasswell was going to be the death of them all. He knew it.

"Perish the thought. Wake him up."

Jason was awake now, and he followed them down the tunnel, torch pointed at their backs like a shotgun. They could feel his eyes on their backs, and, occasionally, Fallon or Morse would turn and look behind them, ostensibly to check if any of the invading creatures were following. Jason Glasswell's eyes glared back at them, cold and grudging, simmering like two hot coals.

The tunnel was as silent and empty as a tomb.

After long minutes of trudging that seemed like hours, they came to the dark empty expanse of Leicester Square.

Morse stopped.

"Wait. Turn your torches off."

Jason tutted loudly as his flicked out. Tom's breath quickened, and he let out a soft, mewling whimper.

"Look at that."

The lights on the platform were glowing a soft, translucent green, sickly and hideous.

"Torches back on. And keep away from the third rail. I think... I think they might be generating their own electricity somehow. No, not electricity. Some kind of alien energy. An alien form of energy, that radiates out from their Queen. From the Palace. *Fuck.*" He considered keeping what he thought quiet. Fuck it. They deserved to know everything. "Something that doesn't follow human physics."

Tom's voice was a high, thin whine. "They don't follow our physics?"

Morse shook his head. "Come on, Tom. We need to keep moving."

"If they don't obey our laws of physics, how... how's your bomb going to work? It could just, I don't know, fizzle out, and we'd be left down there in that bunker of yours in the dark and, and they'll be out there and your bomb won't work and *they'll be crawling at the door* –"

"Shut it!" Morse roared. "I don't know about you, Briscoe, but I'm a citizen of Her Majesty and as far as I'm concerned I obey Her Majesty's proud and noble laws of fucking physics and *so does my bloody bomb*! Now you can throw your wobbly on your own time! Right now we need to get moving so fucking *move*!"

"You don't need to shout." Sharon muttered.

Morse softened. No need to take it out on her in her condition. He thought of Shirley, who that bastard Smith had hung out to dry like a sheet of bloody washing. His Shirley was somewhere out there in this bloody mess, and he'd never know what happened to her. If not for that fucking unspeakable idiot Smith with his bloody thirst for forbidden fucking knowledge, Shirley might be with him now.

He sighed. That would be a fucking tragedy, wouldn't it? Because there was a very good chance that he'd have to watch her die. He'd been spared that, at least. But he didn't have to like it one little bit.

He looked around at Jason. *Take that lemon out of your fucking gob, cunt. My wife's fucking lost to me and yours is right here, and you're too busy pouting to fucking notice.*

Kids today!

He sighed and put an arm around Sharon, giving her shoulder a little squeeze. *Go on, Morse, try to be nice.*

"How are you holding up, my dove?"

She looked up at him, her face pale, smiling slightly, her eyes slightly disconnected. He felt a terrible wave of compassion flooding over him. Her words stumbled gently, as though they were lost or blinded, feeling their way slowly out of her thoughts and into the open air. *Poor kid*, thought Albert Morse. *Poor kid.*

"I think... um, the baby kicked. Or pinched. I don't know. It hurt a bit. Do you think we could rest for a bit?" She half-smiled again, her eyes drifting, roaming. "My Mum will be wondering where I am."

"Your Mum's dead." Jason spat, darkly.

Sharon's face fell. "Oh. Oh yeah. I forgot. Well, could we rest for a little bit anyway? My feet hurt. And the baby kicked." She smiled, and there was a sort of desperation fucking maybe – we won't put you down like the rabid fucking animal you are. Can't say fairer than that, can we? Personally I think I'm offering you a fucking bargain." Morse snarled. "Right now, there's a good chance of you coming out of this alive. I suggest you take it."

Obviously, Morse was going to blow Jason's head off at the first opportunity. But he thought lying might help.

Jason twisted his arm, pressing the barrel of the gun tighter into Charu's temple. Her eyes were massive, blank and vacant with fear – not fear of the gun, or the psychopath holding her hostage. She barely knew they were there.

It was her mobile. She needed her mobile.

Someone might have left a message.

Jason's voice was like cold ashes poured over a grave. Something human might have been in those eyes once – something sympathetic, even decent and loving. It wasn't there now. A thousand thousand petty cruelties and random acts of evil had dampened it until finally it had died altogether.

For Jason Glasswell, the human race had died out long before the aliens came. It had simply faded away until it vanished altogether.

Now the only thing that mattered was what he wanted.

And he wanted to hurt someone.

"Fucking *kill* her..."

"Glass. Well." Morse growled. "I gave Tom that gun because I knew he'd be scared stiff of it unless he needed it. He treated it like a live grenade, Glasswell. He kept that safety pressed on so hard I thought his thumb was going to snap off."

Morse grinned like a skull.

"Have you taken it off yet, you fucking prick?"

in her glazed eyes now. Morse had seen the signs many times before. Her mind was in the first stages of rolling over and giving up. The horror of everything was building up inside her and she was too strong to have hysterics like Tom Briscoe or retreat into her own world of silence like Charu, and she wasn't strong enough to just bear it like Fallon seemed to be doing. She was going to go mad, simply to protect herself from a reality she could no longer bear.

"I'm sorry, love." Morse murmured. Then he put his arm around her again and led her forward into the tunnels, Mickey and Charu following wordlessly behind, then Tom Briscoe looking like a man trapped in Hell. Jason was last, bringing up the rear.

"That's my fucking wife you've got your arm around." He hissed.

Morse said nothing.

Jason Glasswell curled his lip as his knuckles bunched white around the heavy torch. That was his fucking wife he had his arm around. He remembered one time in the King's Arms some poof had been smiling at her. He'd said he was sorry, he didn't mean it, but Jason wasn't having any of that. Didn't show the proper respect, did it?

First he glassed the fucking faggot, then he took his pool cue and smashed it into his ribs until he heard them snap. Then – and this was the bit he was proudest of – he'd held the poof down and carved his cheeks from the corners of his mouth to his ears. And then did his eyes.

Gave him something to smile about. He wouldn't be looking at his bird any more either, would he?

Best night of his life.

He'd given Sharon a black eye when he'd got home 'cause she'd been encouraging the poof, and she'd said sorry and he'd forgiven her. Why wouldn't he? All he wanted was the proper respect he was due. That was all. He'd been willing to wait until they were all in the bunker and Morse was gone, but he'd gone too far now, hadn't he? He was touching Sharon. Nobody touched Sharon. If the cow had tired feet – like none of the rest of them did – she could fucking lump it. She just needed a slap to learn her her fucking place, and Morse...

Morse needed a slap as well.

Time he fucking got one.

Without even breaking his stride, Jason swung the heavy torch around in a short arc. Tom Briscoe had been walking just ahead of him, cradling the gun he'd been given and muttering something about physics, tears running down his ruddy cheeks. He never saw it coming. The torch impacted against the side of his skull, caving it in and crushing the right side of his brain, driving sharp splinters of bone deep into the grey matter. He dropped soundlessly, shuddering, eyes rolling back into his head.

For Tom Briscoe, death was a mercy. If he'd had a chance to think before all the lights in his head went out, he might have wondered why he hadn't tried it himself.

The body hit the floor with a thud. Morse began to turn at the sound.

In one fluid movement, Jason Glasswell reached down and picked up Tom's gun, then strode forward and grabbed hold of Charu Kapur's ponytail, yanking her back against him, then locking his arm around her throat while the barrel of the gun pushed against her head. Her mobile clattered onto the concrete floor of the tunnel. She didn't have time to scream.

Jason did all the screaming for her.

"I will fucking kill her!"

Morse turned and brought up his gun. Sharon gasped and put her hands up to her mouth. "Jason?"

"Shut up, you fucking cow – don't point that gun at me, I'll fucking do her right now, I fucking will –"

Charu started to make high, whining noises in her throat. Her eyes were large and filled with terror as she reached downward, squirming desperately. Her mobile was on the floor. She needed her mobile. She might have got a message from one of her brothers. One of her brothers might have survived or got taken to the hospital or something and tried to leave her a message and because they were in the tunnels she might not have got it and they were alive and if her mobile was broken she'd never know and they'd never find her. She'd been sent a message saying that they were all in the hospital and they were all alive and she just hadn't got it yet. She'd never get it if she didn't get her mobile. She needed her mobile.

"Please, I need my mobile, please –"

"Shut up, you fucking Paki!"

"Jason." Morse's voice was low and clear, punctuated by the hammer of his pistol drawing back with a dry click. "You just killed Tom Briscoe and took his gun away from him, didn't you?"

Jason looked back, eyes brutal, one corner of his mouth twitching slightly into a half-smile. "Yeah. Drop your guns or I'll do her. I will. I've done people before. Done 'em at school. I'll fucking kill her." His mouth twitched again. Then smiled. He had all the cards here. He was in charge.

They were going to give him some respect.

"I've made a real error in judgement saving your life, haven't I? That's what I get for being nice. Let me tell you what's going to happen now, Mr Glasswell. You're going to put the gun down like a good little turd and put your hands behind your head, and maybe – and it's a big

Jason turned white.

He reared back as if a snake had bitten him, taking the gun away from Charu's head and turning it to check the safety, to make sure. His little fingers throbbed.

Charu took her chance, bringing an elbow back into his gut and wiggling free of his grip, dropping to the ground. Her mobile was down there somewhere. She needed her mobile. Someone might have left a message.

Jason snarled like a monster from a horror film and flipped the safety off, bringing the gun down to Charu's back. "Fucking Paki *bitch* –"

And then a small red hole appeared above his right eyebrow.

Jason Glasswell's first memory was when he was four years old and he'd spent a whole day making a card for his grandmother with glue, glitter and old bits of coloured felt his mother had cut out for him. Audrey Glasswell had loved it. She had the kindest grandchild in the whole world, she'd said.

The bullet tore out the back of his skull, dragging all his memories with it in an explosion of red and grey. Jason Glasswell tumbled down on the ground like meat.

No great loss.

Mickey Fallon lowered his smoking gun. He looked over at Morse and nodded once. "It's them computer games what does it. They should ban 'em."

Morse shook his head, lowering his own gun. "Well maybe when you restart civilisation, Mickey, you can take that into account. Jesus fucking Christ." He turned to Sharon, mouth open as if to say something, then shook his head. Her eyes had completely glazed over and her face was expressionless.

She was gone.

Morse looked at Mickey, scratching the back of his

head idly as though he'd just finished putting up a shelf instead of killing a man, and Charu, scrabbling on the ground for a mobile that would never talk to her again. He supposed Tom Briscoe might have been sane – he was frightened enough to be sane – but he doubted it.

I could have done this alone, he thought. *What was the point? What was the point of saving any of them? Anything human in them's gone long ago. You can't see that much horror and stay sane. The Glasswell boy just snapped in a way that was a bit noisy, that's all.* He shook his head, watching Charu scrabbling on the ground.

Near the rails.

"Oh, shit – Charu, love, over here! Over here, it's not safe!"

"I just need my mobile. Someone might have given me a message. I need my mobile." She'd picked up the torch, slippery with Briscoe's blood, and was shining it down at the tunnel floor. Her mobile was bright pink plastic. It had to be here somewhere. It couldn't hide.

Then she noticed a flash of pink in the shadow of the third rail.

She looked up, smiling brightly. "Found it!"

"Get away from the rail, love! It might be—"

He didn't get any further. Charu's body arched grotesquely, the skin crisping as thousands of volts of something that was not quite electricity sizzled through her, stopping her heart in an instant and flinging her back from the rail against the tunnel wall with a sickening crunch. Morse was already moving forward, reaching to take her pulse, knowing he wouldn't find one. Why had he bothered? What was the point?

"Them mobile phones are nothing but trouble. Used to be able to sit on a train in peace." Mickey's voice was flat, emotionless. Morse turned around and looked at him, impotent and incredulous.

"The girl's dead, Mickey. She's been fried alive."

Mickey nodded. "It's them phones. They should ban 'em."

Morse shook his head. "Mickey do me a favour and never say anything again, all right? Come on, we're going to have to leave them here. We can't waste time. We've lost enough to that animalistic prick... no offence, Sharon. Are you all right to walk a bit further, my dove?"

She stared straight ahead.

"Come on, Sharon. It's been a hard day for everyone. You can rest a bit at the next station, I promise." He smiled and put an arm around her shoulder, steering her away from the body of her husband. "Just let me know you're going to be okay, eh? Say something."

Sharon's mouth fell open.

A massive spider's leg pushed up her throat and out of her mouth, waving and tapping, feeling its way. Her eyes gazed forward, sightlessly.

Morse fell back. "Jesus fucking Christ!"

"It's them additives in the food. They should—"

"Ban 'em, I know, quite right, shut up Mickey!" Morse snapped, raising the gun and pointing it at Sharon's head as it tipped back, another spidery leg pushing from between her teeth. "It's not bloody additives, you pillock, it's one of them! They've bloody infected her! I think —" The realisation hit him like a punch in the gut. He wanted to vomit. "Oh no. Oh no, no, no, no, that's just not fucking right..."

Slowly, the skin of Sharon's belly began to tear. Another spider's leg pushed out from inside, widening the rip in the skin and flesh. Inside, Morse could see a single massive eye, wide and red, pulsing with a frightening intelligence.

Morse swallowed bile. "Mickey... I think that used to be her baby."

Mickey nodded once, soberly. "Aye. It's the additives. Should ban 'em."

In the ragged ruin that had once been Sharon Glasswell's womb, the eye throbbed and pulsed, taking everything in. Passing on everything it saw. Another leg pushed out of her belly, as she tottered slightly, her head hanging limply to the side. Something wet and grey began to flow from her ears in thin streams.

Morse was almost surprised when he pulled the trigger. His finger seemed to be working of its own accord, squeezing again and again, punching bullets into the centre of that great, pulsing eye lidded by torn skin. The massive orb burst, sending a torrent of unholy juices cascading down to sizzle gently on the third rail. The stench of a barbecue in the pits of Hell rose and coiled into his nostrils, making his head reel. He realised he was reaching breaking point. He was going to go the way of Mickey Fallon with his *Daily Mail* monotone, Charu and her talisman... or maybe Jason. Mad Jason, the animal, the raging killer... and wouldn't Albert Morse be the best killer of all?

His throat was dry. He couldn't seem to stop firing.

Poor kid.

Poor, poor kid.

Eventually, he noticed the empty gun was clicking in his hand. It sounded like a giant beetle clicking dusty claws together in an ancient tomb. The gun fell from numb fingers, clattering on the concrete.

Sharon Glasswell fell sideways, eyes rolling back into her head as the thing that had eaten her baby and then liquefied the brain in her skull finally stopped twitching.

Morse looked at the mess on the floor for a long moment

before turning to Mickey. "Your gun, please, Mickey. I've got some more business to conduct with this baby-eating piece of shit."

Mickey handed it over without comment. Morse took it from him and aimed it at the seeping, oozing nightmare that had once been Sharon Glasswell's child – and hesitated. That thing had been one big eye – an eye on legs. He knew enough by now that there was a purpose behind every mutation the creatures put their larvae through, no matter how bizarre or hideous. What was the point of an eye on legs?

Surveillance.

"Bad news, Mickey. They know we're down here."

The tunnel around them began to vibrate, the walls shaking, *old plaster* cracking.

Mickey looked back the way they'd come. "Is that a train coming, Mr Morse?" He swung his torch up towards the sound, the sound of something very large and very fast roaring through the tunnels towards them.

His torch lit up row after row of razor sharp teeth.

"*Run!*" bellowed Morse, feet already sprinting along the tunnel, blood pounding, breath burning his lungs. He couldn't outrun that thing. Nobody could. He was a dead man.

He remembered an old joke Selwyn had told him once over a pint in the Prospect, Hilda watching with that cheeky grin she saved for him.

There were these two lads in the jungle, see? And they come across a hungry cheetah who's sizing them up for lunch. It's all right, says the one fellow, I know how to deal with this – we just run over that way as quickly as we can. You're daft, boyo, says his friend, there's no way we can outrun a cheetah! And the first bloke says, no, but I can outrun you.

Sorry, Mickey. But I can outrun you.

His conscience would have lightened a little if he'd known Mickey wasn't running at all.

He was staring at the onrushing tunnel of razor-teeth.

At the Wyrm.

Mickey had grown up in Durham. His Dad had worked down the mines, like his Dad before. Harry Fallon was a big booming man with a great bushy beard and big hairy hands grained black with coal dust. When Mickey'd taken his boy to see *Flash Gordon*, he'd cried silently when the king of the Bird People had gone up on the screen, because he'd missed his Dad so much. When Mickey was only young, Harry Fallon would sit up and read him stories – fairy tales, old tales of goblins and changelings and the creatures that had haunted the land in times gone by. But Mickey's very favourite tale, his very favourite thing of all in the whole wide world, was when Harry Fallon would sit him on his knee, and with Mickey in one big hand and a whisky in the other, he'd sing him his song, his special song, the one his Daddy had taught him and his Daddy before. The song of the Lambton Wyrm.

Whisht! Lads, hold yer gobs,
I'll tell ye all the awful story –
Whisht! Boys! Hold yer gobs!
And I'll tell ye about the Wyrm!

The Wyrm that wrapped himself ten times around Pensher Hill, so large it was, and drank the milk of nine fat cows every day. The terrible worm of legend, and it was here, and it was going to eat him up, whole and all.

Thank God.

Thank God for something that made sense to him at last.

Mickey Fallon closed his eyes and cast his arms wide as he inhaled the breath of the monster, and didn't the wash of stale and fetid air smell of spoiled old milk and his father's whisky-breath?

The thought was almost enough to comfort him as row upon row of whirling razor-teeth sliced and carved his flesh into bloody chunks, to swirl down into the bubbling acid innards of the Wyrm.

Almost.

Albert Morse didn't look back, even when he heard the terrible sound of the old man's scream echoing up the tunnel, keening like a banshee. He just ran harder.

He prayed that the monster had at least slowed down when he chewed Mickey up. But there was no God to hear.

His lungs burned. The acid hissed in his cracking joints. He was an old man and he wasn't made to run like this. There was a terrible temptation deep down inside him to just give up and lie down. Let the monster have him. It would surely only hurt for a second... just one second of pain and then it would all be over...

He kept running. Behind him, there was the sound of obscene flesh slithering against stone.

Morse closed his eyes. Every step felt like his last. His shirt clung to him, dripping wet with sweat. His throat was raw and he could hear the whistling of his breath in his ears. And he was slowing. He was going to die anyway... why not now?

Why not stop running?

Albert Morse opened his eyes. There was light ahead of him.

Charing Cross was lit up – that strange non-electricity the aliens were sending out through the wires of the grid making the lights spasm and flicker obscenely, like glowing fish flitting in the depths of the sea, the platform seeming to veer hideously in the damp glow, a scene from a fevered child's disease-dream.

Morse no longer knew if he was asleep or awake. He hurled himself up onto the platform, inhaling the reek of crusted blood as his eyes took in more severed skins, more sloughed faces. He felt something brushing his heel and turned to see the slimy brown skin of the Wyrm as it slid past him, the flesh thrashing. It couldn't check its momentum in time to get up onto the platform with him, so it had slid on into the tunnel ahead. For a moment, he scrabbled back, one hand in the rubbery, torn remains of a woman's mouth, eyes wide as organs slid under his feet, watching the surreal sight of the massive Wyrm coming slowly to a halt, pulsing and twitching, an obscene, organic version of a tube train... then he was on his feet, running again. It was going to follow him. It had to.

The lights in the station glowed and pulsed like living things, lighting up a scene from a charnel house. People had come here to hide, to cower, to protect themselves against the hell raging above them. Then the larvae had crept and slid and scuttled down towards them, some as big as hubcaps, chewing their way into the bellies of fat men, some small as a fingernail or maybe even a dust mote, waiting to be inhaled.

He thought of Sharon. She'd never been safe. He understood that now. Nobody had ever been safe.

Morse could see what had happened. Once the first grubs had started shifting and gnawing their way through the crowd, that screaming mass of trapped humanity had trampled itself, first in panic and then in the shambling half-life that the wriggling white monsters created when they began to devour the brains of their hosts. Corpse upon corpse littered the station, piles of them stacked and heaped like cordwood. Some were whole, mercifully killed in the first crush, but most were torn open from the inside like burst balloons. Snapped ribs jutted from shredded meat. The cracked remnants of skulls opened up like flowers towards the sun. And everywhere there was the stink of blood, shit, piss and rot - the stench of death.

And that wasn't the worst thing. The worst thing was that somewhere above him there was an army on the march. An army that had burst from the remains of these men, women and children, an army that had slithered and clattered up from the depths of Charing Cross, an army of a thousand different horrors, tentacles and mandibles waving and clattering. They'd surged up out of the station, black insect legs stepping on the dead they left behind, and stalked towards Buckingham Palace like a pack of terrifying, Cthulhuesque Dick Whittingtons, off to do Christ knows what in the service of their terrible Queen. And they'd left this unholy mess, this mass of suppurating meat that had once been Charing Cross, as evidence. Marking their territory. The Apocalypse woz 'ere.

Morse wanted to vomit. His head was spinning and filled with strange thoughts. *Not now, Lord, not now. I can't afford to go mad now.*

He picked his way through the heaped corpse flesh, gingerly at first, trying not to breathe, then moving faster as he heard the sound of something shifting behind him. Something wet and fleshy squeezing itself down into the gaps that presented themselves. The terrible conquering Wyrm, coming to kill.

He ran, boots crunching against the remains of skulls and skeletons, vision swimming under the hellish lights. Behind him, the Wyrm snaked and squeezed through the corridors of the station, hunting. Morse sprinted towards the escalator, the metal stairs shuddering upwards, as sickly as the lights, crusted with blood. Bits of people had been ground into the machinery, but it still ran...

It still ran.

Morse put on a burst of speed, praying to a God who wasn't there as he ran past the staircase to the street, the one with the sign telling you not to climb it unless it was absolutely necessary. Long, glistening ropes of intestines wound around the staircase, shimmering in the flickering light. Had some newly-hatched monstrosity trailed them behind it as it slunk towards light and freedom? Had they been placed deliberately? Maybe they functioned as an antenna, absorbing the strange power that was keeping the station working and flickering.

He couldn't hear the Wyrm behind him as he reached the lifts, hammering the button, knowing that he had seconds at most. His lips moved desperately – *please God, please God, please God...*

But there was no God to hear him.

The doors opened and he burst into the small metal space. If he could get above ground, he could maybe find some higher ground, evade the Wyrm that way. All he had to do was stay alive until the doors closed.

Please God.

Please.

Morse pressed up against the back doors of the elevator, listening to the sound of the Wyrm slithering slowly through the station towards him. Closer and closer...

Then the doors shuddered closed.

Morse breathed out a sigh of relief.

The doors smashed inwards, sparks flying from the metal, reinforced glass shattering as the huge pieces of steel smashed against the wall inches from Morse's soft body. The Wyrm was there, squeezed into the opening – nothing but mouth, a huge open tunnel lined with razor-sharp slivers of bone, coated with glistening slime, alien saliva. Row upon row of sharp teeth stretched back into the depths of the creature's gullet as it pulsed and tensed. It was squeezing itself through the corridors behind, getting enough slack to make a last lunge.

Morse's heart hammered in his chest. His breath whistled, a foreign sound in his throat. He closed his eyes and waited for death.

The lift started into motion.

The beast's head compressed, flattening towards the floor, a terrible keening whine coming from deep within it as the floor of the lift moved up towards the ceiling of the room beyond, crushing the creature. It tried to tug backward, but too late – the razor teeth came together, sinking into the monster's own flesh. The mechanism gave a terrible grinding whine, gears straining – before the face of the Wyrm simply burst, in a gout of black ichor that showered Albert Morse head to toe.

Slowly, the doors behind him glided open.

He blinked, once. He was alive.

He could hide himself. Survive. Better – he could reach Waterloo, arm the bomb. Finish things once and for all.

He could still win this.

If they didn't send anything to stop him.

Slowly, Albert Morse staggered out of the lift, fell to his hands and knees, and vomited.

The Sentinel stood outside the Tower of London. It had not moved since calling the Insect Nation to Earth. Its primary duty had been fulfilled – there was no need of movement now.

It had two duties now. One was to stand in place, defending itself if necessary from any attack. One was to wait for further orders.

It stood.

It waited.

It did both of these things very well indeed.

And eventually, orders came. Orders from the Queen.

There was a potential threat that needed to be dealt with.

The Sentinel turned slowly, on its terrible bone hooves, and began to walk towards Charing Cross.

CHAPTER FOURTEEN

The Little Sister

Her name was Katie, and she was nine years old.

When she was little, she thought monsters didn't exist. She never asked her Mummy and Daddy to check under the bed or in the closet. She never crept into bed with them because she couldn't sleep. When they told her that the monsters would get her if she didn't eat up all her greens, she just laughed. There weren't any such things as monsters. Her parents were just being silly.

Then some bad men had taken her because they wanted her Daddy to give them some money. They'd put her in a crate and joked about shooting her and she had been very, very scared. But they weren't monsters. They were only some very bad men, that was all. She didn't believe in monsters.

Until her Daddy sent the monster to fetch her.

He was a nice monster, and he was very sorry that he'd scared her. He'd explained that he was sorry while he was driving her home, and he was sorry for nearly making her dead as well. But he was a monster, a terrible monster, and she'd understood that it didn't matter how nice he was being just at that moment because he was a monster and monsters ate people. They might go for years and years not eating people, but eventually they would, because that was what monsters did.

Her Daddy and Mummy had paid the monster to get her from the bad men, so she couldn't tell her Mummy and Daddy. And by extension she couldn't tell any adults, because her Mummy and Daddy were adults and if they thought they could trust the monsters then all the other adults would too. So Katie stayed very quiet about what she thought, even about ordinary things, because the monsters might be listening. Even when her Mummy and Daddy sent her to a nice man called an Annielist who seemed very nice and concerned about her and talked in whispers with her Mummy and Daddy using all sorts of big words like post-tror-mat-ick and ort-is-um.

She had to go to a special school where the adults were all very nice and tried to teach her maths and stuff even though she didn't talk about things because the monsters might be listening. There was more than one monster out there, she knew, and when they'd all finished being nice they'd come out and eat everybody up.

Because that was what monsters did.

And when the time came and the monsters ate everybody up, Katie would have to learn to survive on her own.

Albert Morse had his own problems.

The tunnels weren't safe any more, which meant the quickest route was probably over Westminster Bridge. That was about a mile and a half. On a normal day, he wouldn't have thought twice about it.

This wasn't a normal day.

The sky was red. Around him, buildings burned, belching fire. Corpses littered the streets, some burst open, some just dead, killed by the insect-things. The insect-things that might be watching him even now...

Very suddenly, as though a light was turned on in his head, he realised why the Insect Nation were pumping their strange, alien energy into the grid, making the lights glow and the lifts work. It was the cameras. The security cameras on every street corner, in every building. They needed them working. Needed them seeing.

London had the perfect infrastructure in place to spy on people. If you could tap into that, why build your own?

Morse almost smiled, then felt sick again. He kept moving, ducking through the debris, trying to avoid being seen. He would be, though. He couldn't avoid that.

It didn't matter, anyway. All the time he'd been talking to Sharon Glasswell, something alien and terrible had been growing in her belly. Their little spy.

They knew where he was going.

The monsters had come last night.

Katie and her Mummy and Daddy had been on holiday. It hadn't been much of a holiday – Daddy had been drinking again even though Mummy didn't like it. They'd had another discussion – they always called it a discussion, but it sounded like a blazing row to her. When they had their discussions it was usually about Katie, about how she didn't speak now. She couldn't speak, of course – the monsters might be listening – but it still made her feel guilty. Mummy had said she wanted a divorce and Daddy had said that he didn't want anything to do with 'the dummy' anymore. 'The dummy' was Daddy's special name for her when he was drunk. He got drunk a lot.

Katie had been hurt at the time, but she wasn't any more. Her Daddy had probably been under an awful lot of stress. He'd known all about the monsters.

He'd probably known they were coming.

Albert Morse clutched the railing of the Westminster Bridge, knuckles white. The bile rose again in his throat and he felt his knees buckling under him. He shouldn't have looked.

He shouldn't have looked at the Thames.

The water was red – a bloody wash of crimson, unmoving and stagnant as an oxbow lake. Both ends must flow into the sea of mulch left by the ruby force field that glittered overhead, he realised. But it wasn't the stagnant, bloody river that made him sick. It was what floated in it.

Heads, of children and adults. Severed limbs. Scraps of clothing. Occasionally some buoyant personal effect. A handbag. A doll. Even an empty bottle or a can of Special Brew had the power to make his eyes sting with hot, wet tears, marooned as they were in that crimson sea, little reminders of a way of life that was gone forever.

How many people had been in London? How many bodies had ended up in that stagnant water? A small percentage, but still, so many, so many... and every second, more were dying.

How far had the force field spread now, he wondered? America and Russia were probably gone. Even if he stopped things right now, the sea would be most likely uninhabitable by marine life – any stretches of land still with people on them would die soon after that.

There was a real possibility that Albert Morse was the last human being alive. And every friend he'd ever had was dead, and his wife was probably dead, and his dog was dead. Everyone dead, dead, dead... he knew he should be making some snide little comment about it or at least swearing his head off but he just didn't have the energy anymore. Not for any of it.

What was he fighting for, anyway?

What was the point of Albert Morse?

He shook his head and turned his eyes away from the mess below the bridge. He kept an eye on the sky. None of the insect-craft had come overhead yet, but that couldn't last. He had to be out of the open before one did. Or before one of the insect-men appeared at the other end of the bridge, running on skittering chitin feet, racing towards him... or more than one, a horde of them, a crowd, sent by the Palace to tear him to shreds with their sharp claws...

His head was swimming again. Thoughts like that weren't going to get him anywhere.

The facts were simple enough. There were cameras all along the bridge and no way of hiding from them.

They knew where he was.

They knew where he was going.

He had to be ready.

On the other side of the bridge, The Sentinel stood. And waited.

It was good at both of these things.

Katie and her Mummy and Daddy had been on the Eurostar when it had pulled in at Waterloo, late at night. None of them were speaking, and Katie had thought it was because they were angry with each other, or with her. But she knew why, now.

It was because her parents knew that the monsters were listening.

The train had pulled into the station and the doors had

opened, and they were halfway through customs when some men with guns had told them that they should remain where they were because there was a sit-you-ay-shun in London. A man with a moustache asked what the sit-you-ay-shun was, even though it was a grown-up word and he should have known it already. The man with the gun wouldn't say. He said everyone should sit tight and eventually they'd be escorted to safety.

Then something like a big white maggot had scurried into the room and jumped into the man's chest.

All of the adults had started screaming and panicking as more of the big maggots had come into the room, but Katie didn't. She'd known this was coming.

The monsters were here.

And they were eating everybody up.

She'd taken off running, ducking and weaving between the panicky adults and the big maggots. The big maggots didn't seem too interested in her – they seemed to want fat people first, or big muscular people like the man with the gun, and there were so many people about that they could get anyone – but she knew she'd have to find somewhere to hide before they started on her.

Her Mummy and Daddy stayed where they were and screamed for her to come back. But the screams stopped pretty quickly.

It was silly. They'd known all about the monsters. Why didn't they come with her?

She never saw them again.

Morse had slowed to a brisk walk by the time he reached the end of the bridge. He knew he should be running – that every second that passed meant more people were dying, in their hundreds and thousands – but more and more he didn't see the point.

The world was a ball of mulch. Everyone he'd ever known was dead. He'd failed the whole planet and handed it over to a bunch of insects from somewhere that didn't even have bloody physics.

All he wanted to do was lie down and die, and he didn't particularly see a reason why he shouldn't.

The walk slowed to a slouch, and then he stopped altogether. He should have been heading up the York Road, towards Leake Street, but somehow he couldn't be bothered. He could feel the weight of the gun in his pocket – the one he'd taken from Mickey, the one Mickey didn't have when he needed it.

The bomb was a pipe dream. Taking a suitcase nuke across hostile territory? Even detonating it in the station – what would be the point? They had different physics. It had been obvious in the station and it was more obvious outside. His feet were held by something other than gravity. He felt sick in his head and his belly, and the air was hot and seemingly filled with miniature razors. His heart and throat hadn't felt right since the scene in the lift.

He hefted the gun, feeling its weight. It would be easy enough. Just put the barrel in his mouth... close his eyes...

All the troubles of the human race, over with just one squeeze...

He stopped, breathing in deep, feeling the shifting glass of this new air scarring his lungs.

He lifted the gun to his head.

And then he saw the thing standing in front of him.

The Sentinel noted that the human had one of the weapons they'd tried to use against the Insect Nation. It had the weapon pointed to its own head. The Sentinel relayed the data back to the Queen – the massive organic intelligence running the invasion force, ruling the planet. The Sentinel cocked its head slowly, and waited for the answer to come.

Either the human would be allowed to resume killing himself, or the Queen would order the Sentinel to interrupt matters.

By tearing his sharp fingers into the human's belly and pulling out its internal organs.

One by one.

Without killing it.

The answer would return within seconds.

The Sentinel waited patiently.

Morse stared, the gun still halfway towards his open mouth. The thing in front of him was tall – easily nine feet – and spindly, the legs tapering down into thin hooves. It's chest rose and fell like a hummingbird's, the air rushing in and out of a circular mouth lined with teeth. Above the mouth was a single, massive red eye, pulsing with unholy light. The last time Morse had seen an eye like that, it had shone, wet and glistening, from the ragged, ripped belly of poor Sharon Glasswell. At the end of the beast's arms were two sets of ten clawed fingers. It keened softly, a sound on a frequency that made his eyeballs sting and pressure build up in the front of his brain.

It was not the appearance of the thing, or the terrible

sound it made, that caused the bile to rise in Morse's throat – made him want to vomit until he was an empty shell, until there was nothing left in him but his skin.

What made his blood chill in his veins and his mind reel was an almost indefinable quality to the creature's stance. The way it stood – the way it held itself. Even with the grotesque hooves and the quivering, thin fingers, there was no mistaking that body language.

This was John Doe.

This was the one Morse had allowed to slip through his fingers.

The one he'd allowed to destroy the world.

Morse pointed the gun at him and pulled the trigger – once, twice, three times, watching the bullets punch into the vitreous humour of the massive eye and burst it like a water balloon. The creature howled, a sound not so much above the threshold of human hearing as running parallel to it, and then lurched forward, reaching to grab hold of Morse's head in its spindly claws and squeeze hard enough to crush skull and brain.

But Morse was already gone.

By the time Katie had gotten into the station itself, it was clear that the monsters were in charge. They'd turned some of the people on the trains into monsters – lurching, moaning monsters with drool dripping from their mouths and eyes rolled back in their heads, reaching out and hurting anything near them. Like zombies in films. She'd raced down the stairs to the public toilets and hidden there, in the ladies. She could still hear the screams coming from up above. Screams and the noises of things crashing and clattering to the ground.

That lasted for a very long time.

After a while, there wasn't any screaming. Just moaning and the sound of them bumping into things.

Then after a while after that, there weren't even any moans. Just squealing and clicking and chittering.

Insect noises.

And after a while after *that*, there was nothing at all.

The Sentinel had been hurt.

It recorded the extent of the damage and broadcast it to the Palace. Vision had been impaired by a series of projectiles fired from the human weapon it had scanned earlier. Its main ocular unit had been burst – beyond that, damage was minor.

It was easily repaired.

The Sentinel had an advantage over other units, which was why it was rarely used except in emergencies. Unlike these sickly things grown on substandard organics, it was capable of rebuilding itself.

Improving itself.

As its arms reached out automatically to attempt a kill – hands closing on nothing at all – the massive eyeball in its head began to reform itself, coagulating like a scab, the surface repairing and refilling with the obscene fluid. This time, the Sentinel took time to reinforce the fibrous tunic of the bulb of the eye, thickening and strengthening the sclera and cornea until it was capable of withstanding further attacks of that nature.

It took perhaps a minute. The regeneration was the simple part – improvements had to be budgeted from existing areas of the cell-collective. That took time.

But The Sentinel had time.

The human could not possibly escape.

The lungs of Albert Morse no longer burned. The bone-deep weariness that had made him want to put the gun to his head had gone. His legs pounded against the concrete, leaping nimbly over the sundered bodies, boots impacting in pools of not-quite dried blood, spraying globs of dark red.

Adrenaline will do that for you.

He hammered down York Road, turning right onto Leake Street then left again, the station in sight now. He didn't bother looking up to check for the slowly passing insect-craft, or creep through the shadows. There was no point. They'd found him.

He had a sudden, clear understanding that he was the last man on Earth and that he was going to die. He'd been happy to blow his own head off less than a minute ago, and now he was desperately, hopelessly running to stay alive. He was barely capable of thinking, the blood crashing in his brain and his tongue almost hanging out of his mouth like a dog's, dry as dust as he wheezed with every caught breath, but still the irony of it struck him.

It was Doe that was keeping him going.

John Doe. The bastard himself. The one who'd caused all this, who they'd had the chance to carve into little pieces and feed to the wolves, the one they'd let slip through their fingers because the smartest man in the world had been too stupid to kill him when he had the chance. Well, fuck him. There was no way he was going to die at that bastard's hands. He was going to fight him to the last breath in his body and he was going to win. He was going to live. He was going to survive long enough

to get that bomb and blow them all back to the hell they'd come from.

Giving up was no longer an option.

Behind him, he heard the clattering of hooves.

He raced past the entrance to the Tube, down the corridor, then broke right in the station itself, the clattering of the hooves growing louder behind him. He wasn't going to make it to the toilet before the bastard caught up to him. The ridiculousness of that thought almost set him giggling like a schoolboy, but he controlled himself. He knew if he started to laugh he probably wouldn't stop.

The clattering stopped.

Morse threw himself forward, twisting in the air, his back hitting the bloody tile of the station floor as he brought his gun up. The monster was already sailing through the air towards him, razor-toothed mouth impossibly wide. It was going to eat him. It was going to bite his fucking head off while it slit open his belly with those scalpel-claws...

But it was slower than John Doe.

Slower and stupider.

Morse rammed the barrel of the gun into the monster's mouth, his arm disappearing into the Sentinel's gullet up to the mid-elbow. He was screaming, pulling the trigger again and again and again, the bullets slamming into the soft tissue, black ichor running down his arm along with his own blood as the razor teeth carved at his flesh and bone. When the gun stopped jerking back against his hand when he fired, he yanked his arm free, ignoring the pain, and kicked out at the monster hard enough to send it rearing back, vomiting more of the sickly black bile that was its lifeblood. He could no longer feel his hand.

The Sentinel screeched, flapping on the ground like a dying fish, then went still. Morse knew it wouldn't stay

that way for long.

Trying not to look at the ragged, ruined mass that used to be his right hand, Morse started running towards the toilet, leaving a trail of spattered blood.

Bastard, he thought.

Ate my wanking hand.

Katie started awake. She'd been sleeping fitfully in the cubicle she'd been sitting in since the insect-noises had gone away. She didn't feel hungry yet, so she hadn't gone to find any food. She thought the monsters might come back, anyway, so she wasn't going to leave before she got really, really hungry.

She'd heard shots, and a scream. Not a human scream. A monster scream.

Someone was hurting the monsters.

She listened carefully, straining her ears, the way she had late at night when Mummy and Daddy had gone to sleep and she'd listened for the monsters. She'd got very good at listening to things, so she could hear her parents arguing even if they did it in whispers. She could listen to that for hours and never miss a word.

She heard the sound of someone heavy running down the stairs towards the toilets, then slipping and tumbling down – *thumpity-thumpity-thump* – and a sound like a branch breaking.

And then a man shouting a very rude word.

Even her Mummy and Daddy never used that word no matter how loud they argued.

Katie unlocked the door of the cubicle and peeped out to see what was happening.

The Sentinel assessed the damage. It had leapt to kill the human as efficiently as possible but the human had twisted and managed to drive its weapon through The Sentinel's mouth and fire several projectiles into its inner workings.

It had left the weapon sitting inside the Sentinel's body.

If the Sentinel had any concept of emotions, it would have described that as adding insult to injury.

It stood, slowly dissolving the weapon and the projectiles, breaking them down into their composite minerals, then using those minerals to reinforce its internal structure.

The human was weaponless now. It had been injured – one of its manual extremities had been all but destroyed. It would present little threat.

The Sentinel moved forward, hooves clicking deliberately against the tile floor.

Morse had broken his ankle.

Maybe it was the blood loss. Maybe he'd just fucking panicked. But he'd taken the stairs down to the bogs too fast. His ankle had turned and he'd felt something snap and dislocate, and then he'd gone over and over down the bloody steps to land in a heap next to the turnstile.

He could feel his ankle swelling up like a balloon. He was an old man. He wasn't meant for all this kind of running about. The thought made him grin as he dragged himself up on the turnstile, trying to ignore the stabbing, slicing pain in his right arm, trying not to look at the ragged, mangled hand with only a thumb and two fingers.

His left hand dug in his pocket. He was glad he'd

made sure he had fifty pence where he could get to it, but then preparation was everything in an operation like this. *Ha bloody ha, Morse. Keep the British end up. Keep pretending you've still got a hope in Hell.*

The turnstile revolved once, and he swung himself through, leaning against the wall and hopping, leaving behind him a trail of bright, slick blood...

And the slow sound of clattering hooves, coming closer.

Closer.

Katie's eyes widened as she saw the man in the coat come into the Ladies. Men weren't allowed in the Ladies. That was why they were called the Ladies.

She kept herself hidden in the cubicle as the man hopped towards the sinks, trying to support himself against the wall. He was a big man with a broken nose and black hair, greying at the temples, and a big bushy moustache. He looked very grown-up. One of his feet was twisted around, like it was broken, and he'd cut his hand badly. Katie had never seen anyone cut themselves that badly. She didn't think they made sticky plasters big enough to work on cuts like that.

He hopped a couple more paces, and then put his twisty ankle on the ground and said another Very Bad Word and fell over onto the tile floor. He kept dragging himself along towards the sinks, leaving a long wet red trail of blood.

Katie wondered whether she should say something to him.

Then she heard the sound of the turnstile breaking.

It was a sound of metal separating from metal, of bolts and screws being forced from their housings and pinging through the air to clatter against the tiles. Morse closed his eyes and turned himself around to sit against the wall.

Doe was tearing a turnstile right out of the machine to get to him. He was weak, dizzy from blood loss. His right hand was essentially useless and his ankle was broken.

He was finished.

He was going to die in a toilet. In the Ladies, as well. Nice of the Whitehall bigwigs to think that up when they were building the place.

He watched almost dispassionately as the thing clip-clopped into the toilet after him. He knew it would be quick, if not painless. The bastard would probably just come trotting over and rip his throat out. It was all he deserved, anyway. He'd let that twat Smith keep the monster alive. In the end, it was down to him.

"Come on then, fucker." He snarled. "Come and finish me off. What are you waiting for?"

Doe was standing there on his hooves, bent slightly to fit in between the floor and ceiling, his spindly, waving scalpel-fingers twitching and bobbing gently in the air. Slowly, it turned, the great red eye swivelling to look over towards one of the cubicles. Morse's brow furrowed. What was it looking at?

He followed the gaze of the monster, and saw a pair of trainers underneath the door of the stall.

Kids' trainers.

With a kid in them.

"Hey! I'm over here! I'm over here, you fucking bastard!" Morse yelled, his voice cracking. "*I'm over here, you tosser! Come and get me! Come and get me!*"

Ignoring the pain, he pushed himself forward, crawling towards the monster, trying to get it to look back at him. *Kill me, you fucking bastard. Kill me first. Kill me before I have to see somebody else die because of me. Kill me, kill me, kill me, KILL ME —*

And then the door of the cubicle opened, and Katie came out.

The Sentinel was not expecting to find any humans still living apart from the target. It understood that there may have been some humans clinging to life, but they were so few and far between that the chances of it coming across one were tens of thousands to one.

And it recognised this one.

The Sentinel had met it before, when it was following earlier directives. During its chameleon phase.

The cover personality had sustained deep feelings of guilt. The Sentinel did not understand why.

Why should this human be here now, along with the other one? Was it random chance or part of some deeper design by the humans? Were they capable of that level of organisation?

The Sentinel cocked its head, staring down at the small human as it pondered the dilemma.

And then the small human began to speak.

Katie had recognised the monster as soon as it came in. It was wearing its monster-body now, a white maggot-skinned thing with scary claws and lots and lots of scary fangs, but she recognised it anyway because of the way it moved.

It was her monster. The one who had saved her.

And he'd stopped being nice and decided to eat people up. He was probably going to eat the man with the moustache up as well, in one big gulp. But he wouldn't eat her.

"Hello." She smiled and waved. "Hello. Um. Do you remember me?"

The monster looked down at her. The man with the moustache was white as a ghost. He looked very frightened.

"Love." he whispered. "Just run. I'll... I'll keep him busy. You just run and don't look back." He crawled a little closer towards the monster, even though it looked like it really, *really* hurt.

"No. It's okay. I know him. I'll be fine." She looked up at the monster, who was looking down at her with his big red eye. Suddenly he didn't seem so scary. He just seemed a little silly and sad, like someone who kept their Halloween mask on all year. "Um, you saved me from some bad men. I dunno if you remember. You um, you killed them all. And you ate one of them. It was like in a scary film." She looked away for a moment, trying to sum up how she'd felt at the time. "I was really really scared. Um. But you were really nice to me anyway even though I was scared of you." She blushed and looked down at her shoes. This wasn't coming out right.

"Run," wheezed the man with the moustache, like his throat was closing up. He looked like he was going to cry and be sick at the same time. Katie had never seen an adult looking like that.

"It's okay." She smiled at him, then looked back up at the monster. "I know you're only doing what monsters do. I know you want to eat people. But you could be nice if you wanted. That's what I think anyway. And, um, this man here's really hurt badly and I don't know where my Mummy and Daddy are and..." She swallowed. "You could help if you wanted. You could look normal again and be nice and help us. I bet you could. If you wanted to."

She smiled her very best smile.

"I bet you could, though."

Morse thought he was going to be sick. His head was spinning and his vision was greying at the edges. He pulled himself closer to the thing that used to call itself John Doe, hand over hand, dragging his battered body along the tile floor. The girl was standing right in front of him.

Why didn't it do anything?

The Sentinel looked at the small human. Deep in its memory banks, it remembered her.

It.

Her.

The Sentinel had, while obeying its chameleon directive, rescued her from a number of other humans who were attempting to extort money from her father. The small human had been almost catatonic after watching the Sentinel obeying its core directives. Were those core directives flawed in some way?

Why did that thought even occur to The Sentinel?

Why had The Sentinel not contacted the Queen about the small human?

You could be nice if you wanted.

What did that mean?

The cell-collective that made up The Sentinel suddenly seemed to be in flux, at war. Uneasy in the shape it had been assigned. There had been another shape it had taken during chameleon phase. The small human's –

Katie's –

Katie's words were setting The Sentinel's systems out of phase. Why was he even understanding them as anything more than the grunts and squeals of the substandard human species? Was this a weapon they'd developed?

Why had The Sentinel not contacted the Queen?

On the island the humans called Japan, The Sentinel had chosen to remove itself from a community that accepted its existence without suspecting its true nature, in contravention of its basic directives, simply because its cover personality had dictated that it should follow 'a code of honour'.

Why did The Sentinel access such memories now?

Why was it so confused?

You could be nice if you wanted.

The Sentinel looked down at the little girl.

It could be nice.

If it wanted.

Morse swallowed, watching as the monstrosity gently laid its killing hand on Katie's head, ruffling her hair.

Katie smiled and closed her eyes. She *knew* it. She knew that the monster could be nice if it wanted to be. She felt the long, thin, spindly fingers gently ruffling her hair...

...and then The Sentinel tore her head from her body.

CHAPTER FIFTEEN

The Long Goodbye

The first thing I hear is the sound of screaming.

A man screaming, yelling at the top of his lungs, calling me a bastard, calling me a fucking piece of alien shit, calling me everything under the sun... on and on and on.

I can smell disinfectant. Urinal cakes and soap dispensers. And blood. So much blood.

It's like I'm smelling it all through my skin. My breathing's different.

Everything's different.

Every part of me is different. Scents are coming to me through every part of my skin, each seeming to have its own texture. I'm hearing the screaming like I'm underwater – like I have my hands over my ears. My vision's changed. It's flatter, but clearer – like somehow my depth perception's been altered. Colours are different – blues and greens seem washed out, reds seem stronger, more vibrant. Everything I'm seeing seems like a collection of shapes with no connection between them. It's like things aren't coming into focus so much as coalescing.

What am I looking at?

I'm in a toilet. I'm on the floor of a big public toilet. I don't see any urinals, so it's the Ladies. There's blood everywhere – pints of it, all over the floor. Maybe I slipped and fell in it. I can't remember anything since... since the fight with that big-headed doll-guy. And even that's only in flashes.

How long have I been here?

What's happened to me?

First things first. Who's doing the screaming? Some guy bleeding out on the floor...

...is that the Boxer?

I should have worked that out. It's like I'm looking at his organs through his skin, seeing the heat centres pulsing. God, that's strange, that's... Jesus, he's badly hurt. It looks like he's stuck his hand into a woodchipper.

What the hell happened here?

"Mhhhrs...?"

It sounds like something bubbling up from underneath a swamp. My mouth feels weird. It's hard to form words. Try again.

"Mohhrse. Muh. Morse."

It feels like there isn't a tongue in my mouth... like I'm making the sounds with some sort of other organ buried right the way down deep in my throat. He stares at me for a moment, bone-white, like he wasn't expecting me to say anything and now that I have it's the most frightening thing in the world. Then he starts cursing me out again. This is no good. I start to get up off the floor...

...and then I see my hand...

The palm is thin and flat, with ten slender fingers branching off from it, each one ending in a little grey claw like a scalpel. The thumb ends in a merciless hook of bone. It's drenched with red blood, still dripping and oozing.

Whose hand is that? Not mine.

Surely not mine.

My gaze lifts and something else comes into my field of vision and, Jesus Christ, it's the headless body of a child. A little girl by the look of it, in a jumper and jeans. Someone's torn her head off her body. Jesus. Did Morse do that?

"Morrse... dih... dih yuuu..."

That just sets him off again. Bastard this, fucking Godless that. I don't know why –

Oh no.

Oh God. Oh, look at all the blood on my hand.

Look at the hand, for God's sake, it's tailor-made to tear off heads. The heads of little children.

Oh God.

Oh God who would never, never, never make a thing like me...

It was me. I did it.

I look around towards the cubicle stalls and her head's sitting there, on its side, eyes closed, the mouth frozen in a half-smile. A cooling child's head.

She's aged, of course, but I remember that face. From my point of view, I only handed her back to her Dad a couple of days ago. How could I forget?

Little Katie.

And I tore her head off.

And then I remember everything.

I drag myself to my feet, to my *hooves*, and clip-clop over to a mirror. I want to be sick. No, that isn't true – I want to want to be sick. But I can't be sick anymore, of course. Being sick is a human thing. My one big red bug-eye stares back at me, a deep dark pool of blood sitting in white corpse-flesh, a circle-mouth full of shark's teeth opening and closing underneath. No wonder it's so hard to talk. That terrible face leers at me from the mirror. It's so ugly. Grotesque.

When we look at ourselves closely, we always are.

Or is that only true for monsters?

I've never hated myself more than I do now. And I've never hated them more than I do now – the Insects, the Elder Gods who made a thing like me, the monsters who found out they had no use for our world and tore it into pieces so nobody else could have it.

And it is our world. Me included.

I remember everything.

I remember little Katie, her eyes big and wide and mentally damaged – that would be down to me – looking up at me and telling me that I could be nice if I wanted. I remember all my programs fusing and melting together as millennia upon millennia of cover personalities – of individuality and decency and honour and love and all the other stupid human things – crashed against the cold, analytical hive processes of the Insect Intelligence. I remember reaching down and tearing her head off, one last attempt by the Insect to assume dominance. But all that did was make the system crash harder. I remember collapsing on the floor...

It's almost funny. The Insect Nation thought that humans were worthless – biologically backward, unevolved meat-things, not even useful as foodstuffs. But they had a weapon that could beat the Insect Culture, that could infect it, dominate it, take it over. Humanity itself.

What happens when the cover personality is stronger than the 'real' personality? When the imitation becomes more real than the real? Oh, maybe the Insect could take over for a while, long enough to do the damage... but in the end, the weight of humanity, the weight of idiosyncrasy and inconsistency and illogicality and commonality will overwhelm something as simple and stupid as an Insect.

When this started, I thought I was a dead man. I know I'm worse than that now. Infinitely, horrifically worse – but I'm still *me*, for all the evil I've done. I'm still *myself*. Nobody can bury that, not even the things that built me.

And now I remember everything.

I remember calling the Insects here in the first place. Those parts when the Insect Nation were in control are like a dream – like sleepwalking. Like my body is walking and moving and I can't do anything to stop it. Like a nightmare. I remember standing and waiting patiently as buildings burned in front of me and white maggot-things scampered along the streets searching for fresh flesh....

I remember being half-burned to liquid mush by Mister Smith, laying like a charred doll and feeling my flesh reform into something more suited to ending the world.

I remember Sweeney and the wolves and Morse and rescuing little Katie.

I remember performing a string of assassinations around London in 1997. A man named Bristol Terry had made a lot of enemies and wanted them dealt with. He was low on the totem pole, but he had something all the bigger bastards who wanted to kill him didn't – my phone number.

I remember gutting a local paedophile with a kitchen knife in 1989. He was the real thing – he had polaroids. His brain didn't taste any different from any other I'd eaten. I felt like it should have tasted of sick and human shit, but it didn't. It wasn't the only time I was hired by the Neighbourhood Watch. I tried not to kill anybody who hadn't committed a serious crime, though. Overdue library fines didn't cut it.

I remember snapping Emmett Roscoe's neck in an office in a gay club in New York. The Insects won that time. Sorry, Emmett. You were sweet.

I remember solving cases in New York in the fifties. Divorce work, the occasional murder. 'Better Dead Than Red', they said at the time. They might have changed their minds if they'd known about me.

I remember hanging out with Dorothy Parker. That verse of hers that ended 'how lucky are the dead' was written after she met me. Beat that.

I remember walking across America before it was America, from the shores of the Pacific up to what became Canada. I remember being called Wendigo...

I remember living on a cold hill in feudal Japan, taking what offers came my way, keeping the Insect inside under control with a will of frozen iron.

I remember walking from one end of Russia to the other, through snow and ice, eating the brains of wolves and peasants and anyone else who crossed my path.

I remember discussing the existence of the soul with the philosophers of Athens.

I remember building pyramids for Pharaohs.

I remember...

I remember once I saw a man kill a tiger...

Year after year, generation after generation piled one atop the other, so many memories, a lifetime of humanity. And the Insect Nation thought they could lock that away and erase it as though it had never existed.

How you gonna keep 'em down on the farm, now that they seen Paree?

I don't care what I'm made of. I don't care who built me, or what they wanted from me, or what sort of physics I'm meant to operate under. I don't even care about the pulsing red eye I see through or the growled inhuman words that bubble up from the incomprehensible organs inside me.

My name is John.

And I am a human being.

Morse has stopped cursing again. Probably just to catch his breath.

"On yhrr feet, Mhhrs." I growl, trying to get the words out. "Ghht up."

He looks at me. He doesn't understand. But I'll make him understand.

I get down on one knee and haul him up to face me by the scruff of his neck, careful not to do any damage with these scalpel-fingers. I can't help but feel angry with him – he caused this. There was one man on Earth who could have triggered my programming and changed me into an Insect and this idiot brings me within five hundred feet of him.

He could at least have killed me properly when he had the chance.

I fix my great red eye on his and speak slowly.

"I w-wnnt... *want*... the bomb. Mhh... Morse. I want..." It's coming easier now. It almost sounds human. "I want the nuke."

Morse spits. "Go to hell."

"We're already there. I need the bomb, Morse."

"You can torture me all you –"

"And I need to know how to make it go off."

It took a lot to convince Morse I was serious. I think what turned him around in the end wasn't anything I said or did – what can you say or do after you've killed a child in front of a man's eyes? – it was that he didn't have a choice. Arming the thing took two keys – two good hands – and there was no way a man who couldn't even walk was going to get close enough to the Palace to be sure of using it.

What did he have to lose by giving it to me?

In the end, there was no bunker – there was a cache of handguns and one suitcase nuke, hidden in a large room behind a false wall, accessed by inputting a 20-digit code into a unit built inside one of the dryers. No food, no entertainment, no beds – anyone forced to shelter from a nuclear bomb in those circumstances would have died quickly if they were lucky. I asked Morse what he would have said if any of his motley crew had made it through the tunnels alive. He gave me a look and I realised that I shouldn't have spoken. He'd acted on data handed to him by a manipulative Victorian freak – the most he could be accused of was imparting a little false hope. He was trying to save as many people as he possibly could.

People that I murdered.

So I kept my mouth shut while he told me how to arm the bomb and set the timer for half an hour. I considered taking a handgun, but I'm not a hundred per cent sure these hands can actually hold or fire a gun properly – and frankly, these hands look dangerous enough on their own.

So I left one gun with Morse and then cuffed the bomb to my wrist. And then I walked out of there.

There weren't any goodbyes, or pithy comments – I didn't feel much kinship with the Boxer, and he certainly didn't with me. I'd murdered his whole planet and now I was carrying his last hope away with me because he was too weak – or too human – to do the job himself. I don't blame him for being sour.

I took a last look at him on the way out. He didn't look good – he'd lost too much blood, and he'd lost something else as well. There's no way a human being can see the end of the world and stay sane – even someone as strong as Morse had to snap eventually, and his weak spot was his will to live. His responsibility had kept him going for a while, and then his hatred of me had kept him going a while longer, but now all his jobs were done, all his purpose was gone and he wasn't coming back. I asked him what he was going to do and he shrugged and said he'd probably go and see Shirley. She'd gone on ahead of him, but she'd wait for him. She always had. Then he hefted the gun in his left hand.

You don't really get any more unambiguous than that. I just hoped he waited until I was out of earshot. I didn't want yet another death loaded onto my conscience – it was like Buckaroo already.

And now here I am, perfectly-balanced hooves clicking quietly on the steps as I climb up out of that toilet tomb, and I hear a gunshot echoing, bouncing back and forth across tile. And then a slumping body.

Thanks for waiting, Morse.

I straighten up when I'm on the station floor. It's weird having your point of view so far from the ground, but in another way it feels right. I don't know what that says about me. I don't know what sort of person I am now, in this perfect and perfectly alien body.

I've got about twenty-five minutes to find out.

The floor of the concourse is littered with corpses, mostly bits of corpses – the remnants of ribcages and torsos. People torn apart from the inside.

The reproductive cycle of the Insect is pretty simple. Larvae of various sizes are ejected from the motherships into the populace. They chew their way into hosts, taking control of the brainstem and sending the hosts lurching around like – *go on, say it* – like zombies. Then they feed on the flesh and fluids inside, growing along preprogrammed lines of development into soldiers, digger worms, eyes-on-legs and a thousand other slimy forms. And the nastiest of these is the Queen. A big, pulsing command centre, the main link between the Insect Intelligence out there and the creeping little bastards down here. I can feel her scratching away in the back of my mind right now, but it's like Radio 4 left on in another room of the house – just a constant murmur that means nothing to anybody. It's almost soothing.

But it means they're on to me. The Queen doesn't need to send a larva into someone's womb to grow a little surveillance monitor with me. She's got me bugged twenty-four-seven. She's a smart cookie for someone one step up from a cockroach.

She knows what I'm up to at all times. And so do the rest of them.

This is going to be interesting.

There's a skittering sound close behind me. And another from the side. And front.

I'm not surprised that they've come for me so quickly. There can't be much else for them to do. There aren't any humans left to kill, after all. Not in London.

In fact, I might be the last living thing in the world who knows what it's like to be human. Just John Doe – an imitation of a human mind locked in the body of an alien killing machine, strapped to a nuclear bomb counting down from... about twenty-three minutes by now.

The last detective in a world where all crimes have been solved forever.

It'd make a good film if there was anyone left to direct it.

They crawl out of the woodwork, circling slowly,

padding out from watching-places inside Upper Crust and WH Smith, incongruous against the commercial element. Three of them. Black and chitinous. Man-like in proportion, between four and seven feet tall, spurs of black carapace jutting out from shoulders, elbows and knees. Instead of faces, they have masks of black shell with cruel mandibles clicking and clacking slowly – rapping out a who-goes-there in clicks and pheromones. Their ink-black shells seem to ooze under the sickly lighting. Their claws glitter like polished steel. It's their world now, and they know it.

They're the soldiers of the New Insect Order.

I take time in my fist and squeeze it down to a hard point. For a moment, the soldiers freeze still – then they move again, circling at the same slow, steady pace. I start to circle myself, and they blur for a second before I squeeze time tighter, slowing the moment further to catch up with them. They can do what I can do, of course. It's only logical that they'd be able to.

In the back of my mind, I can hear the chittering of the Queen, wheedling, cajoling. The Insects don't understand what's happened to me. They think they can bring me back onto their side by reminding me of the hive, of the Queen, of a world where you do what you do simply because that's what you do, not for any higher reason.

I won't deny it's tempting to live as an Insect. No ego, no emotions, nothing to do but exist and follow the path you're given, without questions, without conscience.

Without guilt.

I speed up slightly. So do they.

I could just let myself go. Let myself embrace the Insect. But I have to ask myself, what sort of person am I?

Am I a bad person?

Am I a monster?

head like a sword from a stone.

Game over.

I let go and time folds back around me like the wings of some terrifying flying creature.

The moment passes.

The shallow cuts on my chest begin to ooze black slime. I concentrate and the wounds seal up, all of my cells moving in concert, working together, a we that is me and mine to control for the first time in my long and ugly life.

If I thought about it, I could even reconfigure my body. Look human again. Be John Doe again, that combination of Bowie and Bogart who looked just unordinary enough not to draw the slightest bit of attention. But there's no place in this world for him anymore.

I can feel the bomb in the case ticking down again. In somewhere around twenty-three minutes, it's going to detonate whatever happens. The closer I am to Buckingham Palace when that happens, the better.

But I don't just want to be close to it. I want to be inside it.

I want to look that bloated Queen, that Insect Intelligence, right in its face before I burn it like an ant through a magnifying glass.

Time locks down again, as tight as I can make it, and I run, my hooves thundering, pounding the floor hard enough to crack the worn tiling. I've got a lot of ground to cover.

And the sooner I get there, the sooner I can finish this once and for all.

The run to the bridge is... not what I was expecting. What was I expecting? A slalom, an obstacle course of

Or do I want to be just like you?

I've never seen a suitcase nuke before. I have a sneaking suspicion that this technology didn't exist back in 2007 when all of this started. The mechanism is delicate, but not so delicate that it goes off when jostled or dropped – otherwise how could you carry it about? Most of that resiliency is down to the carrying case – styled to look like a metallic briefcase – that houses the baby nuke itself. It's a titanium alloy, very solid, thick and hard and very heavy. A normal man would have a difficult time carrying this. The hard titanium shell serves three purposes – one, it intensifies the explosion, in the same way that if you put an M-80 in a matchbox, the resulting bang will be even louder for being contained for a split-second. Two, it keeps all the delicate electronics needed to turn a lump of fissionable uranium into a nuclear blast large enough to destroy a good-sized portion of London in full working order.

And three, it makes a handy mace.

I squeeze time all the way down, to a hard frozen instant, and then in the moment it takes them to react, I swing the case around into the head of the nearest soldier, using all the strength this misshapen body has in it.

The black chitin head of the soldier bursts like an egg, releasing streams of white pus and black fluid that splatter over the silver metal and trickle down the armoured carapace of the thing. It starts to judder, legs and arms spasming, hanging in the air like a suit of clothes on a coat hanger. We're moving too fast for gravity now, so it's not going to fall any time soon.

But it's dead.

In the back of my mind, the voice of the Queen goes still. I've been abandoned.

In a way, this is the moment of truth. This is where I

find out if they can turn me off like a remote drone, if they can send some signal that will cut my strings and send me tumbling to the ground or just dissolve me into a pile of disconnected cells. If they're going to switch me off like defective electronics, this is when it's going to be.

Nothing happens.

Gepetto, I'm a real boy!

The two remaining soldiers look at me with their blank chitin faces, flexing their sharp claws slowly.

Then one leaps for me.

This combat isn't only on the physical level – we're all playing with time, squeezing it further and further down, squeezing more juice out of it, trying to tilt the playing field in one direction or another. It's four-dimensional fighting. And it's a strain, even for this new body they programmed for me, this Ultimate John Doe.

I don't know if aliens get headaches as such, but I'm starting to get one now.

I bring the briefcase up like a shield and the steel-sharp claws screech against the metal, peeling tiny slivers of titanium off it. I push outward, letting the furious momentum of the creature carry it past me. Maybe it'll hit one of the ticket machines and that black skeleton will shatter into fragments. No time to check – the other solider is already leaping, all four limbs bending to slash at me in four different ways. If he gets to finish this move, then I'm going to be divided into about eight pieces. Maybe I'll survive that – I got away with being dissected – but I'm not anxious to find out.

I snap-kick forward, the hard hoof at the end of the leg driving out with the speed and force of a bullet. A big, fat, bullet. It drives into the soldier's midsection – the thorax – crunching and punching through the carapace

and checking the forward momentum. The tips of claws slice close enough to leave a series of tiny cut my soft white maggot-skin, but I don't feel anything.

I'm going to, though.

I shift balance, going for a high kick with my ot foot – my other hoof. The hard bone-like matter sla into the blank face sideways. I squeeze time just that lit bit further to see the hard hoof crushing and distorti the head, a spider web of cracks appearing in the bla chitin, pus spilling in slow motion before the force of t impact cracks the neck and tears the head from the bod sending it tumbling through space, in slow motion to m but so fast and so hard that when it hits the wall all that going to be left is a stain.

Stitch that!

One more. I know for a fact I didn't kill that soldi who flew past me because I'm not that lucky. I use t momentum of the kick to spin around and look behi me, just in time to see flashing black claws of infin sharpness moving right for my big eye...

It takes maybe one hundredth of a second. With ti locked down this far, this tight, there's no leeway speed myself up any further. It's all about being fa than it is.

But in Feudal Japan, I learned the arts of the ninja And he didn't.

My right hand darts out in a perfect snake strike ten long thing fingers folded together so that the scalpel-nails group together into a little forest of k that drives right into the hard surface of its soldier's carapace face, cutting through the hard matter, d in, punching through. The claws that were about to my eyeball like a poisoned boil halt in mid swi start to tremble as I step back, pulling my hand f

monsters – a soldier behind every alleyway, every parked car, leaping and slashing, ganging up to tear me into pieces. But there aren't as many as I was expecting – another five or six at the most. One of them's so short and scrawny it counts as half. It occurs to me that it's about as high as a ten-year-old, and I can't deal with that at all, so I bring my case down on its head hard enough to shatter it and leave it behind me.

They're so *slow* – faster than any other creature on what's left of this planet, but slow all the same. Not nearly as fast as this new, perfect body I'm wearing.

I guess it's logical when you think about it. The Insect Nation created me – and all the other zombies that walked the planet, the cold replica humans – to be both sentinels and weapons of war. We were pure creatures, things folded through space and time from the heart of somewhere else – not the strange hybrid things on the loose in London, grown on substandard human meat and bone. I can outfight the soldiers. Outrun them. Outthink them.

But still, they're not exactly challenging me considering I'm coming to kill them. I reach the end of Westminster Bridge, retracing Morse's faltering steps. I'm wondering about the implications of that. They weren't expecting me to turn on them. They weren't expecting there to be a 'me' ever again – they thought the personality they'd built was just a mask, a cover. And let's not forget that all the other Sentinels – the 'zombies' – were hunted and killed over decades.

If there had been others like me, would we all have become human sooner or later? Could we have driven them away, an army of Sentinels with human minds? What then? Would we have created our own society on the bones of the human race, or just protected what was left, obsessively guarding the last remnants of the species into old age and death? Maybe that's the optimistic view. Maybe I'd just have been taken down the moment I started thinking for myself, torn apart by a platoon of Sentinels loyal to Her Majesty, the Queen of the Insects – there are traitors in every war.

It doesn't matter. You could play 'what if' forever. What if I'd never come to London? What if Mister Smith had never been born? What if Morse had killed me when he'd had the chance?

The only question that matters is what *now*.

Two of the massive alien craft float overhead, watching, keeping me in sight. My hooves clatter and crash on the road. I'm expecting a packed wall of soldiers, waiting to tear me apart, black chitinous creatures clambering over one another to get to me.

But there's nothing at all. Just a red sky and an empty bridge.

How many people were in London? How many of them had those monstrosities burst out of them? How many million soldiers would that make? And they were all crowding towards Buckingham Palace, according to what Sharon's eye-baby picked up from Morse. Simple mathematics says that every square inch of this bridge should be crowded with insect bodies, whether they're after me or not. Where did they go?

If I'm tougher and faster than those black walking things, what were they for? The Sentinels were meant to be the soldiers, clearly. So what are the 'soldiers'?

The back of my mind is silent. Her Majesty isn't speaking to me anymore. I don't know what the plan is beyond the orders I was given. Suddenly I'm feeling nervous, keeping a look out for the other shoe. Overhead, the massive, incomprehensible invasion craft of the Insect

Nation circle like vultures.

There's no sign of any enemies on Bridge Street, Great George Street, Birdcage Walk... the blurring grey-brown stone of the buildings changes to a line of trees whizzing past me – or what were once trees. Dead husks of blackened wood, unable to survive in this new air, under this ruby cage of sky, withered down to nothing but sticks of rotted timber. I'm glad this body doesn't have a nose – I can taste the rotting stench of the acres of dried, dead, rotting grass through my skin as it is. It's horrible.

But I'm nearly there.

I put on a burst of speed, hooves racing, straining every muscle, every cell of this strange and terrible body they've put me into...

...and then the other shoe drops.

Oh.

Oh my God.

Stretching up above me, where Buckingham Palace stood, is a wall of writhing black chitin, a massive tower of gleaming, glistening insect bodies. This is where the soldiers went. All of them. Because they might have had slashing claws and biting mandibles to work with, but they weren't soldiers.

They were workers.

And it looks like they were the bricks too.

The Insect Nation have built their own palace around the old one. They've built it from the husks of their own shock troops, fused together into one mass of millions, stretching right up to the ruby canopy overhead. You can see pus and black fluids oozing down the side of the structure.

It's the most horrible thing I've ever seen in my life.

The most horrible thing of all is how much it looks like

home.

I take a step back, the case of the bomb swinging on its chain as I swing one arm backwards –

– and then it happens. Out of nowhere.

The concrete under my hooves shatters, sending me falling sideways. Instinctively, I grab time, twisting it hard – too late. I'm staring into a cavern of sickly, slimy flesh, a tunnel with rows of razor sharp teeth running all the way down...

Coming up through the concrete at me is one of the Wyrms, the slithering creatures that infested the Tube tunnels. I guess they have a purpose too – ferrying essential minerals to and fro, crunching up corpses and delivering the resultant mash to the Queen to keep it healthy. Something along those lines.

Now it's purpose seems to be to eat me.

Desperately, I break right – and then it veers left and I feel the side of the monster's mouth bumping against my chest, and a terrible tearing sensation in my left arm...

...and then I'm crashing down on the ruined concrete, watching it tunnel away.

It's only when I look at my left arm and see a ragged stump where the elbow used to be that I realise what's happened.

It's got the bomb.

There are a good fifteen to twenty minutes before it blows. That's time enough for the Wyrm to tunnel down below all the concrete and sewers and pipes, further and further down, further and further away from the Palace. Sacrificing itself to carry away the threat.

In about fifteen minutes, we're going to get a hell of

an earthquake.

And that's all we're going to get.

And here I am, stood outside the most terrible monstrosity I've ever imagined, this huge black shell of black insect bone that's going to turn the whole world into a soup of lifeless sludge just because it can, because it's good practice... and I've got one good arm and no weapons.

And I don't have the slightest idea what I'm going to do next.

CHAPTER SIXTEEN

Vengeance is Mine

This is what the end of the world looks like.

Massive spacecraft, from a place without physical laws as we know them, circling in a ruby sky, then folding and crushing through space like paper planes in the hands of a vicious child. Winking out like candles in a church nobody goes to anymore because there is no God.

Why would they stay? There's nothing left for them to do here.

The Insect Nation came here to harvest our world, to gather up a planet full of slaves and foodstuffs. When it turned out that they'd been called too soon, they decided they might as well turn the entire planet into a rich, nutritious ball of mulch. Everyone in London is dead – mostly killed to create the walls of the structure in front of me, a huge spire of living, fused insect tissue, an antenna to broadcast the Insect Way Of Life.

Right now it's broadcasting an ever-expanding disintegrator field that reduces people and buildings and art and culture and life to their component atoms, leaving a roiling, boiling soup where there used to be a world full of human beings.

The only problem the Queen of the Insects has is a malfunctioning Sentinel unit called John Doe. She doesn't seem to be fussing much about it.

I can't get through the wall of black, slimy insect-flesh in front of me. I've been trying – every time I slash at it with the claws on my one good arm, the wounds close over almost before I've made them. Buckingham Palace is sealed forever in a gleaming, glistening cocoon.

It's all over.

I've blown it.

Nothing left to do but stand around and look at the tower, and the ruby sky, and the dozens of corpses. Nothing to do but admire my view of a world that died.

It's funny – I always thought I was dead because I didn't breathe and my heart didn't beat. Because I was a slave to urges I didn't understand. But having a heart that doesn't beat, lungs that don't work – that's not being dead. So long as you're walking around, able to talk to people, do things, *affect* things... how can that be death?

But this is death. Standing here, with the power to stop time, and run at a hundred miles an hour, and tear through walls with my fingernails... and all of it being useless. I can't do anything about this, just like I can't go back in time and stop it from happening. What's done is done. I can't change anything.

Not being able to change anything in the world.

That's what it is to be dead.

Dead and in Hell.

Nothing I've ever done matters. Everything I ever did, all those hundreds of thousands of years of watching people, living among people, changing things in small ways, all the lives I saved and ended, all of it is meaningless. Everything I've ever been, wiped away in one second, because I opened my big monster mouth and ended the world. And I can't even avenge it properly.

It feels like only a day since I took the call from Sweeney.

Twenty-four hours and everything sucks.

I should write that down. A quote from the last human-like being alive.

I look down at my hand, still crusty with Katie's blood. A representative of the countless billions who've left their blood on my hands.

I look at the ragged elbow joint that the Wyrm left when it chewed up my last hope for doing anything other than standing around feeling sorry for myself.

The flesh is twitching on the end of the stump, little tendrils of skin trying to grow a new arm. I watch for a moment, fascinated. I must be doing that myself, on some subconscious level. I suppose if I really thought about it – and if I ate a couple of *you-know-whats* – I could grow a new arm.

Why not? I'm giving the orders now. I decide what this collection of cells, this we that is me, should be used for. Why not get my arm back?

Why stop there?

If I've learnt one thing – one thing about being human, about fighting back against the alien thing I used to be – it's that I don't have to be normal.

I don't *have* to be just like you.

All I have to do is what's right.

Suddenly the feeling of lassitude, of despair, is gone. I can hear Billy Ocean in my head – I met Billy in the eighties – and he's playing his last concert ever, here in my head, and it sounds like victory, like hope, all screaming guitars and crowds waving lighters... *when the going gets tough...*

If this mouth could smile, it would.

I've got things to do. Things to build on this wonderful body, and I'm hungry. And all around me are fallen Londoners, who died without having the insides of their skulls licked clean by invading parasites, Londoners who were lucky enough to be killed by the horde of zombies without becoming one.

I'm salivating. The stump of my elbow is tingling and twitching. And two spots on my side, below my armpits.

And two more spots below that.

I'm hungry. I need to build up some extra body mass. And all around me are brains – delicious, juicy, succulent

BRAINS!

And by God... the God who never made me, the God who might, just might have found a use for me after all...

...do they taste good right now...

Here's a lesson for you – it's okay to commit a massive act of cannibalism if you're saving the world. That said, that wasn't really cannibalism and I did actually end the world first, but try not to point that out. Let me feel good about myself for a minute or two, hey?

And I do feel good about myself. I stretch out with my arms, arching my back, checking the position of the sun. It's been about an hour. Hopefully not too long. At the same time, my other arms reach to feel my ribs, seeing how much mass I've gained from the fifty or sixty brains I ate.

The third pair just flex.

My four new arms have the long scalpel-like nails I'm going to need to tear through that chitin before it reforms itself, but they've got four fingers and one thumb. If there are going to be guns in there, I want to be able to fire them. And the feet have been altered a little as well – once you had toes, back you don't goes. Or something. And I'm seeing through two eyes as well. The depth perception's better.

And when I kill that thing in there, I want it to see something close to a human face.

I'm shorter than I was. Squatter. More human in terms of dimensions, but still alien enough to face down whatever's lurking in there. And I'm feeling more confident than I've ever been. I'm the best of both worlds now, half zombie, half alien.

I, Zombalien.

It's got kind of a ring to it.

And finally – after centuries, after millennia of doing nothing but wasting my time and hurting anybody who ever mattered to me, I'm finally doing something right. Maybe it is too late, but this is what I was meant to do all along. For the first time ever, I'm doing something for my own reasons.

This one's for you, Emmett.

Six clawed hands flex as I move towards the black barrier. I'm humming. There's a part of me that's looking forward to this, a dark part of me that's aching for revenge for a species I was never part of but wanted to join so badly.

Then I take hold of time and crush it, squeeze it with the force of a black hole. I squeeze it until it stops dead, like a broken heart.

And then I attack.

It was intense.

Before, with my one sickly, skinny arm, cutting that wall was like dipping my fingers into a placid lake, then taking them out to leave the surface undamaged. Now, it was like burrowing into sand, having it fall into place behind you as you went. Driving forward, tearing and hacking, all six sets of scalpel-sharp claws slicing deeper into the wound before it could close up, and all the time the insect-flesh wall around me screamed in my mind with a thousand thousand voices, shrieking at me to stop, to turn back, to let myself be swallowed up and infused into their flesh... and then I was carving at old stone, taking chunks out of it with every swipe of steel-hard fingernails...

And then I was through.

And suddenly the Queen of the Insects is taking me seriously again.

She's got a right to. I'm inside her.

I guess when Morse got his information from poor old Callsign Magnet – and when I got my information from poor old Sharon Glasswell – nobody thought about where it might be going. The Queen of England replaced by a twitching Lovecraftian horror, flanked by a troupe of worker-ants with terrifying steel-black claws... that's a grim scenario, but it lets you think you have a chance, that a squad of soldiers could burst in there and take her out if they only got organised quickly enough. That might be survivable.

But of course, the Queen's black-garbed guards were just there as foodstuffs, to help bulk her up. That was why they were all off to the Palace to see the Queen – so she could absorb them into herself.

When I was carving into that big black tower, I was cutting into her skin.

Sometimes it seems like my whole life is based on one critical misunderstanding after another. Maybe that's what life is. Maybe it's at this point, right at the end of everything, right in the final minutes of your time, that you finally get an understanding of just what you're doing and what you've been doing all along.

I don't know. If there's a time for philosophy, then standing inside the internal organs of a massive star-spanning creature that could be described as your mother – or at the very least a second cousin – probably isn't it.

Once upon a time, this might have been an anteroom or a servant's quarters. You can see hints of something that might have been an armchair or a cupboard – but everything's been grown over with slimy, pulsing flesh, shimmering green and slick with alien sweat. The only light comes from clusters of glowing orbs in the ceiling, over a bulge where the light must have been. When I look up at them, a curtain of flesh slides across them for a moment, wetting them, making the noxious light flicker. A blink.

The Queen has grown itself around Buck House, turning the stone and the walls into a kind of makeshift skeleton. Is it using the electrical wiring to send and receive sense-messages? Clever, clever. Maybe I underestimated it.

Maybe not. If it was smart, it could have digested this whole building. But it's just absorbed it and built over it. Which hopefully means it's built over some useful objects. We'll see.

In one wall, there's a rectangular depression about the size of a door. I hope that's what it turns out to be, otherwise I'm going to look pretty stupid.

My new foot – a hoof with flexible toe-like protrusions coming out on three sides – smashes into the covered door, tearing the skin and splintering the wood beneath, and in my head I can hear a mewling screech of pain. It's talking to me again. But I don't need it to.

There's something in my body – in this alien cluster of cells, born to a far-off star in another plane of reality – that recognises its own. I'm being drawn towards the

blunt hands of bone reaching forward to grip me. It's not going to be swinging its fists around in a confined space like this – it's going to try to grab me, tear me into pieces and hurl those pieces onto the walls, where the flagella will helpfully keep me from sticking myself together. I'll be a nice piece of wall art for the rest of eternity.

That's what I'd do if I was in his shoes, anyway.

Eyes narrow. I get hold of time, ready to squeeze, knowing I'll only have a relative split-second of grace before it matches my speed of perception.

I remember Japan.

Choose your moment, Ronin.

Two hands reach for my head, and I lock down time, hard, then reach up and grab all four of his wrists. My body tilts backward, down into the thick black juices that run through the corridor, as my feet drive up, kicking into his midsection, using his own momentum against him.

Judo wasn't invented in Japan until well after I left. But I like to pick things up. And there are a lot of things you pick up after living for a million years.

The Anti-man goes sailing over, smashing into the wall. The flagella catching hold, like I knew they would, sticking to the enamel surface. Too bad for them. The momentum of the Anti-man's flying body is too much for the flesh they're attached to – there's a sound like curtains tearing as it rips a huge swathe of flesh from the wall.

That had to hurt.

I can hear the Queen screeching inside my mind, and I'm betting the Anti-man can too. It rises slowly, clutching its head, then grabs the skin still clinging to its back like a cape and tears it away. It's going to attack again in a second.

If I give it the chance.

I sprint forward and spring into a flying kick. I kept the hooves for a reason, toes or not. They're like having sledgehammers where my feet should be. The sound as one of them makes contact with the Anti-man's face is like a drop hammer smashing a block of concrete.

That's the problem with being made out of bone.

Bone breaks.

The Anti-man staggers back, a deep crack running up the middle of its face. I take the opportunity to insert the long, curved hooks that end my topmost set of thumbs into the gap, digging them in deep, enjoying the way the black blood spurts out to spatter against what's left of my face.

Maybe I shouldn't be enjoying this. This is cruel and sadistic. This is the last gasp against an alien culture that has effectively made the human race extinct. This is probably pointless in the long run – the Insect Nation will carry on, is carrying on, has already carried on, on the shores of no-space and un-time. This is the final nail in the coffin of a failed enterprise for them.

But this is revenge.

Revenge for making me. For letting me spend a million years with the dominant life form of this planet and then coming down and executing them all. Revenge for all the hurt and the pain I've ever felt because I wasn't just like you, and for the love and the sweetness too, because every time I had something even slightly good they programmed me to throw it all away.

I hope this fucking hurts, your Majesty.

The head of the Anti-man cracks open into two neat halves, revealing a cluster of raw nerve endings – what keeps it plugged right into the Insect.

In one swift movement, I lean down and bite the

fuckers. Then I jerk my head back. They tear loose like Velcro popping apart.

The scream in my head in indescribable, and I savour it.

Because the louder you scream, Your Insect Highness, the easier it is for me to find you.

The Anti-man flops down, huge bone body splashing in the stagnant black wash. There'll be more where he came from, and soon. I need something a bit more...

...ah.

Looking back along the flapping swathe of flesh torn from the wall, I see the door I've been looking for.

The one with the little corroded brass plaque that says: ARMOURY. DO NOT ENTER.

Stands to reason there'd be a place for the soldiers and secret service to keep their guns. Let's see what they have.

The door's locked, of course, but one kick takes care of that. Then it's just a matter of looking for a skin-covered bulge and hoping it's a nice metal cabinet rather than a gun rack... here we are. Thumb-hook slits it open. Another little whimper of pain. I hope there's something good here, the Anti-men are going to come...

...running...

Oh yes.

Oh very much yes.

The gun's a Heckler & Koch LA852 sub-machine gun, as used by the army for keeping the peace, which is exactly what I intend to do with it. If keeping the peace translates as killing everything that moves. It fires over 600 rounds a minute if it has to, which means it can use up a magazine in three seconds.

It's a good job I filled a backpack with magazines because I've got four of the bastards.

Yes, since you ask, I do look like a badass.

By this time Her Royal Highness the Queen of Outer Space is shrieking in my brain. It's starting to hurt – as if that constant wail of pain is disrupting my systems. I imagine it's disrupting a few other things as well, judging by how the lights keep flickering.

It's not begging me to stop exactly – there's no emotion there beyond the drive to survive – but it's screaming at me to remember my place, to stand down... to dissolve myself into a nutritious soup for recycling.

It's not that tempting an offer, to be honest.

Out in the corridor, I can hear splashing – more of the Anti-men coming to shut me down for good. I step out of the Armoury to meet them and open up with the HKs. Normally, I'd think twice about spraying the inside of Buckingham Palace with sub-machine gun fire, but this isn't 'normally'. Nothing's ever going to be 'normally' again.

I'm never going to be just like you and I don't care.

There are three of them on either side, trying to sandwich me in. I take hold of time and the rhythm of the bullets slows to the gentle boom, boom, boom of a big bass drum at a parade. It helps me aim better. I can't afford to waste ammo if I'm going to be reloading four guns all the time.

And it's so good to watch those bullets plough into those bone faces, chipping, cracking, shattering them... leaving the vulnerable nerve endings to throb with pain in the damp air. So good watching them fall against the walls, tearing skin off with their weight... so good to hear the screams in my mind as it happens. I'm starting to get a theory about that screaming.

I'm close to the throne room now. Close to the pulsing brain of this monster. There's nothing that's going to stop me. Nothing they can do to even slow me down.

It's time to end this.

Time for Johnny to come marching home.

I don't know what I was expecting when I kicked in the door to the throne room, but this isn't it. But then, what would be?

The brain is massive. A pulsing ball of flesh, glowing with a sickly light, pulsing in slow, random rhythms, the throne embedded somewhere inside it. Coming out from the centre of it are four huge tentacles, covered with writhing, wiggling legs, like millipedes. I keep a sharp eye on them as they weave slowly, protectively, in the air between me and her. If they work like the flagella in the corridor, I don't want to get anywhere near them.

I just look at it.

And it looks at me.

This is the conduit through which the Insect Nation give their orders. This is the means by which they can kill the planet, the driving force behind all the Wyrms and workers and eyes-on-legs swarming through the city.

This is as pure and unadulterated an evil as I've ever seen.

There is no conscience here. No emotion. No reasoning beyond the need to feed, to take, to steal. This is everything humanity fought to rise above, and it would wipe them – wipe us – out in a second.

Because by their standards, we're not just primitive, or inefficient. We're nothing at all. It's not that they think humanity doesn't deserve to live, because that would involve thinking about humanity, thinking about anything besides feeding, eating, the selfish needs of the Insects.

The sound of my own voice surprises me.

"You're not afraid of me, are you? You don't really understand what fear is. But you know. You know that when I end you – when I walk over there and tear you to pieces – everything comes tumbling apart. That ruby dome over our planet is going to dissipate into thin air. All of your children are going to drop down dead. I bet the scream when it happens – that psychic death-scream – is going to be strong enough to reach right back to where you came from and hurt them. Sting them just a little, in their place beyond place and their time beyond time. Maybe burn their fingers enough that they don't come into this universe to play their games anymore.

"I know that's going to kill me as well. You've really been hurting me with all your yelling, and I think when you finally go it's going to melt me down with all the rest of your playthings. I'm never going to get the chance to be normal. I'm never going to be just like them. But I want you to understand that that's fine by me. I don't mind being a zombie any more. I don't mind being dead.

"Because finally – here, at the end of it – I know I've died for something."

The tentacles twitch.

Did it understand me? Does it have any comprehension of what I'm feeling right now?

Of what feelings are?

I shake my head. It's pointless talking to it. I was talking to myself all along. Coming to terms.

Are you out there? Is there anybody left alive? Anybody left to do this for?

It doesn't matter in the end. It's got to be done, so just do it.

Just end it.

I move forward, hooves banging against the old wood, splashing through the thick stagnant mire, raising the guns and firing one long three-second burst – three seconds that stretch out and out as I twist time, gripping it, clamping it with my mind... so that the bullets drift towards the slow-waving tentacles like grey clouds, like a child's balloons... so that the clatter of the gun slows to a sound as regular as the low, slow ticking of a metronome... so that the hollow-point rounds push in slowly, slowly, fragmenting in a beautiful ballet of metal shards, each one finding its place in the grotesque meat of the monster's waving arms.

It doesn't even notice.

I jerk left, hurling myself out of the way of one tentacle, and another comes down, the millipede-legs gripping an arm, then yanking back like a cracked whip. I can feel the tearing sensation as it rips the limb from my body, taking a chunk of my side with it, the gun still chattering in the death-grip of the lost hand, ploughing bullets into the ceiling.

I'm so shocked by that that it manages to tear off two of my left-hand arms before I can twist out of the way. Gouts of black blood spray towards the ceiling in slow motion, falling upwards through the air. It'd probably make a good cigarette advert.

My stomach flips over. This was going to be my big revenge, my big moment when I reclaimed my life, and it's just going to tear me into little bits. If it gets at my head, it's over.

I've got two guns left. I bring them down to aim at the brain itself, sending a slow, beautiful stream of hot lead gliding like fat, lazy birds into the pulsing ball of strange flesh. It's so gratifying to see ragged holes appearing in that massive ball of pus, to see the bright yellow pus shooting out of the wounds, mixing with the black slime filling the room... to hear it shrieking...

I've hurt it. Now I've got to kill it. I power forward, the guns clicking dry in my grip. Then two of the tentacles reach down, each of them snagging one of my thighs –

– there's a yank –

– and I'm up in the air, swinging upside down, dangling from my right leg as the tentacle hangs me over the pulsing brain like a Christmas tree ornament, my other leg and a section of my hip twitching as it hangs from another tentacle far away. The tentacles are already reaching after me. This is where I get torn into tiny pieces and then those pieces get torn into smaller pieces, until all there is of me is a slop of random parts floating in black bile...

But I still have three good hands left.

I hope that's enough claws for this.

I reach down, the nails like razors carving into my own thigh before the tentacles can reach me, cutting and slicing through flesh, through bone, severing the leg just above the knee. My black blood showers down over me as gravity takes over and I fall down, slow and graceful as an elevator...

...right onto the pulsing, glowing surface of the brain itself.

The tentacles are already flicking after me, but too late to catch me before I hit, claws first, touching down like a lunar lander made of razors, slashing my way into the centre of the mass... and starting to eat.

This is probably the first time I've eaten a brain that really, truly deserved it. As I stuff the spongy, glowing matter into my mouth, my other hands tearing and slicing, slashing and stabbing, it tastes of rot, and reek, and foulness, it tastes of poison and bile and everything dark and evil in the world.

It's the best thing I've ever eaten in my life.

Time locks down around me as the screaming starts in earnest, the tentacles thrashing like palsied snakes, darting this way and that, starting to lose their cohesion, pieces flaking off them and drifting down over us like snow. It's almost romantic.

Slow it down enough and anything is beautiful.

And this revenge has been so very slow.

I can feel it, in my mind. I can feel the ruby sky above us flickering, shorting out, letting in the stars. I can feel those few Wyrms and workers dropping, dissolving, dying.

Somewhere, in a place that isn't a place, beyond space, beyond time, I can feel ancient intelligences rearing back, stung.

Stitch that. Stitch that, you bastards. That's been a million years coming and it wasn't anywhere near soon enough. Soak it up, you sons of bitches. That's what the human race thinks of you. That's what it's like to die.

Most of all, I can feel the scream, the death-scream, rising, louder and louder as my own strength fades, my body going slack like it's 1976 all over again, the pain washing through me, burning me cell by cell.

This is what it's like to die. This is agony that makes Morse's torture feel like a picnic in the park. And I love it. Because maybe I earned it, maybe I deserve it, but I chose it.

This death belongs to me.

I could keep it forever. Lock time down so far that I *felt* every cell of myself, of this we that is me, dying one by one. Savour that sweet martyrdom; burning on my cross for the sins I gave to the world...

But a million years is a pretty good run.

And if this is what it's like to die... how did I put it?

At least I've died for something.

I let go of time for the last time and feel it folding around me like the covers of a closing book.

And then...

...the moment passes.

EPILOGUE

Towards Zero

The old man stood on the cliffs, looking out at a brown sea as the tide lapped sluggishly under a clear blue sky.

"G'day!" the voice came from behind him, clear and easy.

"G'day." murmured the old man, sadly.

"Penny for your thoughts? Got an esky here with a few tinnies. Hate drinking with the flies, especially now." It was a young man with sandy-coloured hair, almost white, and very pale skin. He grinned, cracking open the portable cooler beside him and dragging a can of Foster's out of the ice. "Here. Get that down you."

The old man hesitated, then took the cold can and cracked it open, taking a swig. "Ahhh... yer blood's worth bottling, mate. Cheers."

"No drama. Figured in this heat you could probably use a drink." The younger man grinned again, cracking his own tin and taking a gulp. "So – penny for 'em?"

The old man took a drink, then gestured with his can out at the expanse of brown. "What do you reckon, mate?"

"Yeah, I think about the same stuff meself. I figure talking about it helps, but tell me if I'm earbashin' yer." He nodded and smiled, evidently eager for company. "You got family abroad?"

The old man nodded. "Yeah. Had a daughter moved to Connecticut. Me son-in-law's a Yank. Was a Yank. And me ex-wife lived in Brisbane, outside the circle." He sighed, looking at the can in his hand. "Mind if I skull this, mate?"

"Strewth, mate, you'd be a better man than I if you didn't after a story like that."

The old man tilted back the can, draining it in one gulp, then crushed it and tossed it onto the ground. The young man cracked open a second can and handed it to him. "Cheers. Y'know, mate, if you'd told me a month ago Barrow Creek'd be on the coast of the world's first circular country, I'd have called you a bloody galah."

"Yeah," the young man nodded. "One second later we'd be down in the brown ourselves. It's a good thing they learned how to process water from that goop or we'd all have carked it by now. I'm takin' pommy showers as it is."

"I'd tell you not to speak ill of the dead, but the poms started all this, so fuck 'em." There was a long silence. "I'll be honest with you, mate – I came out here to bloody toss meself off, so to speak. I figured I might as well go ahead and cark it with everyone else I knew."

"Still goin' ahead with it?"

"Wouldn't be polite, would it? Besides, don't make much difference. We're all gonna die pretty soon, I reckon. Don't reckon the population can sustain itself. We weren't all that crowded even before we lost the coasts."

The young man shook his head. "Reckon?"

"Fair dinkum, mate. We're stuffed as a species."

The young man grinned and shook his head, cracking open another can. "In a pig's eye, mate. Trust me, there's nowhere to go but up. I'm a great believer in second chances." His eye sparkled. "Who knows where we're all gonna be in a couple million years?"

The old man looked at him. "Bloody hell, you're a bit optimistic! What if all them space fellahs come back?"

The young man smiles. "They won't. Not until we're ready for 'em." He grinned wider. "Trust me on that, mate."

The old man looked at him. "Here, since you're so chipper, lemme put this to yer – how come we survived, eh? Whole bloody planet goes tits up and the bloody outback comes out ripper. How's that work, eh?"

The young man grinned. "Somebody had to live through it, mate. To keep things going, eh?" There was something unsettling about that smile. Something the old man didn't like.

"Yeah... well, I'll be seeing yer, mate. What's your name, anyway?" He stuck out his hand.

"Blow. Joe Blow."

"You're bloody kidding! What's it like to be stuck with that?" The old man laughed as the younger man shook his hand. "Gary Goodall. Christ, you're like ice! Like shakin' hands with a bloody corpse!"

"It's from holdin' the tinnies, mate. You have a good one."

Gary Goodall nodded and waved, then started up the track back to the town.

Joe picked up the cooler and walked to the edge of the cliffs, sitting down and swinging his legs over. It was going to be a long day, and a long day after that one. It might take another couple of thousand years for humanity to pick up and start evolving again.

But Joe could wait.

He had all the time in the world.

THE END

AL EWING crawled from the grave in 1977 and has since shambled around with various bits dropping off him, moaning gutturally and occasionally biting pedestrians. Despite this unfortunate handicap he has managed to write various deeply violent strips for *2000 AD* and the *Judge Dredd Megazine* as well as the novel *El Sombra* for Abaddon's Pax Britannia series. In his spare time, he is a semi-regular guest on the discussion shows Freaky Trigger And The Lollards Of Pop and A Bite Of Stars, A Slug Of Time, And Thou on Resonance FM. Neither of these titles did he make up. If you see Al Ewing, do not panic. Either aim a shotgun blast at his brain or decapitate him, thus separating the brain from the spine and sending him back to the rotting oblivion from whence he should never have emerged.

coming November 2008...

Now read a chapter from the next book in the
Tomes of the Dead series, *Anno Mortis...*

ANNO MORTIS

Rebecca Levene

COMING NOVEMBER 2008 (UK)
JANUARY 2008 (US)

ISBN: 978-1-905437-85-6

£6.99/$7.99

WWW.ABADDONBOOKS.COM

CHAPTER THREE

The beetles were everywhere, small dry legs pattering over his stomach and back and neck, crawling through his hair and under his clothes. They stank of the worst kind of filth. Narcissus froze into horrified immobility. And then, before he'd consciously decided to do it, he ran.

He could see nothing – one hand over his eyes to protect them from the razor-sharp jaws of the beetles – and he hit the far wall with an impact that jarred from his elbows to his backbone. His fingers scrabbled, desperately searching for a door that wasn't there. Splinters of wood lodged painfully beneath his nails and he realised, with a sick shock, that he was making exactly the same sound the beetles had made inside the crate. Mindless creatures fighting to escape.

Sweat was running down his back. He felt some of the beetles there slipping, their legs floundering for purchase in the moisture. It was the most horrible sensation he'd ever experienced. After that he couldn't think at all. He just ran, into another wall, then another, stumbling to his knees halfway across the floor only to push himself upright as a torrent of insects headed towards him.

It was sheer chance that led him to the door, and for a second he didn't realise what it was. He'd almost pushed off again, driven by the overwhelming urge to run, run, run when he realised that it was metal beneath his fingers, not wood. Hinges.

He felt the bodies of beetles squashed to a pulpy liquid beneath his hand as he fumbled, trying to find the handle, trying to get out. But all he found was more wood and eventually he was forced to take his hand away from his eyes.

When he opened them, it was like a vision of Hades. The beetles were everywhere, blunt and brown and clinging. His own body crawled with them, five or ten thick so that he could barely see the skin beneath. He let out a muffled whimper of horror, unable to open his mouth for fear of letting the insects in. But there, finally, he could see it, and he yanked the handle down with the last of his strength and tumbled out into daylight.

All around him the beetles took flight, a black seething cloud heading high into the sky. A moment later they were gone, over the warehouse and away. He drew in a deep, shuddering breath of relief and fell to his knees, lifting his face to the sun and shutting his eyes.

When he opened them, he saw the two guards. They were staring at him with expressions of shock slowly transmuting into rage.

He didn't think there was any strength left in him. But he used what little he had to drive himself to his feet and stumble away, back towards the docks. He could feel runnels of liquid trickling down his cheeks and arms and he knew that not all of it was sweat. The creatures had bitten and scratched him, a thousand wounds that suddenly started to tell him how much they hurt.

He had no breath left to cry for help, even if he'd been certain it would come. He could hear the guards at his heels. He didn't dare waste the time to snatch a look behind him, but he knew they'd be armed. He imagined their swords, poised above their heads for a killing blow, and his heart somehow found the strength to pump a little harder and his legs to run a little faster.

A second later and he was in the maze of port buildings. He dodged right and left, jumping over abandoned barrels and sometimes weaving in and out of the buildings themselves, his breath like fire in his lungs. He didn't know where he was going – nearer the city, further away – only that he had to escape.

Another warehouse loomed straight ahead of him, and he wrenched open the door and flung himself inside. He was so intent on the pursuers behind that he didn't notice the man in front until he'd run straight into him. They fell to the floor together in a tangle of limbs and Narcissus struck out without thinking, the primitive part of him that cared only about living overriding all civilization.

The other man caught his fist in his palm, wincing at the impact. "Easy," he said. "I can help."

Narcissus tried to wrench his hand free, and after a moment the other man let him. "Who are you?" he gasped.

The man laughed. "Does it matter?" He was red-haired, a barbarian, with a hooked nose and a mobile, mocking mouth.

Narcissus scrambled to his feet and the other man followed, moving with a grace that Narcissus couldn't emulate. "It matters to me," he said.

The man bowed. "Then I am Vali, a stranger here. And you are about to be caught, unless you do precisely as I say."

Narcissus opened his mouth to argue – then closed it again as he heard the sound of the warehouse door opening and guttural shouting in Egyptian. More than two voices now; the guards must have found reinforcements.

He turned to Vali, though he didn't know how he could help. The man wasn't even armed.

Vali smiled. "Some fights can't be won – only avoided." And then he stepped aside, and Narcissus saw that there was a crate behind him, half-filled with jars of olive oil. "I threw the rest out earlier. Plenty of room for both of us in here."

There wasn't time to argue. Narcissus scrambled in, bleeding arms and legs jarring painfully against the awkwardly shaped glass, worse when the other man climbed in after, pulling the lid shut behind him.

A second later he heard the Egyptians, moving through the building as they shouted incomprehensibly to each other in their own language. He held his breath, too afraid of being heard to ask Vali the hundred questions clamouring for answers, but they circled in his mind as he crouched and shivered. And the loudest of them was: if Vali had already prepared their hiding place in advance, how had he known that they'd be needing it?

Boda was descending into the darkness beneath the baths without any sign of fear, but Petronius could feel a sour lump of it in his stomach, and threatening to head north. He paused a moment to swallow it back, then scrambled to catch up. The only thing worse than being down here would be being down here alone.

Boda waited for him at the bottom, squatting on her haunches with a look of supreme unconcern. They were in a natural cavern, chill and wet. It was too dark to make out much detail, but he saw the shadows of paintings on the walls, relics of a civilization older than Rome's.

"What is this place?" he whispered.

Boda shrugged. "I don't know. But whoever built the bath house must have known about it."

That was a sobering thought. The bath house had been here as long as Petronius could remember. He vaguely remembered his father telling him that it had been constructed as part of the public works that Emperor Augustus had commissioned in the city. Thirty years ago? Fifty? Whatever Seneca was involved in, it didn't seem likely that it was just smuggling banned books from Egypt.

Boda pointed to the far side of the cavern, where a tunnel could just be seen, snaking up. "The light's coming from that direction."

Petronius was prepared to take her word for it. She seemed to know what she was doing. In fact, she didn't really seem to need him there at all. For a brief moment he entertained the thought of turning round, climbing back up and leaving her to it.

He'd never been this afraid before. He'd thought he had – he thought he was frightened last year when his father very nearly caught him in bed with his business partner's wife. This, though, was the real thing. His father would just have given him a beating. He had no idea what would happen if he was caught snooping around here, but he didn't think it would be good. His body could rot down here a very long time before anyone found it.

Some of what he was thinking must have showed in his face. Boda was staring at him narrow-eyed and impatient. "Are you coming?" she snapped. "Or are you going?"

And then again, he thought, Seneca could have come down here for some innocent – or at least safe – reason. Sexual recreation, perhaps. At the end of that tunnel he might be confronted with nothing more than the sight of the old man balls-deep in a willing woman, which would certainly be unpleasant, but definitely not fatal.

"I'm coming," he said.

She took his arm, guiding him over the uneven floor. His sandals slapped on the wet rock, echoes of the sound bouncing from the walls. She frowned and motioned to her own feet, showing him how she slid them forward without lifting them. He copied her, and as the fear receded he realised that he was starting to enjoy himself. He was having an adventure, something he could tell Flavius about the next time he boasted about his convoy being chased by Gauls all the way to the Rubicon.

She released his arm when the tunnel became too narrow for them to walk side by side. There was a sound from up ahead, a muffled babble of voices that implied more people than the four they'd seen enter, a lot more. Still, their chatter should cover any sound that he and Boda made.

"So," he whispered, "what brings a lovely girl like you to a place like this?"

She turned to frown at him, then said: "Quintus is hiding something, I know it."

"Well, obviously." Her body blocked the dim light that shone back through the tunnel, and he trailed a hand against the wall to guide himself through the darkness. "What exactly do you think he's hiding?"

"A reason why he'd arrange for one of his own gladiators to be killed. And why he'd mutilate the body afterwards."

"Oh." He stopped, suddenly very sure that turning back was a good idea. Dead bodies, mutilated ones – these weren't the sort of adventures he had in mind.

He turned to go, and found her hand clawing at his arm to stop him. He opened his mouth to protest and her other hand clapped over it. Her eyes bored into his, demanding something. Silence, he supposed. When he blinked acknowledgement she released him, dropped to her knees and gesture to him to do the same.

Without her body to block it, he saw what lay ahead.

The tunnel opened into another chamber, broader than the first, its walls carved flat and smooth. He couldn't see Seneca, but that wasn't very surprising. There were at least fifty people here and he recognised a large number of them, the great and the good of Rome. They were chatting, laughing and drinking wine from crystal goblets, as if this was just another social gathering, an informal dinner party for close friends.

But it wasn't. He counted twelve coffins, leaning against the walls at regularly spaced intervals. The guests ignored them, but Petronius was unable to look away, however much he might have wanted to.

The coffins were open. Inside each, he could see bandage-wrapped corpses, and even from his hiding place in the tunnel he could smell the stench of death that wafted from them. All that, though, all that might have been bearable, if the corpses hadn't been moving.

Publia tried not to look inside the coffins. She could see the movement out of the corner of her eye, the white flicker as bandaged arms and legs twitched, but she did her best to ignore it as everyone else seemed to be doing. It wouldn't do to look like naïve yokels gaping in shock at these big city ways.

Which was precisely what her husband was doing. "Antoninus!" she hissed, stamping on his foot to stop him gawping quite so openly.

He turned to her, face blank with shock. "They're alive. They're dead – but they're alive."

"Of course." She laughed gaily, in case anyone more important was listening. "I'm sure this sort of thing goes on in Rome all the time."

"Does it?" He looked a little sick, though it had been his idea to join the Cult of Isis in the first place, and his business partner who'd proposed them for membership. Antoninus had seen it as a way of expanding his network of contacts, perhaps securing a few more lucrative contracts for his slave-importation business.

She'd understood that it could be much more than that. The Cult could be their route to social acceptance, to a class above the one they'd been born to. She couldn't say that she liked everything they stood for. She'd been brought up traditionally, to honour Jupiter and Juno, the divine parents of them all, and steer clear of foreign gods, who were seldom to be trusted. But all around her she could see evidence of the power of the Egyptian deities – and more importantly, of the power of those who worshipped them. If they played it right, her four-year-old son might not grow up to be a merchant like his father. He could be a senator, or even a consul. They just had to ingratiate themselves with the right people.

There was one of them now: Seneca, who was said to have the ear of the Emperor himself. He didn't look like much, skinny and stooped, but Publia put on her best smile as she approached him. "An honour, sir – I can't tell you how thrilled myself and my husband are to be here."

Seneca looked at her and Antoninus a long moment, clearly trying to remember who they were. Then something seemed to click in his memory and he smiled back. "The slave traders, of course. You're most welcome here."

"I've long venerated Isis," Publia said, gesturing to the cow-headed statue behind the altar. "It's such a relief to find others of a like mind."

"Indeed. And for us it was like a blessing from the goddess herself to find a supplicant with such a plentiful supply of slaves."

"I'm sure it was," Antoninus said dryly, and Publia stood on his toe again. She knew that he'd bitterly resented the five slaves they'd been told they needed to offer to the goddess to secure their membership. And a final one als.

And then she saw the smile drop from his face, and eyes darted towards her – just for a moment – before rting away again. He knew she was there and he'd been ld not to show it.

"Move," she said to Petronius. "Get up – we've been een."

A flash of terror crossed his face, already pale from what they'd witnessed, the twitching corpses in their wooden boxes. She knew she was faster and stronger than him. She could outrun him and leave him to slow their pursuers. He was a citizen of Rome, one of those who'd enslaved her, and she owed him nothing.

But she still found herself dragging his arm to get him moving, then pushing him in front of her. Maybe it was because he was still so young. Or maybe it was because no one should be left to those things they'd seen back in the cavern.

They were behind her now. She could smell the death-stench of them and hear the rustle of their bandages as they ran. Petronius stumbled ahead of her on the uneven floor, falling to his knees, and she had to waste precious seconds hauling him back to his feet. She felt the brush of skeletal fingers against her back, and despite herself she cried out in fear, a base animal reaction to a thing that should not be.

The creature behind her answered, its voice a dry rattle. She heard its teeth snapping together, the clash of bone on bone, and she knew that if Petronius fell she wouldn't stop for him again.

But the boy kept his feet and fear drove them both through the tunnel and into the cavern beyond. Petronius was chanting a Latin prayer between desperate pants of breath. She realised she was doing the same, begging Tiu

tomorrow night, before their initiation woul
Expensive in terms of gold, not doubt, but
you thought what it might buy them.

"We were glad to dedicate them to the serv
Publia said. "I hope they've proven useful – w
you our very best."

"Oh yes." A slight smile twitched at the corner of
mouth. "They were exactly what we required."
wandered the room, sweeping over the twitching b
their coffins, and his smile widened.

Publia followed his gaze. There were slaves min
with the crowd, pouring the wine and handing r
small snacks, oysters and stuffed dates, but she di
think any of them were the ones Antoninus had suppli
She distinctly remembered that one of them had been
Nubian – she'd been fascinated by the deep blue black o
his skin – and no one here looked like they hailed from
south of the Mediterranean.

"And now your initiation is almost complete," Seneca
said.

Publia paused, her eye caught by a flicker of movement
to her left, in the entrance tunnel. Was it her imagination,
or were there two figures crouching there?

Seneca raised an enquiring eyebrow.

"I think," she said, "that we have some uninvited
guests."

It took Boda a second too long to realise they'd been
spotted. She'd been watching Quintus as he circulated
through the crowd, trying to figure out his place among
them. Respected, she decided, but not honoured. He
bowed too low and smiled too ingratiatingly to be among

to spare her this death – to grant her any death but this.

When they reached the ladder, she looked behind to see their pursuers for the first time. The bandages had began to loosen in the long flight down the tunnel. She could see skin beneath at shoulder and waist and hip, grey-green and rotting. A hand reached up to grab her ankle, putrid flesh falling away as it grasped, to reveal the white bone beneath.

She kicked out mindlessly. Her foot caught the thing beneath its chin and the head snapped back, spewing corpse fluid through its jagged teeth. Another kick and it fell back to the floor below, leaving its hand still clamped to her leg.

The hand twitched and started to inch its way up her calf, and this time Boda couldn't control the scream that bubbled out of her throat. She scraped her other foot along her leg, peeling skin and not caring because a second kick dislodged the hand to fall and shatter on the rock below. Droplets of blood from the raw scrape on her leg splattered on top of it, falling faster as she pulled herself up the ladder, sending the blood racing through her veins.

And then, finally, she was at the top, pressed against Petronius as he shoved at the underside of the trapdoor. One of the walking dead was only eight rungs below and closing fast. The rest clustered at the foot of the ladder. When the one that was pursuing them pulled them down, the others would be waiting. She couldn't see their eyes beneath the bandages, just the blank white of their faces as they looked up. And still Petronius was pushing against the closed door.

"Hurry!" she shouted.

"I'm trying!" he gasped. Then he gave one final shove and the trapdoor swung open with a hollow thud.

She helped to push him through, ignoring his grunt of

protest. Her own feet wobbled and slipped on the slick wood of the rungs and, for a terrible moment, she thought she was going to fall into the waiting arms of the corpses below. Then Petronius's hand reached through, grasping her wrist and jerking up hard enough to tear the ligaments in her shoulder.

She stifled the cry of pain and used the last of her strength to scrabble for purchase on the marble floor around the trapdoor. Finally she was able to lever herself up and through and she didn't even pause for breath, just slammed the trapdoor shut behind her.

A second later the door bounced on its hinges as the thing below pushed up with inhuman strength. Petroneus flung himself on top of it, an act of bravery that seemed to take him by surprise. His eyes widened in horror as he realised what he'd done.

And it wasn't enough. A decaying hand crept round the edge of the wood to fumble at him. He shuddered and drew back.

Boda stepped over him, ignoring his yelp of pain as his fingers were caught beneath the heel of her sandal. The shelves were even heavier than she remembered and she was at the last of her strength. One tug, two, and they remained stubbornly in place. Then another body was pressed up behind her, two big male hands beside her own, and finally the shelves were moving, grating over the stone floor with a nerve-jangling screech.

Boda had one last, brief glimpse of the undead creature. The bandage had ripped from half its face and she could see the flesh beneath, hanging in decaying lumps from the hinge of its jaw. Its eyes, the milky-white of blindness, glared malevolently at her. Then the weight of the shelves slammed the trapdoor shut.